Ripeness

ALSO BY SARAH MOSS

FICTION

The Fell

Summerwater

Ghost Wall

The Tidal Zone

Signs for Lost Children

Bodies of Light

Night Walking

Cold Earth

NONFICTION

My Good Bright Wolf: A Memoir

Names for the Sea: Strangers in Iceland

Chocolate: A Global History
  (coauthored with Alexander Badenoch)

Spilling the Beans: Eating, Cooking, Reading and Writing in British Women's Fiction, 1770–1830

Ripeness

A NOVEL

Sarah Moss

 FARRAR, STRAUS AND GIROUX | NEW YORK

Farrar, Straus and Giroux
120 Broadway, New York 10271

EU Representative: Macmillan Publishers Ireland Ltd, 1st Floor, The Liffey Trust Centre, 117–126 Sheriff Street Upper, Dublin 1, D01 YC43

Copyright © 2025 by Sarah Moss
All rights reserved
Printed in the United States of America
Originally published in 2025 by Picador, Great Britain
Published in the United States by Farrar, Straus and Giroux
First American edition, 2025

Library of Congress Cataloging-in-Publication Data
Names: Moss, Sarah author
Title: Ripeness : a novel / Sarah Moss.
Description: First American edition. | New York : Farrar, Straus and Giroux, 2025.
Identifiers: LCCN 2025007167 | ISBN 9780374609016 (hardcover)
Subjects: LCGFT: Fiction | Novels
Classification: LCC PR6113.O88 R57 2025 | DDC 823/.92—dc23/eng/20250409
LC record available at https://lccn.loc.gov/2025007167

The publisher of this book does not authorize the use or reproduction of any part of this book in any manner for the purpose of training artificial intelligence technologies or systems. The publisher of this book expressly reserves this book from the Text and Data Mining exception in accordance with Article 4(3) of the European Union Digital Single Market Directive 2019/790.

Our books may be purchased in bulk for specialty retail/wholesale, literacy, corporate/premium, educational, and subscription box use. Please contact MacmillanSpecialMarkets@macmillan.com.

www.fsgbooks.com
Follow us on social media at @fsgbooks

10 9 8 7 6 5 4 3 2 1

This is a work of fiction. Names, characters, places, organizations, and incidents either are products of the author's imagination or are used fictitiously. Any resemblance to actual events, places, organizations, or persons, living or dead, is entirely coincidental.

For Kathy, whose blue boat set out too soon

stories you tell yourself

Yes, Edith says.

Yes, yes. As if he might stop if she stops saying it, as if they were of the generation for whom consent is necessarily verbal and valid only in the moment of utterance, as if her body and his were not already saying it, together, to each other.

Yes, because it is English that comes to hand, to mouth, that comes – because it was English in which she gave birth and English in which she will die. Yes. Oui. Ja. Sì.

His hands, clay-hardened, steel-sinewed, crush the bird bones of her wrists. Break them, she thinks, break me, yes, no, and then thinking stops in soft explosion, no, no, yes, and she holds her mind away from the lines of poetry crossing it like a banner behind an aeroplane. *Every woman adores a Fascist / The boot in the face, the brute / Brute heart of a brute like you.* He lets her arch her back, bridge, every woman should do yoga, deep, deeper, and she hears herself exclaim, wordless.

Afterwards, he lies over her, so she works to breathe, thinks about her ribs trying to expand into him, about her lungs constrained, the air they want, about his hip bone on hers, bone on bone, connective tissue, his hands still closed on her arms and when she tries to move – tissues, her side – he grips. No, he says, and they both feel her quiver.

Of course Gunter's not a Fascist, not unless you wanted to say his politics are so far to the left he's come round the other side, up against the international date line where communism and Fascism border. His veganism is on that border, a purity cult as well as a sacrifice for the collective good. He celebrates poverty as people do only when it is, or was, a choice, and the cottage he bought for a few hundred quid fifty years ago is now a substantial asset. No boots, anyway, he takes off his shoes at the door, which is more than you can say for most local visitors. Not that Gunter isn't local, here all his adult life, but neither of them ever will be counted local, nor their children's children unto the seventh generation. Passports and voting are one thing, who you really are is another. Especially if you're English, especially if you're Jewish. Not that Gunter has children, and her Pat – she'll call him later, or tomorrow – is in London.

Gunter's grip slackens, his skull rolls into hers. Funny, the way men always go to sleep afterwards, whatever needs doing next, however odd the position, like babies. She remembers Pat, pre-school, didn't want a nap, wasn't tired, had better things to do than going to bed and then he'd fall asleep on the wooden floor, a toy car still in his hand. She used to tuck a pillow under his floppy head, put one of those waffle blankets with the silky edging over him, stroke his hair, watch him, the small miracle of his breath and being, and then steal across the room for the book she kept close by just in case the day gave her reading time. No point wasting a child's sleep on housework. She rearranges their limbs, decides she likes the weight of Gunter enough, for now, not to roll him off and wake him. Adjusts the pillow so she can watch the cloud shadows crossing the hill outside, see the weather coming up the valley.

She's not properly English or Jewish, not that being improperly English and Jewish makes her Irish just because she lives here. She's naturalized, officially, has the passport to prove it, but what does that word mean? You wouldn't need to say *naturalized*, would you, if the situation were really natural, you can't by definition make something natural when it's not. Natural from *natare*, to be born, not an act that can be undone or revised. Assimilation from *similis*, same root as similar and simulation, alike but unlike, *unheimlich*, uncanny. And she has three other passports, three other simulations, tucked away just in case. Passports are flags of convenience, Maman used to say, tickets out. Just make sure you show the right one to the right uniform on the right day. Always leave before you're certain, because if you wait until you know, there are boots coming up the stairs and blood on the walls and it's too late. Leave while there's still doubt, while it might be unnecessary.

Maman was uninterested in assimilation and good at leaving: men, children, countries. You can't blame her, Daddy always said, but Edith could and sometimes did blame her, maybe not only for Maman's own desertions but for Lydia's leaving home so thoroughly and so young; maybe, unfairly, for her own divorce, for how good she has turned out to be, at separating from her husband of nearly forty years; for the way neither she nor Lydie could settle. It was the people who felt safe who didn't leave,

Maman said. It was the settled, secure ones who ended up on the cattle trucks, the ones who thought it couldn't happen here, to us. It can always happen here, to you. You won't know until it happens which neighbours will hide you in the attic and who will denounce you to the police, it's rarely as you thought. Keep a bag packed and have an exit strategy, but in Edith's experience, exit strategies like most of the stories you tell yourself tend to be self-fulfilling.

Here she is, Edith, having left and left again if not as often as Maman. Here she is, seventy-three years old, springtime in the year of our Lord – her ex-husband's Lord – 2023, or 5783 by the Jewish reckoning, here in County Clare, in the house she will not leave, no more leaving. Here, under the fascinating naked body of a German potter who also once left, who ran away from Düsseldorf as a young man – imagine him as a young man, the shoulders on him! – and never went back, who was part of the wave of idealistic young northern Europeans coming to, washing up in, the West of Ireland back in the day when property was cheap and the young locals couldn't leave fast enough, leave De Valera's Ireland for London and New York and Sydney and possibly also Düsseldorf, for places where the priest wasn't watching and there was money to be made. Some of them had made money, and had lives, had fun and games, harder to pull off in the Ireland Edith first knew forty years ago. Coming the other way, Gunter had not made money. Mattias farming organically up the hill – goat's milk soap, these days, kale with caterpillars living in it, honey more expensive by the jar than perfume – had not made money. Doro and Will on their smallholding, running the eco B & B in summer and spinning and dyeing and weaving the fleece from their rare-breed sheep in winter, had not made money. They've no pensions, no health insurance, rely on kale and yoga and manual labour to stave off the ailments of old age. Effective enough, mostly, so far, with luck. They'll have to go on forever, until they drop, making things in the old, expensive ways and selling them to people down from Dublin and over from London and New York, people coming back but only to visit, coming home to a place they don't live. Naturalized, maybe.

Their sweat is cooling on her neck, and she can feel friction, stickiness, between her flattened boobs and his ribs. Trickling, below; she clenches her pelvic floor but the sheets will need changing anyway, looks like a good drying day and she wonders did women use to try to avoid it on wet days or with the laundry already backed up, assuming they weren't already avoiding it for the more obvious reasons. The relief of that all being over, nobody tells you. Not that it was ever all that much of a bother for her, living in England, she and her nice GP trying and erring until they found the right pills for her, everything regular and hardly any bleeding. Tie my tubes, she'd said after Pat was born, but even in London in the 1980s they wouldn't do that for a healthy young married woman. You never know, Dr Emmett kept saying, you might want another baby, people change their minds, things happen, I know you think you never will again but you forget, it's like moving house. But it wasn't like moving house, which she's done more times than she bothered to count or can now remember, and it wasn't the birth that put her off, messy and painful but nothing she wasn't expecting, it was motherhood, it was the way her own unfitness was so immediately evident, which was also nothing she wasn't expecting. She loved Pat in the animal way mothers love babies, barring disaster, but early childhood was boring and she has never been good with boredom. At least in London she could go back to work, adult education in the days when local councils still funded English classes that went beyond basic literacy, when the prison education service ran to literary criticism and modern languages. Turns out it's not a compromise, to have one child, especially if you move to Ireland where in her day it was almost deviant to stop at one. Turns out if one of you doesn't want kids, probably best not.

It's not that she regrets Pat's existence – superstition prickles at the thought – but he'd have been better served by a better mother and while there's no control for a life story, she's pretty sure she'd have been a better person as well as a happier one, without a child. She'd have left Mike earlier, decades earlier, all those years wishing he'd have an affair or at least say he'd had an affair so they could end things for a decent reason, all those years thinking she'd have one herself if only so she could tell him about it and liberate them both. A marriage-ending affair would even have been worth all the depilation and polishing and moisturizing she understands that men – men other than German Marxist potters living primitively in County Clare whose tastes were formed in the era when women were expected to have body hair – had come to require. It's not possible, Méabh says, that in four decades no one took a fancy to you, you're an attractive woman. Men have always taken fancies to Méabh, she takes it for granted, a lifetime of fending off attention, though she's coming up forty years married herself and most of the single men of anything like the right age around here are widowed and looking for a replacement woman to wash their socks and cook their dinner or worse yet breakfast, stinky fry-up, or at the very least to tell them when there's soup on their jumper and it's past time the kitchen floor had a wash. Méabh's right that there is sometimes soup on Gunter's jumper and his kitchen floor does want a wash, it's just not Edith's floor and not Edith's problem and the jumper comes off, which is how she prefers him anyway. You must not have noticed, Méabh says, whatever you say you must have been giving off such a strong air of respectability that everyone stayed away, but Edith reckons she's usually pretty tuned-in to people, good at reading mood and repulsion and desire in the way of anyone who grew up as an outsider. No one gave her the eye, not unless you count that man on the train once or Pat's friend Ajay's dad in London but she liked Simran. Sordid, it would have been, to sleep with her friend's husband, fine as he was. She'd used to think someone could probably make a fortune setting up a bureau, an introduction agency, for the unhappily married to pretend to have affairs, like when you could divorce someone only for adultery and people used to have to make a great performance of checking into a hotel and being found by the chambermaid in the morning so the hotel staff could give evidence later, only these days it's not the court that needs to know but your spouse, your friends, the mums at the school gates. Easier to say she went off with another man, he had a thing with a younger woman, more comfortable than we don't like each other anymore, we ran out of conversation years ago, the sight of the hair matted in her hairbrush by the bathroom sink makes me sick, his best hobby is a half-hour crap with his phone and he doesn't even open the window afterwards, all the reasons we should not have married forty years ago have bloomed and spread like mould behind the bath. If mutual dislike were a valid reason for divorce, we'd all be at it and then where would we be? Not in Ireland, anyway, not her generation, who by and large own houses big enough for the many children of couples who were not offered the pill and now, those children having left – London, Berlin, Sydney – big enough to contain their parents' reciprocal disdain. There probably isn't a correlation between the size of your house and how long you can tolerate your spouse, it's probably more complicated than that. We don't divorce, people like us, Dearbhla told her in the first year in Dublin when she'd made the faux pas of inviting a certain couple to dinner, but we may live separate lives, we may not be seen together and it's not mentioned, do you see? She did not, then, see how she was supposed to know what was not mentioned, but she learnt, as immigrants do, as even Maman in her time must have approximately learnt, by keeping quiet, standing back, observing. Be small, migrant, wanderer. Stand in the corner and copy us, though your mimicry will never be quite good enough. So why do you keep trying, Gunther would say, just be who you are, but it's all very well for him, single and devoted to his pots, not setting foot in Dublin from one year to the next. No one ever asked him to give a dinner party.

Right, she thinks, anyway. Sheets in the wash, get them dry by bedtime with a following wind and the longer light these days, and she might go down to the shore while the weather's clear, high tide this afternoon, swimming, stop at the veg stall on the way home, fresh eggs and the first strawberries are in.

Lunch first, she's hungry, not to bother with a shower now if she'll be in the sea later. Bread and cheese, apples, cup of tea over the end of the weekend papers. Time to get this lummox back off to his pots. She pushes his shoulder, shakes him and feels her own ribs flex, feels his wilted softness against her thigh. Gunter, she says, wake up now, come on. I'll make you a coffee and then you can get off home.

somehow astonishing

I took the train to Italy, of course. I was seventeen; it would be twenty years before I boarded my first plane, rushing to my mother's deathbed in Tel Aviv though I knew mine wasn't the hand she longed to hold. I should be clear that I'm not the one you want either. You shouldn't get your hopes up. We'll come to that.

I was meant to be having a year out, to grow up, because I'd been a year ahead of my age all through school. We'd all sat round the table after lunch one day the previous summer, even Dad though it was harvest time, to discuss my future, and Maman had said that however good my marks, even if I were to be offered a place I was too immature to go straight to Oxford. Edith has seen nothing of the world, she'd said, lighting a cigarette which made Gran wince and open the window. She may be able to pass exams and I'm sure she will talk well about books in an interview but her Italian is that of a schoolgirl and even her French could be better, she has been almost nowhere and seen almost nothing, Oxford would be wasted on her. It is a ridiculous plan. I will write to my friends and put together un petit tour, she can go to Teresa in Florence and then perhaps un stage at Marcel's bookshop. An English country childhood is all very well but one does not send one's daughter to Oxford for her to marry a farmer and live on a farm, n'est-ce pas?

I had glanced at Dad, the farmer whose wife Maman in fact was though she could hardly be said to live on the farm, but he had nodded and smiled through worse than that over the years and he said yes, Rachel, I dare say you're right, let's see. Do you want to go travelling, pet, he asked me later when I was helping with the milking, would you like to stay with your mother's friends, and I said yes, I think so, yes, I would, because although of course I disliked being called immature and also I could think of many things I had seen and understood on the farm that I would not have seen and understood elsewhere, I certainly had an appetite for more, for tree-lined city squares and great museums, for parties and lectures, for everywhere and everything.

And then months later, as my exams began, Maman had written to me from the artists' commune in France where she was spending the spring, to say that instead of going to Teresa in Florence I was to go to my sister, who would be staying in a villa in another part of Italy and would need a companion while she had a baby. Maman had followed the letter with a rare international telephone call late one night. I could almost feel the price of the minutes pulsing across the Channel and half of England, through the curly wire in my hand and into the reckoning of my grandmother, hovering behind me in the hall at the farm. Stay on the train from Milan until the end, until Como Lago, Maman said. If you get off at Como San Giovanni, you'll just have to carry your own bags down the hill, don't think I'm springing for a taxi. She produced phrases like 'springing for' with a flourish and an exaggeration of her accent, zink, spreenging, like one of the French mam'zelles in the school stories I loved. Yes, I said, I understand, I will. And you're to look after your sister properly, she said, don't go wandering off, for once she needs help and it will be good for you. As if wandering off were my habit, not hers, as if she had not herself diagnosed in me a deficit of wandering.

I don't suppose, Gran had said at the end of that phone call, your mother thought to ask about your exams? I don't suppose Rachel thought she might go to Lydia herself?

So here I was, on the train as instructed, wandering curtailed or at least redirected by Lydia's misadventures. I carried two bags, an ill-chosen fake-leather handbag already giving at the seams under the strain of three books and a large sandwich I'd bought in Milan and been too shy to eat on the train, and the old Army-issue canvas knapsack Daddy had given me. Not stylish, darling, but if you're not travelling in style it's easier to have your hands free. On the understanding that Italy was hot, I'd rolled up a couple of washed-out cotton frocks that had fitted well enough the summer before, and the bathing suit I'd used for years of school swimming; you'd think even then I might have had the wit to consult a map and notice that Lake Como is nearer Switzerland than the Mediterranean, and I knew fine well my sister's baby wasn't due until the autumn. I would, Maman said, depending on how Lydia did, be needed for perhaps a fortnight or a month after that.

I stood up as we left Como San Giovanni, illogically anxious that I might miss the last stop, swung the canvas sack on my shoulders, the handbag across my body. The various straps bunched my dress, made it even shorter. It was already clear to me that Italian girls did not take trains unaccompanied and that the rising hemlines of the mid-sixties had not reached the thigh of Italy, but here was the lake, absurdly blue, and wooded hills deeply green, stucco buildings absurdly pink, golden afternoon light everywhere, the whole scene at once novel and familiar. Beaker full of the warm South, because it was still obvious to me then that the North was north of our farm in Derbyshire and the South was south of it. The train stopped and I struggled with the door, being accustomed to the English way of opening the window and using the handle on the outside, was helped by a man whose gaze rose from my legs only to my chest, to the solid upholstery I had inherited from Gran's line of hill-farming women. I ignored his offered hand, settled the straw hat from which I'd removed the school ribbon, hurried across the platform towards the water. The boats leave every hour until 8 p.m., Maman had said, and there's no reason you should be later than that. There were unfamiliar smells on the air: flowers, fish, sunshine. If I have to wait, I thought, I will eat the sandwich, I will perhaps treat myself to a cup of tea or even an ice cream, though I knew I didn't really have the nerve for a café alone in Italy and certainly didn't have money to spare.

I crossed the road, looking the wrong way but looking twice, my shadow sharp at my side, saw the piers and the boats waiting and found the ticket office, biglietteria. Senza unica per Lenno, per favore, grazie, the first time I used Italian in the wild somehow astonishing, this code learnt like the formulae in Physics and Chemistry turning out to be a real language producing real ferry tickets after all. Even so, I almost failed to board the boat because I was so unnerved by the absence of a proper queue, so reluctant to push in though I had been waiting as long as anyone else and it wasn't clear what I might be pushing in to. A man in a braided cap and uniform said something to me and when I hesitated said, you go or no? Yes, I said, sì, and let him hand me onto the steamer just before he cast off the ropes. The outdoor seats were still free despite the crowd, so I took the one at the front, shrugged off the knapsack but looped my arm through the strap so it couldn't be stolen while I folded my arms on the railing and rested my chin, waited for the show to begin. I remember feeling the engine's throbbing in my bones, the blend of nausea and thrill. I wanted to tell Nancy, look, here I am, two months ago we were wearing school uniform – well, to be strictly fair I was still wearing a certain amount of school uniform – and inventing humiliating excuses for using the staircase reserved for teachers and prefects, and now I've made my way right across Europe and here I am about to cross Lake Como all alone but more exciting than all alone, in the company of Italians, some of whose Lombardy Italian I can understand.

Don't worry, I'll spare you my nostalgically recalled adolescent raptures over the scenery. I'd just ask you to remember that I'd grown up in post-war Derbyshire, that I was accustomed to bomb craters all over the towns and cities of northern England, by then overrun with brambles and morning glory but sites of explosion none the less, that the rain-hammered ruins of aerial bombardment were ordinary, that rationing meant I'd eaten my first orange when my mother brought them back from Israel in her suitcase, peace-offering or bribe, and here were trees bright with oranges and the scent of their blossom heavy as we came into each small harbour; here were figs, which I knew only dried and chopped in suet puddings, ripening on the trees; lemons weighing down glossy leaves; hillsides silvery with olive groves when I had only read about olives – yes, I know, done before, done to death, but like most clichés there is a reason. I was seventeen and hungry in every way.

Débarques à St Abbondio, Maman's letter said. She always switched to French for disembarkation. Get off, she said, in English you are always getting, food and clothes and ideas and on and off, it's a lazy verb. I alighted. I made landfall. I stepped ashore. I had not expected to be met, we were not that sort of family. Daddy, sometimes, if he remembered your train time – if you had told him your train time – and if he could spare the time and petrol, would drive down to the village and wait in the ancient Land Rover which smelt of manure and dogs, but mostly we stood on our own two feet, even Lydie tottering up the mucky lane in unsuitable shoes with her smart leather case banging against her perfect calves. I hitched the knapsack. My shoes, polished by Daddy and re-soled before I left, had a few miles in them yet. There were pink and red and white geraniums spilling from troughs fixed to the metal railings along the cobbled promenade, railings as exotic to me as the flowers since all the municipal metalwork in England had been torn up for munitions in the early days of the war, before I was born, and never replaced. There were trees of uniform heights planted at uniform distances in stone-lined beds in the pavement and between them wooden benches, freshly painted, unoccupied. I would have liked to sit down a moment, collect myself, but I would have felt conspicuous. Even more conspicuous. There were men sitting at tables in front of what must have been a bar, three little boys who stopped playing on the pebble beach to watch me, two women also disembarking with baskets and packages from their shopping in Como. Turn right and walk straight through the village, the letter said.

The sun was still bright on the promenade. The air and the breeze seemed dry; then as now, I was accustomed to damp. We are half-aquatic, we people of the North Atlantic's unnameable archipelago, Ireland and Northern Ireland and the British Isles, the Republic and the North and the dis-United Kingdom, the smaller island and the bigger one and the tax havens round the edges which tend to be the warmest and driest of the lot. We have, at least, a climate in common. Weather fronts do not divide us. We go out in the rain, we breathe the fog, we swim our chilly waters. You probably don't count yourself among us but maybe you will, after reading this, maybe you will naturalize, though I doubt any story will alter your body's perception of the air, of dryness and humidity. I heard for the first time the shrilling of cicadas, could not yet stop hearing it. There was always birdsong in England then, the quiet of my adult life was not yet falling, and so the Italian birds were less noticeable than they are to me when I travel now, but there were voices I had not heard before in their chorus, unfamiliar wings on the air. The buildings were all a shade of orange-pink I associated with curtains, somehow louche or feminine or not serious enough for outdoor use, and their deep-set windows had white wooden shutters which I had seen only in pictures. My feet slowed as I passed the canopied window of the panificio e pasticceria, displaying piles of prettily shaped biscuits studded with nuts and chocolate; bronzed bread buttoned with olives and tomatoes, gleaming with oil; further back, layer cakes and small creamy confections. I would return, I thought, when I had the lay of the land, when I knew how much money I could spare for such indulgences. If any. I still had my sandwich, after all, a sort of overgrown bread roll exotic enough with its dried beef and peppery salad filling.

I carried on. The pavement ended with the houses. High walls ran between the dusty road and the hillside, and on the other side the lake sparkled and lapped. I would climb some of those hills, and I would swim in the lake which must surely be warm enough, under all this sun. After you leave the village, Maman wrote, take the first turn up the hill and the gate is on your right. Here it was, a large double gate, fancy wrought iron, behind which a gravel drive lined with glossy-leaved pink-flowering bushes curved up daisied grass. Bloody hell, Lydie, I said. Cypress trees towered over the lawns and I couldn't see the house. The villa. I took a deep breath and tried to turn the handle of the gate. Maybe it was just stiff. Maybe I should lift not turn. But the big keyhole was plain, oiled, in use. I looked again for a bell, maybe you were supposed to ring, maybe I was oafish, trying to let myself in. What if it was the wrong house after all, what would they think, some travel-stained foreigner trying to get in? (Always getting, you English, in and out, up and off.) I walked up the road a bit, to see if there was another house, if I could have made a mistake, but there wasn't, not that I could see. After the end of the pink wall there was farmland, cows, and then the mountainside, only one villa to the right of the first road after the end of the village. I tried the gate again, hurt my finger. Trust sodding Lydie to immure herself like Sleeping Beauty. What was I supposed to do, mount my charger and hack through a century's growth of thorns? No mobile phones, of course, in those days; if I'd had a telephone number for the villa, I could perhaps have returned to the village and negotiated the use of the panificio's telephone, but I didn't. Nor, I reflected, did I have anything like enough money for a hotel, let alone a ticket back to England, or even to the South of France where I had a postal address for my mother's hosts but no telephone number. I should have to sleep in an olive grove, hitchhike my way back to Derbyshire, starve to death like Jane Eyre on the moor except that I would be surrounded after all by ripe oranges and figs and I still had my sandwich. I sat down on the grass verge, which I later discovered to have been a mistake, insect bites in places you don't want them, and ate half the sandwich and the last bit of the fruit cake from home, and then I gave thanks again to Daddy for the knapsack and climbed over the gate.

the space required

Edith peers from across the road as she waits to cross alongside an elderly American couple dressed for weather much worse than it is and three young Germans wearing shorts and carrying high-spec backpacks and hiking boots. Summer traffic, now, the tourists whose coming secures the West of Ireland's food and clothes and shelter, tourists to be fed and clothed and sheltered with care and also sometimes disdain. Céad míle fáilte. Put out the flags and strike up the fiddle. Means the café's open longer, anyway, even Sundays, haul in the catch while you can. She nips out in front of Brendan's old tractor, leaving the tourists who'll wait half an hour to get to the other side, returns his grave salute.

You can tell if Méabh's in a room from the street outside. She has presence, Méabh, in the way of an older woman who's spent decades fighting to own the space she occupies and, somewhere along the way, probably not that long ago and perhaps in the absence of her husband's unconditional support, won. Edith remembers Lydia's – well, boyfriend? Housemate?

A choreographer, anyway – talking about the kinesphere, which is the space claimed by bodily movement. Breathing has a little kinesphere, represents the smallest space needed by a living body. Ballet has a very large kinesphere, which is interesting when you think about the restricted size of the bodies that perform it, the ways in which dance allows or commands women to claim space. And the conditions imposed, the price paid. There's Méabh, on the bench at their preferred window table, her kinesphere, the space needed for the action of being Méabh, extending out onto the pavement and back to the counter where it meets the similarly well-established kinesphere of Bríd who owns the place and the bar next door, whose kitchen dances feed half the town and visitors, she likes to say, from across the whole world. No one here seems to notice that this whole world is mostly white folk from the North Atlantic rim.

Méabh stands up, leans across the table to hug and kiss in a waft of silk scarves, tilting vase and bold rose perfume, the sort Edith would like to wear but always decides is too much, too much of one blowsy thing, when she samples it at Duty Free. Darling, Méabh says, you're looking very well, have we Gunter to thank for it? Aye, maybe, says Edith, hearing her old Derbyshire speech rising to Méabh's Clare accent. After a certain age, it's your childhood voice that answers the call. That or I was in the sea this morning, she says. Ah sure, says Méabh, I'll take the sea over a man these days. What will you have? Say what you will about Russia, you should try Nadia's honey cake. Méabh, Edith says, really. Look now, Méabh says, all I'm saying is you should try it. And there are some little dumpling things, I had those for my lunch the other day, and did you hear they want salad with everything, the Ukrainians, no matter what it is they're wanting cucumber and radish on the plate? Seamus can't keep them in the shop. Sounds very healthy, says Edith.

It is known in the village that Nadia who is now cooking for Bríd was a dentist in Kyiv, her qualifications not recognized in the EU. Nadia is smiley, big-eyed, anxious to please, has teeth conspicuously whiter and straighter than is normal around here. Sometimes she makes a kind of fudge and Edith wonders is it an act of suppressed aggression, to put sugar in the mouths of the people who shelter and feed her and her children but don't recognize her, don't see anything but a dispossessed Ukrainian, God love her, a Good Refugee. The Ukrainians, Edith has observed, have a measure of exemption from the requirement for refugees to express gratitude. They are allowed a certain moodiness. Irish people have an ancestral memory of having to flee or fight the aggressor next door who wants the fruits of their labour and their land. Sure how grateful would you be, to share a room in a second-rate hotel with your three kids and have a job waiting tables when you've a postgraduate degree? Eaters of salad and little dumplings, traumatized by exile, longing for home and, importantly, likely to return there when the war ends, if the war ends. And probably Nadia is longing, surely for dentistry and her own house if not for Kyiv. Méabh pushes her plate towards Edith. A generous slice, thin layers of brown cake and pale cream. Oh, says Edith, it's sour cream cake, we used to have it – teenage birthdays, sometimes, bought from the Jewish deli in Sheffield, carried home in a white cardboard box held on someone's lap or nested in hay in the back of the Land Rover. The Jewish deli also sold lox, pickles, chopped herring, occasionally bagels, strange smelly things you didn't want your friends to see. She takes a teaspoon from Méabh's saucer and tries it, a mouthful from the creamy edge. Yes. Walnuts, sour cream, the cinnamon a new but very acceptable addition. A local version, she thinks, might use the hazelnuts that flourish in every crevice of this limestone landscape. It's not Ukrainian, she wants to say, it's Jewish, but of course it's both and neither, because her Jewish food is their Ukrainian food, because some of the great-grandparents of the people now fleeing Russian invasion and taking refuge here in the West of Ireland were the aggressors from whom her great-grandparents fled Ukraine for France. And thence to England, to America, and to Israel. One generation conducts a pogrom, one flees invasion. The grandchildren of survivors instigate genocide in their turn, eyes for eyes, teeth for teeth, the continent of Europe sown east to west and back with eyes and teeth, ploughed into the earth like salt.

She takes another spoonful. People who share recipes, who bake the same birthday cakes, stuff the same flatbreads with the same herbs, are perfectly capable of burning down each other's houses, raping each other's daughters and mutilating each other's sons. The evidence would suggest it's in all of us, both the baking and the bloodlust. What, says Méabh, it's just a cake, let's order another slice. Get your own please, she means, that one's mine. I'll have a scone, Edith says primly, with a pot of tea.

She shrugs off her coat, settles at the other end of the window seat, one foot tucked up so she can turn to see the cobbled harbour, the bobbing boats, the weather coming up the inlet, and face Méabh at the same time. I like your scarf, she says. How are things? Méabh shakes her head and shimmies her shoulders, a dog out of water. No better, she says, worse, really. The kids are fighting all the time and you can't blame them, I do understand, it's barely respectable Conor and the girls together in that little room and Caoimhe's never out of my kitchen, if she's not going through the cupboards she's at the table drinking the good tea and jabbing at that phone and of course it's her childhood home and I'm glad to have her, I've always told all of them never forget there's a bed and a place at the table waiting for you here no matter what but Jesus Mary and Joseph Edith it's coming up to the year they've been with me and – well, of course there's worse suffering in the world and I'm sure the Ukrainians would soon set me right, it's not that I'm not grateful to have them with me and everyone well, you know I missed them away up in Dublin all those years, but poor John now, he barely dares set foot in his own house, can hardly look at the television even for a big game and the way Aoibhinn speaks to him sometimes, you know yourself he can be old-fashioned but if I'd ever dreamt of saying one tenth of the like to my father – well, I wouldn't have dreamt of it, that's all, and it's not as if he's likely to change his mind for being called a Fascist, she should talk to some of her new friends up at the school if she wants to know what Fascism looks like. Edith thinks about another spoonful of Méabh's cake, and thinks better of it. She's a lovely girl, I'm not saying she's not, says Méabh, and I know it's better they have ideas and the confidence to speak up – I know, Edith says, you bring them up to be independent and strong-minded and then look what happens. Pat and Mike used to argue horribly, I hated it, and it was obviously stags clashing horns across the kitchen table, neither of them actually cared about the political stuff, or certainly not enough to take action. It was kind of disturbingly primal and I just used to get up and clear the dishes and neither of them noticed even when they were arguing about women's rights. Oh, Edith, says Méabh, I do know, I didn't forget you've Pat so much further away than Dublin, I know you miss him – London's fine, Edith says, London's about the right distance. I like hearing about his life there and I love the visits, I wouldn't have your patience if he came to live with me, let alone bringing three teenagers. I know there isn't anywhere, I know we have this conversation every time, but is there really nowhere they can go? I mean, you know everyone, surely someone knows someone who has an empty house, what about that Moloney place, the Americans are there, what, two weeks a year, couldn't you rent that, what about that one on the back road to Carran? Ah sure, Méabh says, they'll never let those, the Moloneys are back every summer and the Flanagan cousins'll never come to terms, not in this generation, why do you think they left in the first place? No, there's nothing habitable left and don't think I haven't thought of some of the ruins too, at least for the kids come summer, the whole three months of it with no school, Edith, how will I manage? Tell them at least to go away for a weekend, says Edith, no one's going to win if you lose your mind. Aoibhinn could work in the hotel, couldn't she, she wouldn't have to be behind the bar, haven't we all made beds in our time? Sure there's the coffee van down at the beach, or would she not go visit her old friends in Dublin?

The oxygen mask thing, she thinks, save yourself, Méabh, but it's never been obvious to her why the recommended course of action during a sudden loss of cabin pressure on a plane should be the model for behaviour under all other circumstances, and anyway she's pretty sure she would have fitted Pat's mask first, come the hour. Does anyone really leave their child blue and choking and falling through the sky while securing their own air supply? Maman, maybe, but that too would have been instinct rather than rule-following.

Nadia brings a tray holding one of Gunter's teapots, steam twining from the spout, one of his good hefty mugs, a small china milk jug of no relevance to either Gunter's pots or mint tea, a plump bronzed scone dimpled with berries, butter in the lavish Irish quantity, a generous puddle of green jam. Nadia has remembered Edith's preference for the rhubarb and ginger made by Brídʼs daughter-in-law over the strawberry jam served to tourists. Thank you, says Edith, that looks great.

They can't go away, Méabh says, she really is saving every penny for a house, or trying to at least and you can't blame her for treating the kids sometimes, it's not as if not buying a dress means they can buy a house any decade soon, you know yourself the prices are just a joke, who has that kind of money? We do, Edith thinks, we who were young when the young could buy houses. The house in Dun Laoghaire that she learnt to call the Marital Home sold for an absurd sum, a number she will never mention to anyone, thirty times what they paid for it when they moved from London thirty years ago. Her pension's derisory – piecework, long gaps – and she's not rich (does anyone think herself rich?) but with the divorce agreement she has and is likely to continue to have the cottage, health insurance, her car, enough money to pay the bills, a monthly subscription at the yoga studio, going out for coffee when she feels like it. (All right, maybe she is rich. But not very rich.) She is likely to die in comfort and leave Pat enough to do likewise. You do know, she nearly says to Méabh, there's always a bed for you at my house, you know the spare room is always made up and no one in it, if Caoimhe can't go away for a few days why don't you come and stay with me. But she doesn't say it. Because of Gunter. Because Méabh is her friend and she tends to like people less when she lives with them. Because, Edith thinks, she is not a generous person, and she learnt long ago that – barring certain necessities such as nappy-changing, wearing a mask during a pandemic and waiting your turn – you should do nothing resentfully.

Anyway, Méabh says, there's nothing to be done about it, will you look at the sunshine now, enough of this, when you've finished that scone let's go say hello to Columcille, maybe he can do something for Caoimhe. I think, says Edith, if the saints were able and willing to intervene in the Irish property market things would be looking very different, but let's ask him, why not. I'm sorry, going on about it, says Méabh, you're very good to listen. Not at all, says Edith, inadequate, aware that there's an Irish response, more courteous and more loving, just beyond her grasp. Here, she says, have some of this scone, I ate a fair bit of your cake.

They take Méabh's car up the hill. Edith winds down the window, because it's that kind of car, and the smell of cut grass and cows blows in. Probably with the window closed the car wouldn't be sounding as if something's about to fall off the undercarriage. The afternoon has settled into blue and green, a few cotton-wool clouds casting shadows on the stony hills. There are big lambs in the roadside fields, hawthorn in bloom, but even at this time of year the valley's velvet greens fade into the limestone upland. There's still spring up there, but it's tiny, flowering in the crevices and rain-cups of sedimentary rock, in the pinprick markings of the planet's bone. Will we look for the invisible flower, she asks. Too early, says Méabh, next month. One of Edith's guides to the local flora describes a white flower unique to the Burren and observed, or at least recorded, only three times in the last century, which may be, the book says, because it is too small to see; this is one of Edith's favourite facts about the Burren. This landscape is as fragile and as much menaced as any and all others, but there's something about the nakedness of limestone, something about the encounter of body and stone, that makes her feel safe. No concealment, no adornment. She said once to Méabh, maybe the first time Méabh brought her to the well here, you know I persuaded Mike to buy the cottage because I feel so much at ease here, something about the limestone maybe, it was limestone where I grew up, I love the big skies and the tiny flora, just thinking about this place used to cheer me up when I was in Dublin. And then she heard herself and said sorry, I'm romanticizing where you live, I know you can't eat the view, but Méabh said ah sure, you've come home, girl, you were always meant to be here. And though Edith knows she isn't home, not in the way that Méabh is, not here and not anywhere, the words were an embrace, hearing them like feeling the first glass of wine filtering into your blood, like sun on your back after rain, benediction.

Méabh, driving as ever with verve, almost swipes a car – black, over-sized, Dublin plates – coming over the hill. Feckers, she says, it's a superpower, not caring if your car gets scratched. Never mind the car, I care if we get scratched, Edith decides not to say. Méabh hurls them into a bend, guns the engine up the hill which admittedly isn't just for show, with the two of them on board a few bags of groceries are enough to make the old engine falter up here. Will you look at that tree now, Méabh says; the big hawthorn at the top of the field, twisted and sculpted by the north wind, fluorescent, green and foaming white, sun-soaking. You get to know the trees individually round here, the way Edith once knew the shops and cafés in Dublin. Springtime, she says.

There are no other cars in Columcille's lay-by. A fresh wind, and only April after all; Edith fastens her coat, checks for gloves in the pockets. Méabh's pulling on a knitted hat in a shade of rowanberry orange that does not suit her, nor possibly anyone. They climb over the stone stile into the green lane. Look at the sunlight through that wall, Edith says. For centuries the drystone walls around here have been built with spaces, windows – wind eyes – to let the wind through, because things last longer with less resistance, because permeability, in the West of Ireland, is a virtue. They're a kind of stone lace, those walls, a tracery. Bare ruin'd choirs, she thinks. To love that well which thou must leave ere long. Enough of that. See those lambs, she says, is she feeding three, the one by the wall?

They stop to watch. The lambs are past the staggering stage now, playing their annual games on the mounds and dips of their field, knowledge somehow passed down like the skipping rhymes at school. Gallop to the top, quarter-jump, bleat, run away. It's like watching the kids in the playground, says Méabh,

Junior Infants. They won't see the age of five, says Edith, nor even two. Some of them, the boys – males – have crosses sprayed on their backs. They don't know, she thinks, sheep don't signify. One hopes. Not that that stops her eating lamb once in a while. Did you know, she says, that the French for a clover-leaf junction is saut de mouton, jump of a sheep? Do you think some civil engineer back in the day grew up on a sheep farm? She imagines him, the civil engineer, running a toy car around a toy motorway junction laid out on a shiny table in some French mairie, explaining to men in 1950s suits how cars will change direction at a hundred kilometres an hour without bumping into each other, the way lambs leap. What's a clover-leaf junction, Méabh says, and when Edith explains Méabh says there aren't any in Ireland which is, Edith says, not true, there's at least one on the M50, and then she starts to say that you can tell it's an unfamiliar idea because of the way they slow traffic to thirty as it merges with traffic going at a hundred and twenty and it's no wonder – shut up, she thinks, my lady, memsahib, in your English accent, you can go back where you came from if you don't like it here, if you want to give up Irish decency and democracy for English motorway junctions not designed to kill you. And she does like it here, very much, with Méabh, the sunlight dappling through the hazel trees, the cloud shadows drifting across the hills, even the slash of the Famine road across the valley, blurred now by rowan and birch, edges softening as old scars do. I see you, she thinks: starving men wasting the last of their blood on roads to nowhere, stones still now where skin-and-bone arms set them down two centuries ago; overseers who keep tongues like hers in their heads, well-dressed, sitting on restless horses. We are all descended from the survivors, who are not, Primo Levi who ought to know tells us, the true witnesses.

Stop tormenting yourself, says Méabh, I can see it in your face, you get a look. It's not the Famine road again, is it? It's a bit self-centred, you know, to take personal responsibility. We do know you haven't been stealing the wheat yourself. Sorry, says Edith, though she's not at all sure an English person, a person one of whose four passports is English, should be sorry for tormenting herself in the sight of the Famine road, though on the other hand maybe it's another act of colonial self-aggrandizement, the idea that her guilt is relevant, isn't colonial guilt part of the self-centred pathology of being white and English? And stop apologizing, says Méabh, it's very English, and Edith catches herself in time, which doesn't mean she's not sorry for being sorry. Englishness is Englishness, she thinks, and we all have to live with it, within and without. What's done is done.

They go on, up the green road, and then through the skewed iron gate into the hazel wood, where it's almost bluebell time, almost garlic time. Another week or two, says Edith, for the ramps, do you remember that pesto last year? She made it with hazelnuts, a gesture towards the local though the hazelnuts were from the supermarket and imported, Irish nuts not ripening with the garlic, and anyway served it with buckwheat pasta, pan-European, not really pesto at all. Of course, says Méabh, teach me this year?

The path is deeply worn between tree roots, slippery with mud as they make their way down towards the well. Ribbons flutter from the branches along the way, some ragged and faded, some new. There are prayer cards tied among the leaves, and laminated photos hanging like Christmas decorations. Edith waits for Méabh to step carefully down to the water, gleaming under the leaning grass. It's a spring, not a well, rising and bubbling from the earth. There are more personal objects in the trees overhanging the water, necklaces, scarves, hair-ties, handwritten prayers. Women's things, never a man's tie. They never see anyone else here. Méabh unhooks the cup from its nail, dips, drinks. Covid be damned. Edith offers a hand to help her back up the path, steps down herself as Méabh begins to pace seven clockwise circles, which is what you do here, what, Edith likes to imagine, people were doing here long before the Romans crucified a troublemaker at the other end of the sea. She doesn't go to church anymore, Méabh, but she's murmuring Hail Marys all the same.

my sister's habitat

I hung about inside the gate for a bit, because I wasn't entirely sure I had the right house and if there was a dog I wanted to be able to get back over sharpish, and then I jumped on the gravel a few times so that any dog would hear me and show up when I was expecting it, but the birdsong and the crickets went on and nothing changed so I set off up the drive, trying to remember that I was allowed to be there, that I was expected and in any case had nowhere else to go. The cedars were taller than any tree I'd ever seen, but the flowers in the grass were familiar: buttercups, daisies, clover, a scattering of purple orchids. The drive curved up the hill to another wrought-iron gate set into another pink stucco wall, and I stopped again to look for a bell but again there wasn't one, and this gate was ajar although loose on the hinges and heavy to open. I danced my jig on the gravel again. Still no dog, nor gatekeeper nor elf nor wizard. Even so, I approached the house on the grass, circumspect. The turquoise of a circular swimming pool blotted the lawn and there were orange and lemon trees along the terrace, fruiting and flowering at the same time. I paused to touch and smell – fancy having oranges growing outside your house like blackberries! What I had read about brides carrying bouquets of orange blossom made sense; their scent would recall any fainting soul. Glancing around, I picked a couple of oranges and stuffed them into my pack, so that if I did find myself sleeping rough I'd have something to eat. The house loomed before me, a lump of pink like a monstrous fancy cake, doors and windows narrow and arched. The shutters were open but I could see no movement within. I'll have to go back, I thought, I'll have to sleep under a hedge and hitch-hike my way back to Derbyshire and then what will I do, hang around the farm for the rest of the year. Or make my way to my mother, but though staying in a French artists' commune had some appeal she was not reliably pleased to see me even when she had arranged a meeting, and I understood that the unexpected arrival of a scruffy, hungry and patently English daughter might cause embarrassment. It was obviously necessary to be thorough in eliminating Maman's original plan first. And also, if Lydie is not here, where is she? Even so, I thought, back door for the likes of me.

There was a knocker, a shapely iron dolphin, on the back door, and a bell beside it, but I passed the windows of a kitchen first – pans hanging from a rack, shelves of plates and bowls to feed an army or at least a dinner larger than I'd ever attended – and saw someone inside. Not my sister. Kitchens were not my sister's habitat. I hesitated. An elderly woman, black headscarf, white apron, opened the window and said buon giorno, not apparently surprised but hardly welcoming. Buon giorno, I said, I am Lydia's sister. From England. Yes, she said, one moment.

The apron was gone when she opened the back door, which had not been locked. So, she said, come in. I am Signora Pilone. You can't tell, in Italian or for the matter of that any language I know other than English, if a woman's title indicates marriage or only maturity. I am Edith, I said, offering a hand which she did not take. It was dim and chilly in the hall. Marble floor, dark wood panelling, coat stand, could have been an English country house not that I'd been in many of those. Is my sister here, I asked. She was looking me up and down, grubby and crumpled, skirt too short, worn shoes. Army knapsack. You try, I thought, coming straight through by third-class train from London and we'll see how white your apron is when you get there. Signora Lydia is sleeping, she said, but from somewhere above my sister called Edith, you've come, I'll be down in a minute, I meant to come and meet you but I fell asleep. You wish to wash, said Signora Pilone, opening a section of the panelling to show me a lavatory, and when I saw myself in the mirror I could only agree.

I knew, of course, that Lydie would look different. The last time I'd seen her was at the party for the last night of Swan Lake, when she must have been already pregnant but only just, not showing and apparently unaware. But when she came into the sitting room where Signora Pilone had sent me, all trompe l'oeil nymphs and alarmingly large and low chandelier – nightmare to dust, surely – it was her familiarity that surprised me. She looked like the Lydia of six months earlier with a football under her frock, as if her condition were merely another stage prop. Naturally I had not seen many women so late in pregnancy and had perhaps overestimated its effect, but my sister crossed the room as lightly and neatly as ever, duck-footed still, her limbs and neck slender and poised. I'd often found her carriage annoying, thought it pretentious to take the laundry basket to the garden or cut bread for sandwiches as if you were miming for the Albert Hall, but for now affection welled. I pushed myself off the low sofa and leant over the bump for the bisous which were our habit, but I couldn't reach her cheek without our bellies touching and hers kicked mine. Bloody hell, our Lyd, I said, is that – Lovely to see you too, she said, yes, obviously it is. It kicks all the time. Keeps me awake. I stepped back, looked her up and down. Hoped I hadn't been secretly thinking that I might for a few weeks be prettier than my sister and only partly because I wasn't, because even weeks before giving birth she was untouchably glamorous, wearing a pleated black linen thing that on most people might have looked like a lampshade, the strands of hair falling from her chignon an artful softening of the severity of black linen and russet hair that looks implausible but is natural, seen also on Dad in my childhood and Gran in her youth, neither of whom could be suspected of dye. She'd refreshed her lipstick for me, which I found funny, but I looked away from her brutalized bare feet. How does it feel, I asked, the kicking? She shrugged. As you'd expect. As if there's an alien being trying to get out from under my ribs. Did she offer you tea, Mrs P? No, I said, it's all right, I don't want to give trouble. I had the sudden bleak thought that I would not be allowed to make myself a cup of tea when I wanted one, not for weeks or months. Nonsense, she said, that's what she's there for, she doesn't have anything else to do. If she's looking after this whole house, I wanted to say, she certainly does, but I wanted the tea too much and I let Lydia ring the bell, which was a mistake, it was obvious that Signora Pilone was no maidservant and when she appeared it was through the double doors from the next room, as if from the wings, in character, and the character was more Lady Macbeth than serving wench. I started stammering in Italian, if the signora would not be too much inconvenienced, if it might be possible, conditional tense creaking into action, but Lydie sighed and said tea, please, Mrs Pilone, on the terrace. She understands a bit of English, Lydie said as the doors closed behind the signora, enough to take orders, it's not as if Igor speaks Italian. When had my sister become someone who spoke so easily of giving orders? Come on, she said, you'll like the terrace, there's a lovely view and you can pick the oranges. I did not tell her that I had already picked the oranges.

The terrace ran the length of the house, a marble stage overlooking an arrangement of flower beds, the pool and well-groomed lawns dropping down to the lake, across the water to the mountains on the other side. The cypresses hid the road, and any other sign of humans on this side of the lake. Orange trees stood straight, about my height, in terracotta pots. There was a trellis; roses, blood-red, musk on the air. A cuckoo called, insistent as a ringing telephone. The sun had already dropped below the hill behind the house. I am an upland person. Our farm is high on the moor, nothing between us and the sky. It occurred to me that winter days on the lakeshore would be short, the sun's passage between the mountains brief. Lydie braced her hands on the arms of a metal chair and lowered herself, the kind of movement I had never seen her make before. Is it uncomfortable, I asked. She shrugged. Dancers, of course, are accustomed to discomfort. Pain is their bread and butter. Those little ones are called kumquats, she said, you can eat them whole, quite marmalade-y. Peel and all, I asked; I thought we'd outgrown playing tricks on each other but she's always enjoyed my provincialism. My naïveté. Cross my heart, she said, and I was leaning over the bush to pick the fruit as I had previously leant over my sister's belly to embrace her when Signora Pilone came carrying the tea-tray. Scusi, I said, going to help, passing cups and saucers, noting regretfully that there was no milk and only four small biscuits. She did not, I think, excuse me.

Lydia pulled around another chair and put her feet on it, where we both looked at them, twisted and scarred like the exposed roots of a tree. Is it uncomfortable, I wanted to ask again, but I said are they better for not dancing? Nothing is better for not dancing, she said, pass the biscuits please. I knew her well enough to take my share before passing the plate. Dad sends love, I said, and he said to tell you remember you can go home any time, no matter what, and Gran said, you'd not be the first nor last village girl to leave for London and come back with her tail between her legs and a bun in the oven, we'd manage. Lydie gestured, flickered her tail obscenely into being and we grinned at each other. She sipped her tea. Village girl, she said, yes, and also no, here is fine. Fair enough, I said, only I promised I'd tell you. Now you have, she said, and by the way the others will be back soon, they went for a walk. Others, I said, I thought – I mean, no one said – You didn't think I'd spend weeks here on my own, did you, she said, what on earth would I do, I'd go out of my mind, me and Mrs Pillars. They're my friends. I told them about the villa and there's a barn with a sprung floor, you'll see, meals and beds found, who wouldn't want to come? And me, I did not say, isn't that what I'm here for, to stop you going out of your mind? Does Igor know they're here, I asked. She shrugged. I'm sure Mrs Pillars has told him, she said, and he can't think I'd just sit here watching the clouds and waiting, they're all part of the company anyway. How many of them, I asked. Four, she said, at the moment, you've met Katja and Louise, and then there's Ed and Tom. Oh, I said, I'm not sure I remember. I had met lots of dancers at the party and been introduced to none of them. The whole point of the corps de ballet is that they all look the same, and their party clothes were almost as similar as their costumes, dull red or green dresses, collared and trendily trapezoid or egg-shaped in ways that only a dancer could wear. Lydie had left a biscuit and I took it. I was going to eat that, she said. Do you dress for dinner, I asked, though apart from the bare feet she seemed already dressed for dinner, or indeed for the opera or a particularly smart funeral. Tiaras will be worn, she said, penguin suits and décolleté all round. Is that your school hat? Tell you what, darling, why don't you have a bath and put on a fresh frock before the others come back. It was an uncharacteristically kind way for her to tell me that I smelt.

I had, Lydie told me, my own bathroom, or at least all the other bedrooms had en-suite bathrooms which meant that no one else would be using the one off the hall. The bathroom looked as I imagined a Turkish bath might, marble walls and floor and a marble bathtub that reminded me of the tomb of the third Lord Houghton in the church at home, though happily without the effigy. At least the loo and basin were made of ordinary stuff, but the overall impression was still that of a room carved out of Stilton cheese. The window was an uncurtained balcony door opening onto a stone terrace. I stepped out, exploring, and found that the adjacent bedroom also gave onto the terrace. I peered in; it looked like a stage set for Romeo and Juliet, with a draped four-poster bed, a generous fainting couch and a collection of imposing wardrobes and tables leaving plenty of room for a modest sword-fight and a pas de deux. One of my sister's entourage must have been staying there, but the only signs of occupation were a pair of men's shoes by the wardrobe, a bunch of the pink roses from the terrace in a glass vase on the bedside table and a red dressing gown hanging from the door.

The taps in my bathroom were set into the wall above the marble sarcophagus, looking more like a fountain than indoor plumbing. The hot water gushed almost immediately and at a volume that suggested plenty, but I had never filled a bath higher than my ankles in my life and this one was so large that even a very modest depth must mean a considerable cost in heating. It was a hot day, anyway, no need for more than taking the chill off cold water. I checked more than once that the door was locked and pulled off my clothes, which did indeed smell and looked very shabby thrown onto the deal chair. I'd mended some holes in my underthings but they were getting so worn that more darning would just make more holes, and the gingham dress showed where it had been let out and down as I finished growing. The other set were cleaner, but 'fresh' was an overstatement. Maybe Lydia would have some glamorous castoffs, maybe once she'd had the baby she'd discard her maternity clothes and I could somehow make them longer and narrower though I wasn't that good with my needle, a competent plain sewer, Gran said. And a competent plain knitter and a plain cook. I helped myself to a generous handful of what appeared to be lavender bath salts.

There was a full-length mirror behind the bathroom door. It can't have been the first time I saw my whole body naked, but it might have been the first time in some years. I cupped my breasts – they should fit, Lydie said, in a champagne coupe, but I had not seen a champagne coupe and imagined an ordinary wine glass, which seemed an unlikely and uncomfortable proceeding for which they were obviously too big. If you weren't a dancer, Lydie said, for most men too big was better than too small, especially if the rest of you wasn't fat. I'd always been built on a bigger scale than her, taller and broader in the hips and shoulders, taking after my father's Derbyshire farming folk while she, presumably, followed the maternal line for which we had only Maman's evidence. I ran my hands over the curve of my hips, up the softness of my inner thighs. Strong, I thought. Built for fells and weather, which you could say was better than being built for spinning in circles on your tiptoes and being carried around a stage holding your arms in a very straight line. I got into the bath with the water still running, leant back to put my head under the polished brass tap and let the cool water run into my eyes and ears and mouth.

I heard the others come in while I was arranging things in my room and I stayed where I was, not unpacking – it had taken me all of three minutes to hang up two dresses and put two jerseys and my remaining underwear in a drawer – but looking at all the knickknacks and ornaments, and at the pictures on the wall, none of which seemed likely to have been chosen by Igor. The room was elegant of course, parquet flooring, stone-mullioned arched door to a small balcony over the front door and sharing the view from the terrace, but the elaborate plasterwork ceiling was higher than the room's width and the walls were papered with a dark trellis pattern giving the impression of mesh fencing. The kidney-shaped dressing table was protected by a sheet of glass, on which clustered tarnished candlesticks, a brown glass tree with purple glass fruit hanging from it on metal hooks, some glass paperweights like overgrown marbles. If I'd had brushes and makeup and scent, there would have been nowhere to put them. Even the bedside table was covered in bronze ornaments, elephants and palm trees four inches high. I ran my finger along the sharp edge of a leaf. I wished I could put them all away, bundle them into the mirror-fronted wardrobe that loomed in the corner beside the narrow bed. I did not much want to go down and meet Lydia's glamorous friends, but nor was the room any refuge, and I was hungry. I'd write to Nancy: lucky I've more sense than to go looking for laundry lists and dead wives. I sniffed my wrist, which I'd sprayed with some perfume I found in the bathroom, lilies and overripe fruit, not Lydie's. I wandered out onto the balcony and hitched myself up to sit on the stone parapet, rough and warm through my skirt. The drop onto the marble terrace below was long enough. I could hear voices, the clink of glasses, laughter that was not English from the room below. The light was fading but the cicadas were still loud. Home felt very far away.

antiphonal

Edith wakes at dawn. She usually does; her bedroom faces east and there are no curtains in the cottage, so if there's morning sun it shines on her face. Her friends, here and visiting from Dublin, are dismayed: windows should be dressed, said Dearbhla, anyone could be looking in at you. Really, said Méabh, not even the bathroom? There's hillside outside her bedroom, just grass and rock, the bathroom window is high so a person would have to be very deliberate in his intention to glimpse the nakedness of an old woman, and for the other rooms she has never understood why people worry about passers-by – not that there are many passers-by – seeing clothed domestic life in progress. Better to have all the daylight you can get, better to have rooms clean and bare, than to hide your tea-making, your reading, your typing, from people who surely do the same things in the same way in their own houses. What is the shame in your daily business, that you fear your neighbour's glance? It's just nicer to have some privacy, Dearbhla says, that's all, and Edith thinks that privacy is a commodity only where there is belonging, that for the outsider whose neighbours already know her strangeness it is nicer to have sunlight. Mike used to insist that he couldn't sleep if there was morning light, if there was fresh air. He liked heavy dusty curtains, bedclothes over his head, blankets tucked in instead of duvets that could be kicked off, frowst and stuffiness. It had seemed exotic to her at the beginning, so much stuff, so much investment in bodily comfort. Only later, too late, had she returned to her own taste, the cold plainness of her childhood home. When he started to complain of draughts, she thinks, was the beginning of the end, though she is aware that she assigns this moment to different events according to her mood, and also he presumably has his own accounting. He was obviously more relieved than surprised when she said it at last, after another half-hearted disagreement neither of them could be bothered to win: I don't want to spend the remaining years of my life like this and I don't think you do either, we may not have long but we have long enough to try something else. Will we let each other go? Yes, he said, yes, all right, fine, it's a good thing we married in England, makes things much easier. I suppose we'll sell the house then, will we, half each and you can have the cottage if we keep the lawyers out of it? As if he too had already thought about it, had had Plan A in his back pocket all along, waiting only for her to take responsibility for saying it. Or more kindly, maybe more plausibly, he was not wanting to cause pain. How much earlier could they have freed each other? When he started to grunt every time he stood up. When he started to pick his ears in her presence. When she let him see her dipping her unwashed hand in the muesli jar to take more than a fair ratio of nuts, when she told him she'd do her laundry and he could do his own, when she stopped even bothering to tell him her plans for the weekend. Further back, when they stopped arguing, which was after they stopped having sex. There was probably a point where they chose or accepted the marriage's death sentence, where they could have sought counselling or gone travelling or taken tango lessons, only they didn't want to so there you go. They were able to part peacefully, which isn't nothing, as testament to a relationship. They don't hate each other. Plan A: always leave with regret.

She kicks off the duvet, gets up and opens the French window. There was rain in the night, wind singing under the eaves, and the grass is still sequinned but there's sunshine for now, even though she can see the next shower coming over the hill. She steps out, bare feet on cold stone flags, wind through rough silk pyjamas, breathes in for five heartbeats and out for five. The call and response of lambs and ewes sings across the valley, antiphonal. In for six, out for six. Rooks flustering around their tree. In for seven, out for seven. Kenny's tractor coming down the road, Mary's dogs barking. Her feet begin to hurt with the cold and she breathes into the pain for a bit, because she can, for practice, because pain isn't fear when you know what's causing it and when it's going to stop but at her age it's no bad thing to have the odd trick on hand for other kinds of pain which she doesn't pretend aren't coming her way. Yoga and sex don't give you immortality and that, she thinks, is quite enough of that for one day, memento mori, death greeted, now let's grind some beans. And then perhaps down to the beach, greet life in the North Atlantic.

bees had gathered

Sunrise so far south was late. I'd slept with the balcony doors open, imagining being woken by dawn coming over the mountain, but a cuckoo began to call before there was colour in the landscape, still too dark to see anything but the mesh of the wallpaper and the gleam of the mirrored wardrobe and the glassy possessions on the table at the end of the bed. I had slept fitfully, afraid of falling from the narrow, high bed, prodded by springs sticking through the mattress, bothered by the musty smell of a pillow softer than we had at home and by a bellyful of late and unfamiliar food, meat and oil and cheese. The cuckoo called again, very near. Cuckoo in the nest, I thought, my sister's nestling.

You'll go to Lydia at the end of the summer, Maman had written, in what must have been the aftermath of an announcement that largely passed me by. I was deep in revision for my A-levels, hadn't raised my head to see that there would be a summer after my exams, saw Lydie's news as the adults' concern, until Maman made it mine. *Je t'envoie*, she wrote; Igor is sending her to his house in Italy until it's all over. *Igor la met*. As if we were both corps de ballet, to be sent and put where it suited our directors, as if she had raised us to be passive. It will still be good for your Italian, Maman said, even if not as much as a few weeks with Teresa, I don't know how you passed the Oxford entrance exam but I suppose you're better at reading and writing than speaking. Lydie has been a fool about this, I can't think why she didn't sort herself out while there was time. *Mettre de l'ordre*, set things in order, tidy up. Her friends must know someone, it's a dance company. It occurred to me for the first time that perhaps my mother had also known someone, that she would, in Lydia's circumstances, have had no compunction about sorting herself out, bringing order. Even married and settled, simulating being settled, on the farm, it seemed unlikely that my mother had regarded babies with any enthusiasm. I would have gone looking for them after the war, she said once, I would not have given up, only I was pregnant and it was not permitted. She meant looking for her parents and her sister, who had followed the order to board the train to the camps. I wondered who in those days had been able to forbid Maman's wandering, because in my memory she acknowledged no authority. But it's illegal, I had wanted to say, to sort oneself out; I could imagine Maman's shrug. The law is made by men, she'd have said, the law is an ass. Rachel is carrying on, I'd overheard Gran say to Dad, like something out of a French novel, there's no reason our Lydie can't just come home and have her baby, we're in the 1960s not the 1860s, no call for all this nonsense about villas in Italy, for once in your life will you not tell her to stop play-acting? If it's what Lydia wants, Dad said, and then they heard me and stopped. If Gran read French novels, she did it when I wasn't there.

I sat up. The light was strong over the mountains to the east, a pale yellow glow edging the clouds above, but the trees were still dim and grey. The cuckoo called again, further away. I have made arrangements for the child, Maman had written. Call this number when it is born and ask for Sœur Mathilde. She will tell you how to proceed. I had seen a telephone in the hall, fixed to the wall like stag's antlers. I imagined myself standing there, making the call, Signora Pilone listening from the kitchen. And a baby, I supposed, crying upstairs.

I pushed back the scratchy sheet and the blankets and went out onto the balcony. From there I could see the lake, still as a pond, crepuscular, and the gardens where the roses and oranges were pale clusters on the dark shapes of trees and bushes. There was no wind, and then the edge of the sun breasted the summit opposite. Light cracked the sky and seeped into the woods and water. The wind began to breathe and the lake rippled pewter. Morning can be such a relief.

I went back into the room, where it was still night, and pressed the switch by the door which made something buzz and click before the electric light came on, yellow and dim. I tugged the wardrobe door, which also made a noise, and took out last night's clothes because I didn't know what the laundry arrangements might be and wanted to postpone asking for as long as possible. If laundry was sent out, I had no means of paying for mine, though the bath was plenty big enough for me to sort myself out. So to speak.

It's easy, I discovered, to move silently around a stone-floored house. The front door was locked but the heavy iron key was in it and the lock well oiled, though there was nothing I could do about the gravel path. I should have put on a cardigan. Brisk walk, I thought, soon warm you up. There was sunlight on the hillside now, my shadow taking shape, somehow comforting. I walked on the neat grass, leaving footprints in the dew, to the nearer gate, and then turned onto a track up the hill, found myself creeping past a cottage beside the empty stables, maybe where Signora Pilone lived. The crickets and birds had started their conversations and the air already seemed drier than it had on the balcony. I wasn't going far, not climbing the mountain, I just wanted the lay of the land. And to be away from the villa for a bit.

The track turned into a cobbled path, well made. The trees were too tall for me to see where the path went so I followed it to find out. Uphill, hairpins, and at the first bend a shrine before which someone had left a bunch of cornflowers and white roses in a blue glass. I stopped to look, remembered having read something about stations of the cross, though I had them confused with the Apostles, a baker's dozen, more or less, in both cases. My Christian education had been cursory, mostly daily hymn-singing at school with the Lord's Prayer twice a week, and occasionally I'd join Granny's more regular attendance if I fancied an hour or so in our medieval village church, incense-scented, dimly lit through sixteenth-century stained glass, Mr Galton the choirmaster and organist generally said to be far too good for us, a Cambridge organ scholar who had not been right since he came back from the war. When I went to church, I assumed when any thinking person went to church, it was for the beauty of holiness rather than because I believed any of it, though how I reconciled my passion for the poetry of Donne and Cranmer with my conviction that no intelligent person could ever have held the basic tenets of Christianity to be true I do not now recollect. There were, after all, plenty of mysteries in the adult world, plenty of hypocrisies no one tried to resolve.

The shrine was something between a signpost and an overgrown stone picture frame, holding a painting of men in robes doing, as far as I could see, nothing in particular, which was the subject of very many of the pictures and statues Maman had asked us to admire in art galleries and probably broadly the subject of Western art, give or take some bosoms and babies and the odd battle scene. I moved on briskly, humming, thinking how much easier it was to be alone than in company though also how much I would have liked Nancy to be there. And Dad would have liked to see this hillside, and would have been curious about the meadows I had seen on the mountains across the lake. Of course he couldn't leave the farm. I sometimes wondered if Maman had deliberately married a man who would never be able to accompany her roaming, but though she had brought us up on the story of their romance, his chivalrous rescue of the Jewish Cinderella, Lydia had planted in me the suspicion that she had married him mostly because she found almost anything preferable to paid domestic service. And fair enough, really. Maman had been my age when her place at the Sorbonne was replaced by a job as a live-in cook for a family in Sheffield as the ticket to safe passage out of wartime France. Her parents, having themselves been born in Kyiv and fled to Paris, were not among those who thought it couldn't happen there and to them.

Get the children out, at least, though in the event her sister, the first Lydia, left but then returned to her parents and was caught there, with them; she had fled only as far as Amsterdam where she would probably have met the same fate. There were British visas for domestic servants, not for philosophy students, and so my mother became a domestic servant despite her enduring ignorance of every form of housework and cooking. As my Lydia said, marrying anyone would have looked like a good plan, but Dad wasn't just anyone and he did love her, even Lydie couldn't doubt that. I didn't want to think about how I'd feel if someone – everyone – took away my Oxford place and made me choose between skivvying in another country and trying to survive Nazi occupation. Enough, there was the cuckoo again, and a rustling through the trees that was probably just a deer but could be a wild boar, un cinghiale, or even a bear. Orso, Latin ursus. If I ever had a son, I'd call him Orsino. Would Lydie be able to name her child, would Lydie's name go with the baby wherever the baby was going, like a token in a Shakespearean comedy? Could she, could we, give the child a locket or a ring? The cuckoo, again, sweat prickling on my back, and here was the next shrine, this time obviously Jesus dragging a cross too heavy to lift, and I wondered, if they were going to crucify him anyway, why go along with the ritual? It's not as if it would have been worse if he'd refused the whole performance, sat down on the ground and said go ahead then, kill me, make the sacrifice here and now, I'm not playing, the show won't go on. Maybe other saviours did, the ones we don't hear about.

I didn't bother to look at the other shrines. Who needs to see more tortured bodies, or the same body more tortured? I turned instead to the sunlight now filtering through the leaves, to the flowers at my feet and the butterflies attending to them, and when the cobbled path ended at a whitewashed chapel high on the hill I sat with my back to the church and looked down to the villa, to its miniature garden and round sapphire pool, the cypresses hardly the size of the plaster fir trees Granny and I used every year on the Christmas cake. Boats drew lines across the lake below like pins dragged over silk and I could feel my arms and legs and face drinking in sunshine, bathing in Italian light.

On the way down, I could see that the valley had woken up. Light flashed off the occasional car windscreen along the road. The ferries gathered at Bellagio where the Y-shape of the lake divides. The wind was warm now, hay and flowers on the air. I had noticed on the way up that the orchard above the house was weighted with apples, pears and plums; I stood on tiptoe for a huge pear, yellower than any I knew, heavy and sun-warm. I rubbed it on my dress. Not worth the growing, Dad said of pears, hard as granite until they rot, only good for chutney. I took a bite. Juice ran. Honey and some green, herbal flavour, a texture between liquid and firmness I'd never tasted before. I leant forward, so the juice would fall onto the grass and not my dress, understood why the bees had gathered with such passion about a windfall.

Morning, said a voice. Pear went the wrong way. Sorry, he said, oh dear. It was Lydie's friend Edmund, who'd sat beside me at dinner last night and taken a kindly interest. As long as I can cough, I reminded myself, my airway is not blocked. In my last term at school we could choose First Aid instead of tennis. I tried to inhale. Ed swung out of the plum tree and banged my back, which helped. I managed to swallow and started coughing again, wiped my streaming nose on the back of my hand. My lungs tasted pear. Sorry, he said, only it seemed ruder to stay up there watching you. I'm all right, I wheezed, then another paroxysm came and he banged my back again, until masticated pear fell out of my mouth. There we go, he said, better out than in, as the actress said to the vicar. Recovering now? Yes, I said, thank you. I was still holding the rest of the pear. I swallowed, breathed, took a cautious bite. They are good, aren't they, he said, and you must have a plum. Or three. Only they're so ripe some of them burst when you pick them. Ripeness is all, I said. Men must endure their going hence even as their coming hither. I'd managed to get it into my Oxford entrance exam, my idea that Lear is a darker play than Hamlet. Readiness is all, Hamlet says, and readiness is voluntary, an act of will, where Lear's ripeness happens to us as to plums and pears, regardless of agency or volition. Though the idea had limits, I realized standing in the orchard; it's all very well for Edgar to talk to elderly Gloucester about ripeness but Hamlet dies young, unripe, in which case maybe readiness is the best you can do but still more submission to the inevitable than volition. The inevitability of Hamlet's death was a matter about which I could have talked for a long time, but probably not, I thought, with Ed; I had tried him on poetry at dinner. Dancers, in my experience, aren't much interested in words and don't sit still long enough to read. That's Shakespeare, he said, isn't it? Lydie said you're brainy. I'm going to Oxford next year, I wanted to say, because it still didn't seem real to me. I'm going to wear a gown and spend my days reading in beautiful old buildings. I just like reading, I said, and I can't dance, I don't even really like music. I shooed a wasp away from my pear and took a bigger bite. Everyone likes music, Ed said, you mean you don't like ballet music, there must be something else. No, I said, I mean I prefer silence, I prefer silence to all music. I wait for it to stop. I quite like watching ballet and I see you need the music to keep time but I wouldn't want to sit there and listen with nothing to watch. Folk songs, he said, popular music, jazz, hymns? Christmas carols? I could feel the coughing wanting to start again. The pear was so soft I went ahead and ate the core, leaving just the stalk to twirl in my fingers. No, I said, jazz induces murderous inclinations, the way it plinks about and never goes anywhere. I like some carols and hymns but mostly for the words. What about birdsong, he said, waves on the shore, wind in the trees, I bet you don't mean real silence. I don't think you ever get real silence, I said, and we both listened. The silence of the grave, I thought, the rest is silence, and I wondered what Lydie's baby could hear. Another of her friends, Tom, had played the grand piano in the villa's sitting room after dinner and she'd said the baby moved to the beat, that it seemed to have a better sense of rhythm than I, for example, did, and Katja had said it must be used to Lydie's heart, which I thought unkind under the circumstances. I think liking or not liking those sounds would be like liking or not liking air or water, I said, they're life, of course I like them. Have a plum, he said, and I took one, warm as a new-laid egg, from his hand. But you probably don't like sirens, he said, or drilling, or the through train going past you on the platform, and you might really hate people chewing or scrumpling paper. Sawing, actually, I said, especially if it squawks. There you go then, he said, you do like music, you have preferences. And I bet you can dance. He looked me up and down, that awful dress and I hadn't brushed my hair. Not before breakfast, anyway, I said.

Back at the villa, I followed Ed round to the terrace, avoiding passing Signora Pilone's lair. The morning sun was strong on the gardens and the pool twinkled. Come for a swim, Ed said, after breakfast? I thought of my swimming costume, which still had my house badge sewn above the breast, and covered me from mid-thigh to neck though I was aware that on any close inspection worn patches undermined the modest impression. One of the girls will lend you a bathing suit, he said. Not if they want it back in wearable condition, I said, I'm twice their size, and then I minded when he didn't object.

My sister sat at the table where we'd had tea, her feet up on another chair. She wore a pale pink silk dressing gown that I remembered Maman giving her for Christmas – I had flannel pyjamas – necessarily open over a patently-not-virginal white lawn nightie. Tom, more or less properly dressed, sat opposite, neither of them watching Katja and Louise who were dancing, or at least practising, barefoot on the lawn below. Pliés, I thought – I had got that far myself, at Mrs Fanning's Saturday classes which Maman wanted me to take too. Her mother, she said, had insisted on dance lessons for her and the first Lydia, ballet along with piano and violin in the Haussmann apartment in 1930s Paris, a rare glimpse of her girlhood. Not everyone will be a dancer, she said, but every woman can learn to move gracefully, it is always possible to be elegant, the kind of statement I wanted to contradict – what about stuffing a chicken, what about brushing your teeth – until I remembered what 'always' meant to Maman. Mothers danced and sang with their children in the queues for the gas chambers, did you know that? Elegance can be the counterweight to fear. We defy augury. Morning, said Tom, don't tell me you've climbed a mountain already. There's coffee in the pot.

We had coffee at home only when Maman was there, and I hadn't overcome its bitterness. There didn't seem to be tea, and I didn't like to ask, so I let Ed pour coffee and filled up the cup with milk and three spoons of sugar. Breakfast appeared to be a large sponge cake and bread rolls with pale butter and apricot jam. Poor Edie, said Lydia, all she wants is a nice cup of tea and a kipper with a boiled egg. Not kippers, I said, that's just for Sundays and special occasions. If the men hadn't been there, I'd have said what's wrong with eggs for breakfast anyway, you grew up eating them same as I did, you used to go out to the henhouse with the basket. You used to eat like the rest of us, speak like the rest of us.

Katja and Louise moved together, as if pulled by one set of strings, left legs sweeping above their shoulders, arms brushing the blue sky. Practice clothes, tights and leotards, tiny skirts. Poor Lydie. They're just playing, said Ed, there's a proper sprung floor and a barre in the old barn. Just showing off, I thought, more like, but Lydia swigged her coffee, stood up and made her way down the steps. Lydie, I called, don't. Lydie, please, you'll hurt yourself. Or hurt the baby, but I wasn't sure how much she might mind about the baby.

She dropped the silk gown on the grass, and after a horrible moment I saw – we all saw – that at least she had her knickers on under the nightie, and though it looked indecent one had to remember that she'd appeared on stage before royalty wearing less. Katja and Louise moved apart, flanked her. The three of them, their three shadows beside them, dipped and rose. Don't run, Lydie, I said, don't jump, please don't jump, because it seemed obvious that she and the baby would come apart if she jumped, unravel like a badly made parcel, and also, as three legs twisted, three backs curved, three arms reached, that the dance would lift her, that she must fly as she had flown, that she almost as much as her baby was being danced, but there was no jump, only flowing and shimmering, the white nightdress fluttering at her belly, and soon all three linked hands, real smiles replaced the dancers' rictus and they dropped into deep curtseys among the buttercups. Lydie, I said, you mustn't, really, surely your doctor said – hush, said Ed, drink your coffee, Edith, that's enough.

I saw that there was something I had not understood, some grown-up or dancing thing, and I shut up, but as my sister returned breathless to her chair and the others resumed their routine, the idea of the doctor persisted. There must be someone, in the village or the next village. Women, after all, have babies everywhere. But as far as I knew, Lydie had no Italian; was it part of my job, to translate? There would be words I hardly knew in English, words for what I had never named. Maman was in Israel when I first had the curse, and it was Gran who showed me what to do. My down-theres. My underneaths. You couldn't grow up on a farm and not know how mammals are conceived and born, but it was hard to imagine my sister about that bloody process. I watched her stretch her arms over her head, tilt her pretty neck one way and then the other, full of grace.

those unheard

She doesn't often see Gunter outside. Only on the doorstep, hail and farewell, but she recognizes him half a mile off, the height and the walk long before the face or the clothes, which are more colourful than is the way of men around here. He swoops along, his steps wing-beats, as if the compromise is the touch of his boots on the ground rather than the motion through air, fast, of course, he was always fast, never knew the ballast of wife or child though the pots, surely, are heavy enough, enough years at the wheel. A man of earth and fire, she supposes, though you wouldn't think it to look at him. She picks up her own pace, waves, suffers a sudden doubt, perhaps not him after all, though no one else walks like that and even if they do if he's a local man they'll be stopping for a chat anyway and if he's a visitor she'll never see him again so who cares, really, and look it is Gunter, red coat, that stride. She catches herself arranging her face and tries not to. Rain's coming on but it's salt spray in her hair. Sea pinks ruffle along the roadside, and the light on the sea shifts as if a stagehand in the gods has changed it. Birds, incoming across the waves, and across the water the cliffs fall dark as the weather moves in. Here's her favourite stone bench, one of her favourite stone benches, where she can sit a long time watching but she doesn't, somehow, want to sit and watch with him so she keeps going, into the wind. Hallo, he says, still after all these decades the German vowel, and she says hello, good afternoon – not in your studio then, she doesn't say, because it's not a job, is it, he can be there when he feels like it, only somehow that's where she keeps him, in her mind, during the day. He puts his arm around her shoulder, bends to kiss her cheek, bristles and cold and damp. One of the big green vases broke in the kiln, he says, and it broke some of its neighbours. So he left.

It happens, with pots. Probably with most of the plastic arts, the material follows its own rules, there's an air bubble or a flaw in the rock or the wood formed in a way you hadn't fully understood and so your idea cannot take shape, and she wonders, as she hugs him back, what the dancer's equivalent is. She never heard Lydia, or any other dancer, speak contentedly of her own performance, always there was some mistake, some failure, some small betrayal of muscle or nerve, rarely apparent to any but the most expert audience. Was Lydia's body her material or her instrument? If the dancer's body is her instrument then her material is the performance; transient, traceless movement through time and space. And clay, she thinks, lives in its own relation to time, earth preserved by fire, dissolution aborted, pots outlasting makers and owners, urns outlasting mourners and ashes, by centuries, by millennia. Foster child of silence and slow time, cold pastoral; as Keats saw, the Grecian urn is almost-dead in its almost-changelessness. She hadn't thought of that poem as quite so literally about the potter's art. Or the potter's craft or even science, really, glazing and firing, technology against death. Or against life, if change is life and perfection death, because the problem with the urn is its perfection. Heard melodies are sweet, but those unheard are sweeter. The best art is what you can't make. Thank God for a memory furnished before the internet took over remembering, because it's all very well, knowing where to look, but the internet won't tell you what you're looking for, the internet isn't going to suggest Keats when you're standing by the Flaggy Shore talking about a mishap in a kiln. I'm sorry, she says, but isn't it also a bit reassuring, that even pots participate in brokenness? I mean, think of all the potsherds in the ground from all the things humans have broken pretty much since we started controlling fire, it must be one of the oldest makers' experiences. Fucking frustrating, he says. Do you know how many hours I spent on that vase? And it took out at least two hundred euro of jugs and mugs for the gallery.

He takes her hand and they walk on, his direction, back the way she came, which she doesn't mind, not really, she was only going over to town to buy boring things from the supermarket and who wouldn't rather have a while longer on this shore? Slow down, she's too proud to say, wouldn't mind so much feeling like a child trotting at his side but does mind feeling like a hurried old lady. Lengthen her stride, deep breaths, she can keep up.

She sings as she drives. The car has a radio but nothing can replace Radio 3, and even after thirty years she'd rather have nothing than an ersatz substitute. I can set it up for you, Méabh said, you just stream via your phone, it's not hard. It will be hard and anyway she doesn't drive enough to bother; rarely, these days, leaves North Clare. Jerusalem the Golden, with milk and honey blest. There's a particular pleasure in belting out English patriotism in the privacy of the car, singing the old numbers from Hymns Ancient and Modern at which she would wince and whimper under all other circumstances. Devil has all the best tunes, though sometimes she sings the Devil's other playlists, songs to which she has no right, with indiscriminate defiance. Up the Ra, Come Out ye Black and Tans. Glorious things of thee are spoken, Zion city of our God to the tune of Deutschland über Alles. Allons enfants de la Patrie, which she used to sing to provoke Pat when he was slow leaving the house or getting out of the car. (You English, always getting.) I vow to thee my country, not that she can hit the high notes but the attempt reminds her of the Queen of the Night so she has a go at that while she's about it and makes a noise that even she doesn't enjoy. And for a rousing finale, did those feet in ancient time. Always, she thinks, suspect the word *ancient*. Like *natural*, it means there's mischief afoot. It means politics. Natural, must remember the yogurt, not that the other kind is unnatural.

Speaking of which, what's this? People in the road, here? It's miles from town, miles from anywhere. She slows down. Tractors, a crowd, placards. In Ireland, especially this part of Ireland, the absence of people of colour doesn't necessarily mean the mob is frightening the way it would in most of Europe. A community will turn out to prevent an eviction and it works, often enough. Sometimes you have to take to the streets. Miners' strike, though looking back she wonders a bit about that, fossil fuels, coal smoke, Pat in the pram, the lovely old coach-built pram, jumble sale, wouldn't have fitted in any car. Poll tax. Maggie Maggie Maggie, out out out. Better songs at Greenham Common, for sure, back in the days before she turned to Mike and the consolations of bourgeois security. Good thing his mother never heard about Greenham, not that she'd have understood, and Mike in those days liked her bolshiness, her actually very mild and probably hereditary urge to épater la bourgeoisie. In some ways, given where she'd come from, marrying Mike and settling down in the Marital Home in South County Dublin was among the most rebellious choices she could have made. Thatcher and the Falklands, she and Priya chanting and pushing Pat and Priya's twins in their prams past Marble Arch, a man scolding them for putting anti-war badges on the pram hoods, inflicting politics on their children, he'd said, as if any child could avoid politics. She pulls over, maybe someone needs help, though it's not likely she can provide any assistance not already available at younger and stronger hands. Unless someone needs protecting from those hands, lend her white lady privilege, what else is it for? Repeal the Eighth, she still has the T-shirt. They can bury her in it, give the churchyard worms a shock, and she wonders, in this country where people visit the dead before burial, where caskets are open until the last minute, does anyone ever wear a protest T-shirt? Motorbiking leathers, surely team kits for sports? Suits for men, she's seen always, women in their dullest dresses, usually a rosary around cold fingers. Bury me in scarlet, she thinks, in my dancing shoes, though she gave away the last of her party clothes after lockdown, no more dancing for the cocooning generation, no more silk around the legs or unseemly cleavage. She gives them a little squeeze as she gets out of the car, always had nice tits and they haven't gone as far south as— How are ye, he says, the nearest man. Jeans, plaid shirt, forties, could be anyone but that's a Dublin accent, which is a shame because to many of the locals in these rebel counties her own voice could as easily be South Dublin as Derbyshire, West Brit as Brit, she can almost pass, but he will know. Grand, she says, how are ye. It's not a question. How do you do, comment allez-vous, no one wants to know. What do we have here, she wants to ask, what's going on, what do you think you're doing, but they're not questions she can ask in her English voice. Lady Muck. It's a damp day, she says, to be out. They're people of a certain age, this crowd, not habitual protestors. She could teach them a thing or two. One woman went to Greenham, went to Greenham Common, one woman and her Co-op bag, went to Greenham Common. Back when a supermarket bag was innocent, when the bomb still seemed like a decision that might be unmade. One of the placards, held at an uncertain angle, says Locals Only. Hay bales wrapped in tattered black plastic block the boreen which leads, she thinks, only around the fields, must be a farm or two along it, has there been one of those rural murders that slashes the community and takes generations to heal, some man, some jealous brother or son, ending the argument about who inherits the farm with a gun? The Irish zeal for land ownership is postcolonial. Few rights of way, no public access to the hills, living in apartments is for immigrants, Irish people want to own the ground under their feet and to say who is allowed to go there. Who is allowed to see in. We know whose fault that is, eight centuries of dispossession. Oh, and it's Méabh. Méabh, what's going on, what's happened?

Hello to you too, says Méabh, air-kissing, damp cagoule, hair electric, but she looks uncomfortable. Sheepish, even. Not part of her natural range, like a dodgy alto tackling the Queen of the Night. Edith recognizes some of the others, Seamus from the shop and Eilidh who sometimes comes to yoga. Isn't it our turn for some sunshine, Méabh says, even an hour or two to lift the spirits? Sure, Edith says, but what's with the signs? Méabh fiddles with her hair. There's a bit of an issue, she says, looking away. Right, says Edith. Well, says Méabh, they're after bussing seventy-five poor lads down from Dublin and putting them in the old hotel, and it's not safe, you know yourself how it is walking these roads and how else are they to go anywhere, and it's a septic tank down there, not been maintained since the hotel closed, imagine when it leaks, and the doctor already run off her feet, people she's been seeing all their lives waiting days for appointments and they'll be needing all sorts, won't they, won't have seen a doctor in years, it's not right, there's been no consultation. Eimear and her friends train up and down this lane, says Eilidh, and I'm not being funny, I'm sure they're nice enough lads but lads all the same, watching our girls in their shorts. Coming from Africa, you know yourself the ideas they have about women over there. The Ukrainians are one thing, women and kids, we all understood that, but this— The place is just already full, that's the long and short of it, why don't they keep them up in Dublin if they're so welcome? Edith closes her eyes. This. This. This again, here.

Edith, says Méabh, Edith, it's for the lads themselves as much as anything. I doubt they mean our girls any harm, no more than any other men would, cooped up without women, but they've nothing to do and we've nothing for them, you know that, we can't house our own. Imagine being stuck out here, what are they to do? There's no shop, no pub, and the hotel's a wreck, holes in the roof, you know the chimney came down over the winter, they shouldn't be asking anyone to live like that, you know they're not allowed to work, they'll be so isolated. There've been suicides, you know, in some of these places.

Edith knows her lines, should have known that sooner or later she'd have to say them here. Africa, she says to Eilidh, is larger and more culturally diverse than Europe, I have no idea what these young men think about women and nor do you, but I would imagine they have more urgent things to worry about than the Holy Cross under-sixteen camogie team. And you must be able to see the area isn't full, it's been depopulated for the last century and more, aren't there derelict houses and pubs closed everywhere and schools about to close until the Ukrainians came? These young men are here, she says, because it's better for them than the alternative, because there is no alternative. No one becomes a refugee for fun. What if the places they're coming from are so dangerous, so impossible, that a derelict hotel on a dangerous road in a place you're not wanted is obviously better? Then it's still not good enough, says Méabh, they shouldn't be here, it's wrong for them and wrong for us.

Us, Edith says.

Yes, us. Including the Ukrainians. They didn't try to put them out here, did they, the government, they put them in the towns, even though some of them have cars, they put them where the kids could go to school and the mothers could find work and they could walk to the shops and the church if they wanted it and the GAA, why shouldn't these ones get the same? Because there's no more of the same, Edith thinks, because we, whoever we are, prioritized the white Christian mothers and children, and here we are back in the story of scarcity, as if there isn't enough to go round though the country's rich, among the richest, taxes in surplus, like most shortages the problem is distribution not supply. But Méabh's not wrong about the doctor and as far as she knows there simply isn't another building available and it's the same all over the country, hotels closed for tourists which was all very well during the pandemic when they weren't coming anyway, suited everyone, income for the hotels and accommodation for the Ukrainians even though no one really wants to live in a hotel, especially not with kids and not for weeks becoming months becoming years, but now – everyone needs the tourists and the tourists need the hotels and every house is full and no one can afford to build partly because of the war in Ukraine affecting supply chains and partly because we're running out of oil to transport the materials and what are we to do? But Méabh, she says, imagine those lads in there, how cold and scared they must be, they must have come down the road and found you here. They have, says Méabh. No one threatened them. No one even said anything. It's not personal, no one wishes them any harm. They saw us and they went back in. She lifts her chin.

How long are you planning to stay here, Edith wants to ask, what will you do next, what do you expect them to do, and she wonders about going up the road, if they'll let her through, if she's local enough, maybe on the way back, take some food to the young men, scones or brown bread, something Irish. Would it do any good, help anyone? They don't need scones, certainly don't need an old white lady saviour, they need a place of safety, and then healthcare, education, work. Dignity, independence, inasmuch as any of us has or should have independence. What Maman needed when she arrived in Sheffield in 1941, probably the same age as some of these unseen lads, probably carrying the same shame and fear, probably similarly feeling that she had abandoned and also been abandoned by her parents. It runs in families, abandonment, once established. Oh, shut up, she thinks, this isn't all about you, their drama is not yours.

I don't think it's OK, she says to Méabh, any of it. It's not good.

She finds herself shaky, nauseous. What words to set upon the air, between friends! *It's not good*. Especially here, where direct speech is not done. The Irish have registers of expression above the range of immigrants' hearing and that's where they say you're wrong, what you're doing is bad. She's spent half her adult life not saying what she thinks, not speaking as she finds, standing quietly in corners compromising and colluding as fast as she learnt how. And here she is crude, English, colonial. And right. What has she done to Méabh, to their friendship, but also what else could she have done? There are, it seems, lines she will not cross. There are, must be, limits.

She gets back into her car and sets off, changing gear too fast, before Méabh can say, it's all very well for you to say that, isn't it, with two bedrooms and a bathroom sitting empty in your house.

he giveth his beloved

I had, it seemed, nothing to do, which had never happened before. Dad didn't exactly expect me to work on the farm but I had my jobs – hens, mostly – and there was always something needing done. Granny did most of the housework and cooking during term but expected my participation at weekends and in the holidays. You'll have to look after this place or another eventually, she said, easier if you know how, and anyway these bones aren't getting any younger. Don't want you turning out like your mother, she meant, higher education's all well and good but someone has to be able to put a meal on the table and wash the clothes. The Devil finds work for idle hands, and neither women's nor farmers' work is ever done, and between that and my school work I had never been at a loss. It wasn't that Dad and Granny disapproved of reading, but I learnt early that it was best to take a novel up to the attic, where I had a nest of cushions by the chimney breast, or in summer out onto the moor Brontë-fashion, to avoid someone suggesting a more productive activity. When you finish that chapter, Edie, I could use a hand in the barn. If you've time to sit about this afternoon, the hall floor wants a wash. We left the sitting about to Maman and Lydie, who appeared as unexpectedly as angels and were about as much practical use.

And now at the villa there was a girl, I thought younger than me, who came from the village to wash floors and help Signora Pilone with the laundry. You put your dirty clothes, Lydie instructed me, in the basket in your bathroom, see? And in a day or two you'll find them washed and ironed and folded on your bed. Honestly, haven't you been anywhere? She knew I had not been anywhere, only sometimes to stay with her in her digs in London, and therefore she knew also that I knew that she washed her clothes in her landlady's scullery, put them through the mangle and hung them to dry in the sooty garden, where the whites turned grey, or over the radiator in her room where they often began to smell damp and she wore them anyway. Igor might buy her perfume and take her out for champagne but she mended her own stockings and walked to save the bus fare like everyone else.

I had not even tried to go into the kitchen, though I would have liked to make some toast, salt the butter and boil an egg the way I wanted it, without slime, for breakfast. The doors were always closed, and if ever I knocked – when one of the others sent me to ask for an unscheduled sandwich or glass of milk, because dancers are always hungry and Lydie's appetite was capricious – Signora Pilone stood blocking the way. Sì, signorina, lo porterò. She would bring it. There was no call for me to hang around. I would have liked to be able to write to Granny about the kitchen, which would have interested her much more than my lyrical accounts of sunrise and birdsong. Granny was a creative cook, had never allowed kitchen work to become mere drudgery. She had always kept a herb bed, asked Maman for details she couldn't give about the food she ate in France and Israel, read the Elizabeth David Maman gave her for Christmas with interest although she had no access to most of the ingredients required. Her standby cake for the WI teas was a nut-filled gingerbread passed on by a Dutch neighbour who'd married one of my grandfather's friends after he was involved in liberating Amsterdam. I might one day see if I could soften Signora Pilone by asking her how she made a cheesecake oddly similar to Granny's curd tart, but whenever I actually encountered her that day receded. I could have fed the hens who lived in a well-defended henhouse by the orchard, or gathered their eggs. I'd have quite liked to polish the brass handles on the sideboards in the dining and drawing rooms, because they were mucky and it annoyed me, but I didn't dare ask. While I was taking my exams I would have said that several weeks in an Italian villa with nothing in particular to do would be heavenly, beyond imagining, but in the event it took me only a couple of days to achieve boredom, the first of many new experiences that summer.

Help your sister, Maman had instructed, but I could not see what help was required. Lydie seemed remote, replete. She liked to sit on one of the wickerwork chaises longues in the sun on the terrace, somnolent as a reptile, with her feet up, her belly growing like rising bread. She had several pots and tubes of scented creams which she rubbed over her arms and legs, around her neck. Another dancer in the company had left to have a baby, a married woman for whom it was no scandal though Lydie and her friends seemed scandalized. Alice, Lydie reported, had developed varicose veins, even though she was only twenty-five. She and Katja and Louise shuddered, shimmied their shoulders in synchronized horror. The veins seemed more upsetting than the baby. Alice had returned afterwards but for only one season. She said it was too tiring, Katja said, she said her husband didn't see the point, but – well, she made her choice. I'll be back, Lydie said, craning over her stomach to put the cream on her calves. Nutcracker, remember?

Lyd, I said, let me do that for you, you'll do yourself a mischief squashing it like that. Do yourself a mischief, repeated Katja. She had grown up in Lyons with Russian Jewish parents who had got out just in time and her accent reminded me of Maman. Northern phrase, I said, another one for your collection, do give over, our Lyd. Stop being annoying, Lydia said, but sure, you can do it if you like. She passed me the pot, opaque glass like a bathroom window, heavy as a paperweight, and I perched at her feet and dipped my fingers. The smell delighted me, more herbal than floral, bright green. Not that much, she said, Igor's generous but there are limits. Oh yes, said Louise, very generous indeed, and they all giggled. I know what you mean, I wanted to say, I'm not stupid, but I had no idea what they meant and I was hourly reminded that despite the evidence of my Oxford entrance exam there were ways in which I was very stupid. Igor gave this to you then, I said, as if Igor had not given her almost everything she possessed, including her place in the company and the promise of a soloist's part in the winter's Nutcracker, which seemed to me an odd exchange for a baby. Who else, she said, gentle upward strokes, darling, and whatever it is you're about to say about my feet, don't. I didn't.

Katja stood up. I'm off to practise in the barn, she said. Lydie never went there, but I watched them sometimes. The barn was like a church, high-windowed, full of light and air, and even I could tell as I walked across the floor that the gravity it held was less than elsewhere, that it had been built to launch and spring. I liked to watch the girls, to marvel at what their bodies could do that mine could not, but more than that I liked to watch Tom and especially Ed, whose jumps seemed even more remarkable than the way Louise could spin and spin en pointe, the way Katja flew in Tom's hands, as if it was his job to keep her airborne on his fingers. Ed, I thought, could almost take flight along the beams of the afternoon sun with his shadow kingfisher-swift across the whitewashed wall. I saw exactly why my grounded, landlocked sister did not go there. I moved my finger pads in small circles up from her ankle and reached the other hand towards my own calf, wondering how different it could be, how legs made by walking were different from legs made by dancing. I'll be off too, said Louise, see you at dinner.

I watched her cross the lawn. Whatever Maman said about elegance, ballet dancers walk like waterfowl. Earth is not their element. I screwed the lid back onto the pot of lotion. Lyd, I said, could you swim, are you allowed? She leant back, lifted her newly ample chest towards the sky. There would, I thought, be an issue about milk, wouldn't there? Would she feed the child herself? Either way we would have a problem sooner or later; I had seen cows with mastitis. I wish you'd stop talking about what's allowed, she said, I'm a grown woman, I do what I like.

And I don't want to go swimming, you go ahead. Don't you think it would feel nice, I said, kind of weightless? She closed her eyes. You can't be kind of weightless, she said, you're the one who's supposed to be good with words. A thing is either weightless or not and I'm definitely not. You swim if you want to.

I hesitated. Help your sister, aide ta sœur. I didn't think I'd been much use at all, so far, and leaving her lying on her own in the sun like a stranded whale didn't seem particularly like help. Not that my sister usually found succour in the fact of my company. Go on, she said, swim. I stood up. Would you like me to, I don't know, read to you or something? She sighed, half-opened her eyes. I'm pregnant, she said, not blind or stupid, if I want to read I'll read, it's probably about the only thing I can do just as easily now as before. Go swim, Edie, leave me alone. I'll keep an eye on you in case you need rescuing.

I went in to change. It was cooler in the house, and seemed dark after the sharp light outside. The girl from the village was sweeping the stairs. Buon giorno, I said, and she startled. Scusi, I said. I wanted to introduce myself, ask her about her life. Did she go to school, was this her summer job? Was there a school in the village or did she, enviably, take the boat across the lake every morning? Did she walk with her friends sometimes on Saturday afternoons, as Nancy and I did? Mi chiamo Edith, I said. My name works in French, which is why Maman agreed to Dad's choice, Lydia for her sister who died in Belsen and then Edith for his aunt, Granny's sister who died more comfortably of cancer the year I was born. But the Anglo-Saxon 'th' has no Italian rendition. Editta. Dita. Maybe at Oxford I would say, my friends call me Dita. The girl glanced up, nodded and returned

73

to her sweeping. I lacked the courage to persevere, and continued to my marble bathroom where I put on my swimsuit and then paused. Surely, in this house of dancers, it would be all right to cross the house and garden in a suit that was after all more modest than many ballet costumes? All right for the dancers, maybe, who breakfasted in their dressing gowns and wandered around in practice clothes at all hours, but there was the girl on the stairs, who was wearing a skirt longer than any I owned with a long-sleeved blouse on a hot day, and Signora Pilone who was invariably dressed in black from neck to ankle. I dropped my frock back over the swimsuit.

Lydie pushed herself up on her elbows to watch me, barefoot, trying to cross the gravel between the terrace and the pool. The stones were hot as well as sharp underfoot and every instinct told me not to take another step. You'd make a terrible dancer, she said, it's just a bit of pain, it won't even last. I would that, I said, things hurt for a reason. That particular thing will hurt a lot longer if you faff about like that, she said, but I did it my way, and when I came to the water I did that my way too, inch by inch, because though it wasn't exactly cold it was a lot colder than both the air and my skin. Just jump in, she said, dive, why don't you, it's deep enough, you're like a little old woman. You've lived in London too long, I said. Little old woman indeed, have you met Granny? Or any of the WI, come to that? I'd never seen Granny swim, but she went about her business, including walking the mile to the village, in all the weathers and seasons of the High Peak, as did almost all the older women thereabouts. If they'd seen reason to walk into icy water it would have been done without hesitation. OK, Lydia said, then you're like a little girl, mincing and creeping, just get in. Shut up, I muttered, knowing she was too far away to hear. What was that, she said. I took another step, which brought the water to my waist and made me suck in my diaphragm, as if I could hold my skin from the water into which I was walking. Shut up, I said, louder. God, you really are a little girl, she said, can you imagine what people will think of you at Oxford if that's your idea of debate. I turned back to face her. That's not my idea of debate, I said, what would be the point in trying to have a debate with a— with a fat ballerina, I was about to say, but I saw Tom coming around the corner from the barn and stopped myself. I put my hands in the water and stroked its surface, which was deceptively warm. Brava, Tom called, you're really going in. I let myself fall backwards. Cold splashed over my brain. The pool wasn't big enough to get going but I did a few strokes on my back and then balanced my arms and legs and head on the water and floated, chill at my back and sun on my front, eyes clenched against the light, getting used to it. Tom's shape stood above me and I flipped onto my front, let my legs sink through the layers of coolness, kicked. How bad is it, he asked. Lovely, I said, once you're in. And probably very good for you. His feet were at my eye level, and I thought I'd never looked properly at a man's feet before, wondered were they different from women's, would a doctor or an archaeologist know from a foot what was at the top of the leg – my gaze began to follow my mind upwards before I blushed, pushed off, swam a splashy width. Across the terrace, Lydie had sat up, belly resting between her spread legs on the chaise longue. Poor Lyd, of all the people to find herself distended, grounded like a broken bird. Hapless, I thought, flightless, as if waiting for the predator to turn up, no wonder she was grumpy. I turned around to see Tom pull off his sleeveless vest, sweat-stained from dancing. Stand back, he said, pointed his hands above his head, bowed down and glided under the surface without a splash, like a needle pushed into fabric, and as if completing the stitch he barely disturbed the flickering pattern of light and water as his head emerged at the other side. Bloody hell, he said, they make them tough in Yorkshire. Derbyshire, I said, and I made a lot more fuss getting in. He shook his head, spraying water. You're right though, he said, it's starting to feel good. I swam across, breaststroke, ladylike. I liked being waterborne, liked the ease of movement and the way I could feel the currents, the energy of my own action, brushing past. I braced my hands and feet against the side and pushed off on my back, making an ungainly wave that left me drifting towards the other side. There she blows, called Lydia, and Tom dived beneath me like a grebe upending itself and reappeared at my side. It's quite deep, he said, at this end, must have been built for diving. Igor, I asked. He shrugged, treading water. I don't know him very well. He would build a pool. And probably a helipad. Well, I said, it's a nice pool, I expect I would too. What else would you do, he asked, with a whole lot of money?

I thought briefly of pretending to be so unworldly that I had never considered the matter, but I knew only one person who could plausibly say such a thing, a saintly girl from my class at school, and she was dreadful. Dreadful company, I mean, the kind of person who makes you think since she's obviously bound for a life of usefulness and an afterlife of eternal peace you might rather go the other way. Buy a whole lot of books, I said, and a very old house with a library to put them in. Which house, he said, which was perspicacious of him. Next village over from us, I said, 1640s, stone. It's halfway up the hill, so apart but not as isolated as we are, and it has a huge lintel stone with a verse carved in it. I went inside once, carol-singing, and I don't think it's changed much at all in three centuries, even the furniture looked Jacobean. Dad always says you'd spend all your time worrying about the roof but I expect if you had a whole lot of money you wouldn't. Well, that or a Venetian palazzo, anyway, but I've never been to Venice, I just like the idea.

I knew he was about to tell me what Venice was like, that it wasn't all that beautiful, that there were mosquitos and bad drains or something, but he stretched his arms along the edge of the pool and let his legs lift. Hair under the arms but not, oddly, on the legs; I supposed he must shave them. I've never been either, he said, but I'd like to. Maybe one day you'll tour there, I said. Lydie had been to Paris and Copenhagen and even, closely chaperoned and before Igor defected, what was then Leningrad. Milan, he said, is more likely. And less romantic. What's the verse then? Except the Lord keep the city, I said, the watchman waketh but in vain. I always wondered why they chose that, if they were reminding themselves not to worry about their new house or warning burglars that God was watching, only I doubt seventeenth-century burglars could read and it was never anywhere near a city. Tom stood up, water streaming down his fine shoulders, lifted his chin and sang something that sounded like a dance, stately. His voice was high, higher than he spoke, and it seemed that the wind and birds paused to listen. Bloody hell, said Lydie, that's a party trick and a half. It's beautiful, I said, but what – Vivaldi, he said, Nisi Dominus. That's your Psalm. Except that the Lord build the house, they labour in vain that build it; except the Lord keepeth the city, the watchman waketh but in vain. He sank back, let his legs float again. But Vivaldi, he said, regrettably lacking the King James Version, sang it in Latin: Vanum est vobis ante lucem surgere. He looked to me. It is vain for you to rise before the light, I said. Excellent, he said, surgite, post quam sederitis, qui manducatis panem doloris. After which something, I couldn't do the middle bit. Something about eating the bread of sorrow, I said, or bread of pain. That you go so late to your rest, and eat the bread of carefulness, he said. For so he giveth his beloved sleep. Definitely about not worrying, then, I said, how nice to have a lullaby over your front door, I always thought the 1640s were quite a lively time to be building a house, specially round our way, though I suppose most times are. But Tom, how on earth – choirboy, he said, vicar's son, somebody has to be, those Psalms won't sing themselves. Lydia had pushed herself off her chair and toddled over to us. She was wearing the black dress again but today it looked too formal for her unwashed hair and bare legs, as if she were trying on another woman's clothes. Vicar, she said, or bishop? Because that didn't sound like a parish church to me. And forgive me, I said, but you didn't learn Latin at ballet school. They learnt, as far as I could see, very little beyond dancing at ballet school, though the promise was a complete English education. Maybe Lydie was just resistant.

He stood up again, folded his hands over the pale fluff on his chest, focused his gaze on the fig tree and sang again, absurd, exquisite. I applauded and he swept his hand to his shoulder to bow, dipping his forehead in the water. Lo, children are an heritage of the Lord, he said, and the fruit of the womb— oh God, sorry, Lyd. Never mind. Forget about it. Why don't you come for a swim? For about the twenty-eighth time of asking, she said, because I don't want to, I don't feel like it and I don't have to.

I pitched myself underwater, left them to it.

After my swim I was sad to realize that the glamour of my marble bathtub had already worn off. Nothing in my subsequent life would have taught me that marble remains cold even when covered for some time with hot water. I found some cheer in thinking that this fact can't have been common knowledge in Europe since the fall of the Roman Empire, and it was not uninteresting to learn that wealth and glamour did not mean comfort. There were many intriguing potions and bottles in the bathroom but none of them seemed to contain shampoo, so I washed my hair with soap. The worn linen towel did a poor job of drying it and the whole experience, I thought, pulling my clothes back over damp skin, was less satisfactory than the mundane arrangements at home. I was hungry but there were another two hours until dinner and I wasn't, would never be, hungry enough to importune Signora Pilone on my own account. I went into my room and leant over the balustrade, alternately watching the boats on the lake – which couldn't after all actually go anywhere, couldn't leave this narrow valley – and watching the drips from my hair falling onto the terrace below. I saw Signora Pilone coming from her cottage with a covered basket. I noticed a column of ants passing up and down the wall and craned to trace their path down to the orange tree outside the sitting room and up, as far as I could see, all the way to the roof. I supposed it wasn't practical for ants to be afraid of heights. Nancy and I had watched them wrestle picnic crumbs the equivalent of miles across rocks at home, but none of these seemed to be carrying anything and it was hard to imagine the purpose of their procession.

Edie, called Tom. I looked back down. He was on the terrace, conventionally and in fact rather well dressed in un-English linen trousers and a soft white shirt. Lydia's chaise longue was empty. Evening, I said. You weren't thinking of jumping, were you, he said. No, I said, watching ants, I'm mildly bored but not suicidal. In that case, I can help, he said, come into the village with me? I'm posting letters but mostly I fancied going somewhere else for a bit. I'll buy you an ice cream. I'm not a child, I said. You're as bad as your sister, he said, how about thank you, Tom, that's very kind. Sorry, I said, I'll be down in a minute.

I tugged open the wardrobe, as if some casually elegant new thing might have eventuated in there since I last looked, cast a despondent glance at my dress and shoes and was halfway down the stairs when it occurred to me that one of the bottles in my bathroom contained a perfume I hadn't yet tried and if it was already open like most of the others, no one would know if I availed myself. I nipped back up and sprayed my neck and wrists with something called Eau Folle, which I hoped wasn't a pun but at least was obviously designed for a woman; there was one in a dark glass bottle I liked more but I thought it might be aftershave and for some seventeen-year-old reason that was important.

There you are, said Tom, goodness, all scented! Too much, I asked. He nodded. Just a little, I'd say, they're probably not used to it in the pasticceria. To be honest, I said, I've never worn scent before I came here, it's just it was there in the bathroom and I feel such a fright in this dress. You look nice, he said, but maybe a touch of the damp flannel before we go out.

I trailed back up to the bathroom, sniffing my wrist, discovering that once you've put on perfume you lose all sense of how much is enough. My hair had made a damp patch down my back and I could feel the dress sticking over my bra straps. I had no flannel but I ran water over my arms and splashed my neck. It wasn't as if the dress would get any wetter.

I went back down. I had been wrong about the dress not getting wetter. Tom was balancing on one leg and doing something generally considered impossible with the other. Is this better, I said. He lowered the leg. Perfect, he said, only aren't you a trifle damp. It'll dry, I said, it's a warm enough day and I'm not made of sugar. What, he said. Granny says it, I said, means I won't melt in the rain or in this case the bathwater, do let's go.

We walked briskly, almost scurrying, as if we were running away, not talking until we reached the road and I closed the gate behind us. The weather and light were unchanged, bright and hot, as if the planet's tilt had stopped. I wanted to go home. 'S a bit of a relief, isn't it, Tom said, getting away. We set off down towards the glinting lake. It shouldn't be, I said, we're in the lap of luxury, but yes, it is, a bit, I suppose the lap of luxury doesn't suit everyone. I'd give it a bit more of a try, he said, before concluding that, and there are other kinds of luxury you know, hotels and cars and clothes. I shrugged. I don't know, I said, more Lydie's thing than mine, I like books and walking. I was so sure, in those days, that I wanted a life of noble simplicity, plain living and high thinking. I dare say, he said, but have you tried fast cars and Parisian evening gowns? Oh yes, obviously, I said, life on a Derbyshire hill farm is rife with such things, what about you?

We came down to the main road, where I looked the wrong way. Have you swum in the lake, I asked. I liked the idea but it looked cold, something about its pewter colour even under blue skies. There were still patches of snow on some of the mountaintops. No, he said, and I haven't seen anyone else swimming, not that I've been out much. I think most of the hotels have pools. But I'll watch you from the beach if you want to try. Not today, anyway, I said.

We came to the first pink houses. I could feel my hair and clothes warming and drying in the sunlight reflecting between their walls and the stone pavement, and I began to feel better. So, I said, fast cars and French frocks for you? If you're offering, he said, sure. As far as I know, I said, my dad's Land Rover is as we speak running with one of Gran's stockings as a fan belt, but I'm sure we could give you the other. And Maman does buy her clothes and some of Lydie's in Paris though I doubt she has anything you could call an evening gown. I used to get the cast-offs until I got too big. So she doesn't live with you, he said, your mother?

We passed the bar outside which men in clothes you'd think would be too hot sat smoking over their drinks. They should have been at work. I tugged my dress down. She comes and goes, I said, what about yours? She stays, he said, except occasionally she goes to my sister, usually when there's a new baby or the children have mumps. Older sister, I asked. Four years older, he said, lives near Bristol, three children, married a curate the way clergy daughters do, all very respectable, no fast cars involved. And you ran away to join the circus, I said. More or less, he said, yes, they weren't pleased, still aren't, really. No job for a man, throwing away your opportunities, what on earth will you do in middle age, hardly dignified prancing about dressed like that. I don't visit very often. Have they seen you dance, I asked. I couldn't imagine how anyone could see him jump and think he should do anything else. Once, he said, Mother said she knows it's an art form but she still doesn't think it's quite right and she wonders how the girls' mothers feel watching the men handling them like that and Father said you're very strong, that's clear, but you know you could have gone to university and done rowing or even tennis. When I got into Oxford, I said, Maman said brains would only get me so far and however clever a woman might be she still needs to pay attention to her appearance and manner. As if I might not have noticed that it's not enough for a girl to be clever. And Dad said Rachel, it's not just brains, she worked very hard for it, which was nice of him I know but— Always tell a clever girl she's beautiful and a beautiful girl she's clever, said Tom, that's what they say. Will you have an ice cream after all? Yes, please, I said.

I followed him into the pasticceria, wanting to say, aren't we more than that, isn't there something beyond being beautiful or clever, having a job for a man or a job for a woman, tell me the world is big enough for more. It was not apparent to me that for Lydia, for your mother, there was more. Ballet might have been an escape of sorts for the boys, but it seemed to me then that the more I saw of it, the more it seemed a deeper hole, a harder trap, for the girls, who simply had to be even more beautiful, even slimmer, even more controlled and contained, than the rest of us, and especially than those of us who had whatever exemption intelligence bought. I was not, I understand now, allowing for the joy, the vocation, of lives made around the making of art, but even so I think the price paid for that joy by Lydia and her friends was very high.

day and age

At her age, she finds herself thinking, there is comfort in living where you can see the sun rise and set, which is ridiculous because the sunrise and sunset are obviously, globally, constant, available to all, and if anything the passage of the days should be more discomfiting when a person has fewer of them left – all things being equal which they're not – but she knows what she means. It focuses the mind, seeing the sun come over the hill or at least the hill come over the sun if we're going to be Galilean about it; seeing the shadows shorten, turn, lengthen, at least on days when there are shadows which are also not to be taken for granted on the wet coast of a wet North Atlantic island; seeing the sun sink into the sea. Or give that appearance.

She could walk to the beach but she drives, wearing an expensive fleece-lined waterproof robe over red swim-shorts sold for the use of teenage boys, and a red bikini bra promising lift and separation. Old habits stick and she takes the keys, even though she's only going to leave them in the pocket of the robe, but doesn't lock the car. She walks through the dunes, which are a precious and threatened ecosystem but not one she enjoys, always moving and changing, like geology on fast-forward, slithery underfoot, mysteriously capable of hiding the sea even though it is, must be, just there, a landscape of disorientation. In England, she remembers, dunes were often informal nudist colonies, or places where people who couldn't afford or weren't allowed indoor privacy went to have sex. She and her sister had come on such a couple once, Cattersty Sands, a rare day out for Dad, maybe his birthday, he and Maman sitting boringly on a blanket watching the sea doing nothing unusual, she and Lydie wandering off, scrambling up a sandy knoll and sliding down, sharp marram grass and stones in the warm sand, and there was a bare pink behind going up and down and bare legs sticking out and they'd stood there a while, probably not that long really, hand in hand, sundressed shoulders, watching. Méabh says that in her childhood the priest used to patrol the beach here like a lifeguard on summer afternoons, but probably, she thinks, he wasn't scrambling in the dunes, not with a long black dress, though it's surprising where they manage to go, people in long dresses, Victorian lady explorers and Irish priests alike. Doughty, that's the word, though not one she's ever heard anyone say, one of the now surely tiny collection she can use in writing but not pronounce. Dorty, dowty?

The tide's near the top, just where you want it for a quick swim. She pushes off her runners, even though that means she'll have to unknot the laces later when she's cold and wet, sheds the robe, walks down to where the waves are spreading up the sand. It's the only beach between the cliffs on this coastline and even at this time of year there are a few heads in the water and three surfers out beyond them.

She keeps the same pace as she walks into the sea. Box breathing, in two three four, hold two three four, out two three four, hold two three four. Breathe into the base of your spine, says her yoga teacher, which used to sound idiotic and now makes perfect sense. A wave splashes her chest, salt-slap to the face. She leans into it as it recedes and she's swimming, eyeline is waterline, feet weed-wreathed, ribbons of cold stroking breast and thigh and there's another wave, salt-nose, salt-eye, trickling in her head, salt-throat. She strikes out, make the most of it, can't stay in long this time of year, arm-beat foot-beat heartbeat breathe, wave, arm-beat foot-beat heartbeat breathe, sea, here to America, to Scotland, Cornwall, Spain, dolphins and submarines, oil platforms, wrecks, guns and bombs, bones of coral made, shoals and fleets, schools of mackerel, flocks of birds but not so many now, fewer every year and the cliffs silent as the oceans get louder, hum and buzz, submarine reverberations until the whales can't hear themselves think and the dolphins swim onto the shore, hotter and hotter, they say, not frankly that you can tell but if we're waiting until the human body feels the climate – well, already happening, some places, blood pressure up from salt in the water, rising sea levels, forest fires, city fires, you think you're safe here, cold wet coast of a cold wet island, rain to be treasured, this day and age, water given from the sky, you'd think it a miracle almost if you weren't in the way of it—

Fingers numbing, weed gone or not felt by the toes, time's up, body for the dry land again, turn, water-pull, ocean-pull, beach-pull, foot grazes sand, stumbles, swim on, a while yet, wave, no salt-slap now, face already salt, already cold, already sea, hair-weed on salt-neck, grounding, grounding, feet meet sand, sand meet feet, bodyweight, lift, walk. Hello, air, earth, element.

the one doing the cooking

Igor had left the platform of the old hayloft in the barn when he had the building converted into a ballet studio. I liked the hayloft. It reminded me of the attic at home, where I could see, curl up in, the bones of the house, not exactly hiding but well out of the way. An old ladder, made of the same dark wood as the rafters, probably from trees that were green in Dante's day, ran up the wall. I took a book there sometimes when they weren't dancing, when the light and quiet of the place reminded me of the pool with no one in it, both self-contained and inviting, but I especially liked to sit there while the dancers danced. Circle, front row. No one minded if I watched. We're used to it, Katja said, and mostly it's people who are there to tell us what we're doing wrong. But are you really that bored? I'm a bit bored, I said, I'm not used to not being busy, but this isn't at all boring, in some ways it's actually more interesting than just watching a finished performance in a theatre. Not that I had in fact seen many of those, only the last year or two after Lydie joined the company and had free tickets sometimes and I was old enough to go to London on my own. Katja shrugged. We're not even really rehearsing anything, you know, it's just practice. Fine by me, anyway.

They would be dancing Giselle in the autumn. Louise had told me the story, which was about as awful as ballet stories come, a bit like Tess of the D'Urbervilles with tutus and extra foot pain. Beautiful peasant girl Giselle is seduced by Glamorous Count who is also in love with and engaged to beautiful princess. Handsome Gamekeeper, more suitably in love with peasant girl, tells her about the princess, whereupon – being more fragile than her station in life indicates – peasant girl goes mad, dies and is somewhat surprisingly buried in the forest, no reason given but ballet doesn't really do reasons. Because it looks nice, because it's traditional. Dead Giselle joins all the other girls who died of premarital betrayal, luring wayfarers to dance with them until the wayfarers die of dancing all night. Handsome Gamekeeper is caught by the Queen of Dead Girls mourning at Giselle's grave and danced to death, whereupon dead Giselle emerges to save Glamorous Count from the same fate. The end, Giselle still dead, Count free to marry beautiful princess and live happily ever after. Tom would be Handsome Gamekeeper, Lydie would have been Queen of Dead Girls but now it was Louise, Katja was one of the other dead girls. Igor, of course, would be the Count. None of it really existed yet, which intrigued me. There's no notation of ballet. It has to be passed on in real time, one living body to another. If a dancer dies without teaching the dance, the dance dies too. Of course there were films of people dancing Giselle, but for over a hundred years it had been passed between muscle and bone, and no version was present except in the moment of dancing. Dance, I thought, is presence, it is movement in the absence of past and future time, and also it is a form of storytelling and although narrative time and dance time are different, have different forms of the present tense, the ideas of pure presence and narrative are not compatible. I was beginning to understand that truths can be incompatible, that we live and think and especially make art between impossibilities.

I sat dangling my feet over the dance floor, thinking about all this. Maybe the silly story wasn't the point, though if it wasn't the point I didn't see why there couldn't be a story in which Prince Charming fell in love with a clever scullery maid and lost his mind when she said terribly sorry but actually I'm engaged to the butler, lots of dancing with mops and silver trays because kitchen work can be a form of dance, I used to think Granny and I were dancing when we made pies together, and I wondered about suggesting it, if they were just practising, not rehearsing. Do a pastry-making dance for me, I'd say, and what about sheep-shearing, and if you've ever seen the dogs herding sheep off a fell you've seen ballet, principals and corps and all, but what would they know about that, these city dancers in their silk shoes?

I had observed that dancers could build a private space around themselves. Louisa and Tom were each working alone, communing with themselves and their bodies in a way that reminded me of Billy in the village at home, who was harmless but often absent from himself and the people and business around him and often engaged in repetitive movements, flapping or circling or, I thought for the first time, dancing with himself or for himself. Louisa was working on a particular turn, schooling herself in some detail invisible to me, and I wasn't sure if Tom was stretching a large muscle group or testing the margins of his balance and flexibility in a pose, but both of them were somehow solitary, had taken possession of space around them. And in the middle of the room, taking up all the space, Ed made Katja fly and swoop. They were one body, two again, one again. His hands worked her legs, her arms led his feet. Whose head governed, I wondered, but you could tell, really – Katja was the one who had to trust, on whose behalf he fought gravity. Was he the strings and she the puppet? I remembered Lydia saying she'd heard Igor complain that when he partnered Mariane de Martes, she behaved as if it were his job to carry her around the stage, as if he were a machine for keeping her airborne, and he remade the choreography so she spent more time standing in pretty attitudes while he danced and flew and the company let him because audiences loved his flights as much as they loved her beauty. Ed lifted Katja above his head and she, back arched, wings spread, hovered. Morning's minion, I thought, rung upon the rein of a wimpling wing. Gerard Manley Hopkins' poems were in the glorious kingdom of things I didn't yet understand, but I liked the sounds. Katja dove across Ed's body, what they called a swan dive though in fact swans are no more dignified than ducks when upending themselves, bound herself to him with one leg while they spread their four arms and smiled. He carried her off the imaginary stage as I applauded.

I walked back to the villa with her. I'm starving, she said. If you don't mind my saying so, I said, dancers always are. Why would I mind, she said, it's true, we use a lot of energy. Madame once said that was why she took the company to America so much just after the war, to feed her dancers, they had oranges and steak and eggs there and they'd been dancing ten shows a week on carrots and the national loaf, there were extra rations for miners but not dancers. Though of course in Amsterdam and Petersburg there was no bread and no dancing. And in Belsen, I thought— Well, I said, people needed coal more than ballet. Maybe, she said, but you know in England they danced right through the war, on tour and in London? My mother always quotes the sign about air raids in the theatres, I said, when she's feeling affectionate she says it tells you all you need to know about England. *If you wish to leave for home or an official Air Raid shelter you are at liberty to do so. All we ask is that if you feel you must go you will depart quietly and without excitement.* And when she's not feeling affectionate she says poor people were dying like rats in cellars while the rich enjoyed their death cult and you only have to eat English food for a week to understand why they don't care if they live or die. She sounds fun, your mother, said Katja. I shrugged. Several of my friends found Maman intriguing, glamorous, iconoclastic, all of which she was, none of which appeased my friends' parents. It's easy to say that kind of thing, I said, when you're not the one doing the cooking. I sometimes thought that Maman's employers in Sheffield when she first arrived in England claiming to be a cook were not the last on the list of characters deserving sympathy in that story. They had tried, she said, to speak French, the husband and son had gone out to pick wild garlic because they knew that French people liked garlic, and when her abject incompetence in the kitchen became apparent they had encouraged their friends to employ her as a tutor of French and violin while allowing her to live rent-free in their attic. She married Dad from their house, a quick war wedding a few weeks after meeting him at a dance hall; farmers, of course, were exempt from active service, though Dad had signed up towards the end, leaving Gran in charge of the farm and Maman, which hardly bears thinking about. Maman used to tell us about their romance, how she'd known the moment she saw him, so English, so red-haired and blue-eyed, so kind and so strong. So safe, Lydie said to me years later, as much in admiration as judgement; so adoring, the owner of so much land, so ready to accept and excuse her vagabond ways, his mother so willing to keep his house and raise his daughters while she wandered Europe. They meant well, that Sheffield family, Maman said, there were plenty of stories of young refugee women who had it very much worse, but even so, not one book in the house, no piano and mon Dieu the pictures on the wall – She had not stayed in touch with them. She was not a Good Refugee, not prostrate with gratitude for food and shelter and work of any kind, not willing to forget the education and expectations of her people.

We passed the window of the kitchen, where Signora Pilone stood rolling out pastry or dough. At home I usually made the pastry. Some women, Granny said, just had good hands for it, the way some had a feel for plants. Would you ask her for a sandwich for me, asked Katja, or just a plate of biscuits, maybe the lemon ones? And a cold drink? Sandwich is panino, I said, or tramezzino, depending, and biscuits are biscotti, but she understands enough English. I know, she said, but please, she doesn't always understand my English, or maybe pretends not to. Fair enough, I thought, Katja was already living in her second or maybe third language and I liked to be useful. Yes, I said, all right, which would you prefer? Don't mind, she said, maybe some of each? And a little fruit? You could pick your own fruit, I wanted to say. I could see that someone tired and hungry from diving and flying and spinning wouldn't want to walk up the hill to reach and clamber after plums, but she'd only have to stretch out a hand for an orange.

I knocked at the kitchen door, preparing my Italian sentence. I hoped Signora Pilone was used to the prodigious appetites and odd hours of dancers. Igor, Lydie said, had bought the villa a few years ago, but she didn't think he'd spent much time there. Much of the year, Signora Pilone must have the place to herself, which might be spooky if you were the kind of person who is spooked. I remembered Mrs Fairfax in Jane Eyre, keeping Thornfield ready in case Mr Rochester turns up at short notice, but at least she has the madwoman in the attic and the French child in the nursery and their attendants to feed and manage, and anyway she's nicer than Signora Pilone. She came out and looked me up and down. No apron, how could she keep her black dress black while handling flour? Buon giorno, I said, though I'd already seen her and said that several times that day. Would it be possible to ask for a small snack for the dancers? Spuntino, let her decide how much trouble to take, cut sandwiches or put some biscuits on a plate. I knew that once the others saw Katja's food, they'd want some too, and if they didn't I would. I could also well imagine how it would feel to be in the middle of making pies and have someone come to the door demanding snacks. She didn't smile, sighed as she nodded. Yes, in a minute. Scusi, I heard myself say, posso aiutarla? Can I help you? I felt myself flush, wished I hadn't asked. She had the village girl, didn't she, if she wanted help, and why would she want a stupid foreigner bumbling around her kitchen? Sai cucinare, she asked. Can you cook? In the English fashion, I said, a little, my grandmother teaches me. Our eyes met. Your grandmother? Yes, I said, we live in the hills, a bit like here. On a farm. I paused to build the sentence. Mia nonna dice che sono brava a fare la pasticceria. My grandmother says I am good at making pastry, though A-level vocabulary wasn't much interested in food and I might have said I was good at making a bakery. That's good, she said. Not today. I'll bring food for the dancers.

I found Katja where they all tended to settle between bouts of exertion, in the chairs on the terrace. She was lying back on a chaise longue, eyes closed but feet crossed at the ankle, toes pointed, hands behind her head, as if she were performing a tired dancer. Food's coming, I said. The wind ruffled the trees. Cloud shadows played across the hillside opposite, and the cuckoo called again, though I'd remembered that magpies can imitate a cuckoo call and there were magpies around, there are always magpies around. If it wasn't a real cuckoo, was it more or less theatrical? Katja, I said, what's it like, dancing like that? With a man, I mean? She opened her eyes. What do you mean, she asked. Dancers and words, I thought again, sometimes there's almost no point trying to talk to them. I mean, how does it feel? What do you think when you're being – well, manhandled like that? Nothing much, she said, you're just thinking about the dancing. I sat on the foot of the chaise longue I thought of as Lydie's. I noticed that the ants' procession up the side of the house came out from the dining room, through a hole at the bottom of the French window. It looks rather intimate, I said, some of the places he puts his hands.

She craned her head to look at me. It is, I suppose, she said, if you think about it that way, but we really don't. He puts his hands where they have to go to keep you in the right position for the choreography. That's all anyone's thinking about. She lay down again. Though, she added, I was once in a partnering class where one of the girls said something and the teacher said, sweetie, he'll put his hand up you like a bloody glove puppet if that's what he has to do and if you don't like it there are plenty of girls who would, I thought that was a bit much. Yes, I said, so do I. Did she leave? A few months later, she said, she wasn't really committed, you can always tell, people who are late to class or don't watch their figure or take time off for every little injury, it's just not a job for the half-hearted, there's no point, it has to be your whole life. Yes, I said, I see that, but I thought what about Lydia, what about when your little injury is a baby and you're off for six months?

rocking chair she's carried

She checks her phone again. She keeps all the notifications switched off, doesn't want to be at the beck and call of a machine, but sometimes she wonders if it wouldn't be better to know that it will tell her if there's anything she wants to know, if she might check less often if silence meant there was no reason to look.

Still nothing. She takes another sip of the tea made from the Rose Pouchong she brings in her suitcase from England. There's rain moving across the hill outside, pattering on her roof. A good day to be curling up in Maman's cane rocking chair she's carried from house to house and over two seas these last thirty years, a good day for the new novel from a writer in whom she has confidence. It's not as if she and Méabh are always, maybe even usually, in daily contact. Their text conversations bloom and wilt, effervesce and run out, bloom again. But three days is unusual, four or now five says something's wrong.

She goes back to her book, which is good, deserves her full attention.

Rain falls.

The fridge sighs.

She remembers the first time she met Méabh, down at the Flaggy Shore, before the divorce, when this was still their summer cottage though once Pat was old enough to manage after school by himself she'd come here alone far more than with Mike. Escape, a small-scale version of Maman's disappearances; it's not that she thinks it was always easy for Mike, being married to her, having to introduce his friends and family to a difficult not-quite-Englishwoman from a broken home when he could have had his pick of the Mount Anville and Loreto girls. He should have stayed in character, married one of his friends' sisters or his father's colleagues' daughters, a woman who would have given him three or four kids, never thought of sending the boys anywhere but his old school and the girls anywhere but hers. She knew them, the women he might have married, the women his friends and brothers had married; for years she had exchanged dinner parties, sat by while they spoke of skincare and summer camps and spa days for the girls. None of them would have dreamt of helping herself to a few days' solitude because she felt like it. Most of them were, as far as she could see, pack animals who showed no desire for solitude, though probably she is unjust, probably she could have tried harder or differently to join the tribe, probably if she had she would have found individuals and allies. Instead she had Dearbhla from the Samaritans and, for fifteen years of shared hilarity, Clare from a short-lived Dante reading group, Clare who was from the North via Modern Languages at Cambridge and to a lesser extent also an outsider.

That particular trip was partly because it was the first anniversary of Clare's death and she'd wanted to grieve in peace, without Mike saying Clare was only a friend wasn't she, you don't make this much fuss about your own sister or your mother. Clare had said once, towards the end, funerals are for the living, let the boys do whatever they want, I won't be here to care. They might like, Edith had said, to think that they're doing what you wanted, a last act of love, it might help them, to have directions, and Clare had said oh in that case push me out to sea in a burning boat, Viking-style. Administrative nightmare, Edith said, you'd never get permission. Might distract them, Clare said, a last act of parental annoyance, and between them they constructed a brief fantasy about just how much of a nuisance one might posthumously be, what outlandish last requests could be made. Edith told Clare about the first time Maman had taken her and Lydie to Paris – the time Maman stood under the window of the apartment where she'd grown up, until she turned and fled from a neighbour she remembered – and Lydie, passing the statue of the vicomte de Turenne as a child, looking not unlike her eleven-year-old self, all legs and wavy hair, had said Maman, when I die I want a statue like that, where everyone sees it. But I want a fountain too, and the street named after me. Put it in your will, chérie, Maman said, Maman whose sister and parents had been incinerated, obliterated. Ça ne serait pas mon problème, which turned out to be wrong. Maman outlived Lydie by five years, though Lydie's death intestate, overseas, and also more or less without assets was mostly Edith's problem because Maman returned to the kibbutz straight from the funeral. But you can see why, can't you, said Dad, losing her daughter as well as her parents and her sister, you can see why she'd want her own people now. I suppose so, said Edith, having by then understood for some years that she and Dad were not Maman's own people, that the kibbutz was the closest thing to home left on earth for Maman, that she and Dad would have to console each other inasmuch as consolation was possible.

Oh, Edith, Clare had said, I don't know whether to laugh or cry, God rest their souls, Lydia and – Rachel, is it, your mother? Laugh and cry both, Edith said, neither, and Clare opened her arms and they held each other a moment, Clare smelling of medicine and antiseptic, her hacked hair dry against Edith's cheek. Of course in the event, less than a month later, her family buried Clare decently, properly, beside her parents, let the undertaker make up her face for the viewing as it had never been made up before, dressed her in a strange mother-of-the-bride outfit that could only have come from a section of her wardrobe reserved for mistakes, and of course Edith went along, behaved herself, wept only decorously. But for Clare's anniversary she made a paper boat and took it and a box of matches down to the shore at sunset. The Vikings must have used some form of accelerant on these occasions. Wooden boats, unlike paper, are big enough to burn satisfactorily before they sink, and also Viking mourners must have paid attention to wind and tide and current. There were people around, summer sunset, barbecues, campervans, and eventually a woman wearing floaty orange trousers and a turquoise shirt left her group sitting on the wall and crunched over the stones to where Edith crouched tearful and frustrated over her singed paper. Are you all right, she said, can I help? It's for my friend, Edith said, my friend Clare who died, it doesn't work. Méabh lowered herself to sit beside Edith. Ah, she said, tell me then, about your friend Clare, and when

Edith had told her Méabh had waved to the people she'd left on the wall and they'd come over with their bottle of wine and toasted Clare, a spontaneous wake for a woman they'd never met, and Edith had thought only in Ireland, I love it here and I cannot rise to the kindness of the Irish, I can only give thanks to end my days among them and I will never leave.

The kindness of the Irish.

Céad míle fáilte.

It's not fair, is it, to hold people to such a standard. Why should Ireland be different from the rest of Europe, from Paris and Kyiv?

She keeps reading.

Maybe she should be the one to start.

Can she still be friends with someone who thinks the problem is refugees?

Rain falls.

She keeps reading.

all red over London

We'd drunk wine that night. I was cautious, not wanting to make a fool of myself – any more of a fool of myself – in front of the dancers, and also frankly not liking the taste. Did anyone like it, really? Wouldn't they rather have the lemonade Signora Pilone occasionally made for us, with fruit from the terrace and mint from the garden? I had learnt to like coffee and I would learn to like wine, hoped to arrive in Oxford able to tell one grape from another better than anyone would expect from a girl with my accent, but it wasn't coming easily. There had also been fried sausages so highly salted and spiced I could hardly eat them, and a rich sherry-flavoured egg custard for dessert. I was not surprised to wake in the dark.

I slept with the balcony doors open, to enjoy the coolness of the night and because I found the room's narrowness and criss-cross wallpaper oppressive. It was a room you needed to be able to leave. I woke thirsty and hot, kicked off the blankets, drank the whole glass of water on the bedside table, pulled off my nightdress to let the breeze cool my skin. I fell back into uneasy sleep, woke again cold and needing to pee. I put the nightdress back on, pulled the blankets back up and lay there reluctant, arguing with myself, maybe it could wait, probably I would forget about it if I went back to sleep, perhaps if I lay on my side I wouldn't notice – I pushed off the blankets again, feet on the cold stone floor. Always best not to look at mirrors in the dark, even at home, what you don't know won't hurt you though even then I knew that was rubbish, it's exactly what you don't know that hurts you. The wardrobe sighed as I passed it and the bedroom door creaked, nothing I could do about that.

The hall floor was gritty underfoot and a breeze moved along the corridor. It occurred to me that you wouldn't hear a ghost on a stone floor. At Nancy's house, which was only Victorian, much newer than the farm, they had one that walked down the first four stairs and ran down the rest. I hadn't really believed her until I heard it myself, but at least you knew where it was, and therefore where it wasn't. On stone they could be anywhere and you wouldn't know until— There was a light on downstairs. First things first. Knowing the orchestral capacities of the plumbing, I didn't flush, washed my hands under a careful dribble but took a moment's comfort in the jasmine soap before I went quietly down the stairs. If we had left a light on, Signora Pilone would be annoyed, and though there was no sign of fire, if they'd left the light on they might also have left the candles on the dining table aflame.

The light came from the drawing room, a room so formal we rarely went in. No voices, but liquid pouring into a glass, furniture creaking. A secret drinker? Ballet's not a job for the half-hearted, I remembered, it has to be your whole life. I was young enough to believe that dedication must be incompatible with what I would have considered weakness. I peered around the door and saw my sister curled up on the sofa, wearing the white nightdress, holding a glass of something pale. There were bottles on the coffee table, and the exact angles and reflective surfaces of the room's arrangements made her dissolution stark. What on earth are you doing, I wanted to say, do you want to hurt the baby, but I took a deep breath. Lydie, I said, are you all right, are you not well? Oh, hello you, she said, what are you doing up? Needed the lav, I said, and I saw the light, can't you sleep?

Come in, she said, have a drink, it's quite nice, there's no tonic but I'm mixing gin with that fizzy yellow stuff, I've even sliced up a lemon. It's sweet, you'll like it. Gin, I thought, hot baths, jumping down the stairs, but she didn't seem to be intent on destruction. I didn't say I thought pregnant women weren't supposed to have gin. I'll mix my own, I said, you stay there. There was a drinks cupboard in the corner, including a fridge kept stocked with cans of an Italian pop I liked, sweet and herbaceous. I poured some into a glass and then knelt at the coffee table with my back to Lydie as I took some of her lemon and pretended to add gin.

No one could sleep, she said, when there's an alien kicking them in the ribs and they're so big they have to wake up to turn over, not to mention needing to pee hourly, and my hips hurt when I lie on my side and I can't breathe when I lie on my back and I haven't even tried lying on my front, not for months. No, I said, good, don't do that. I wondered what would happen if she did – presumably the baby's waters would stop her squashing it and she surely wouldn't actually burst, although it looked that way. Ewes in lamb and cows in calf lie more or less normally. I sat at the other end of the sofa, tucked my cold feet under my nightie. So are you down here every night, I asked, meaning, are you drinking alone every night. No, she said, well, sometimes, it's pretty boring, you know, being awake all night. It goes on a long time. Not all night, I said, surely. She was always the last down in the mornings. Most of it, she said.

I sipped my drink, turned the cold glass in my hand, noticed again how even my fingers were thicker and stronger than hers. Lyd, I said, how did it happen, the baby? The usual way, she said, you don't need me to tell you, do you, about the birds and the bees? As far as I know, I said, the point about birds and bees is that they have other arrangements. No, I understand the principles of mammalian reproduction. I have even, I did not say, kissed three boys from the other Grammar School and rather enjoyably allowed one of them to unfasten my bra although I kept my school blouse on throughout the occasion. I didn't know you had a boyfriend, I said.

She turned and stretched out her legs along the sofa. I didn't, she said, or at least, not exactly. So who, I asked. Did Maman know? Could she really have got this far without anyone asking? Are you sure you want to know, she said. Chin up, challenging. I thought if you didn't have a boyfriend it was probably Igor, I said, hence the house. Yes, she said, it probably was. Probably, I said, Lyd, don't you know?

She looked away, rested her elbow on the back of the sofa and her head in her hand. No, she said, not for sure.

I remembered to close my mouth. I had no idea what to say.

I'll tell you, she said, if you want, probably only because I've had a drink. Or two. But you can't tell anyone, Edith, you have to promise me that, not one soul, I swear I'd kill you and then myself. I mean it.

No, I thought, don't tell me. Whatever it is, I don't want to know.

Her hair came down over her face. Promise me, Edie.

Does Maman know, I asked. No one, she said, no one at all. Maman thinks it's Igor, she didn't ask for details.

Then not me, I thought, I'm not old enough, I don't want it. I promise, I said, Lydie of course I promise.

I don't know how much of this you want to know either. I don't know what you might think you want to know and then wish you didn't know. You'll be old enough yourself now, to see how times change, how something you do or say or think can be perfectly ordinary and reasonable and ten or twenty years later deviant or even criminal, how none of us can know now which of our normalities will seem depraved when today's children grow up – driving cars, probably, eating meat. I'd hope it's obvious that the circumstances of your conception are not your fault. But I see that a story like this might change what you think, or how you feel, about yourself. I understand how guilt can run in your blood, once you know about it. You could stop here, stay innocent.

No? No, I wouldn't either. I'd always rather know. But don't say I didn't etc.

*

I was sleeping with Igor, she said. To be honest quite a few of us do, or have, or certainly would. I didn't think I was the only one. I'm not the only one to get pregnant, either, but the others— He was kind about it. He is kind. I mean, of course he's an arrogant bastard but if anyone has a right to be, it's him, he does have things to be arrogant about, you've seen him dance and maybe more to the point you've seen how even English audiences react so you can imagine what it's like in America. People say he acts like someone who can have anything he wants but even if that's true he's not wrong, and especially when you think about his childhood I'd say he behaves rather well, considering. He saw his father and his brother killed, you know, in Leningrad before the war, they made him and his mother and sisters watch. He has nightmares. He told me one night, horrible, I won't haunt you with it. And he's nice. He was nice to me. Still is, obviously, I mean here we are.

There we were, reflected in the uncurtained window, wavering in the wavering glass. I drew a circle in the dew on my cold drink. I could just hear the bubbles still.

He took me out to dinner, she said, several nights a week, and he bought me nice dresses, I don't know if you remember the blue one, and of course I knew it was mostly just my turn, it wasn't that I ever imagined he'd marry me or anything like that, but it was fun, I'd never have been able to go to restaurants like that otherwise and they're great, if you ever get the chance take it, not just the food though that was wonderful, steak almost every time because Igor's not like some men, he understands that dancers have to eat, and he really knows how to order wine. I learnt a lot from him. And I liked going to bed with him. I don't suppose you'd know about that, I hope you get to find out at Oxford, but – well, I liked it. She finished her drink. At least I liked it most of the time, there were some things – and I learnt a fair amount there too.

I drank some of my fizz, which was less fizzy and warmer now. But Lyd, I said, surely he knew to use – I didn't know what to call it. A French letter. A prophylactic.

Men don't like them, she said, you can see why they wouldn't. No, but he sent me to a doctor. There's a thing called a Dutch cap. Rubber, you put it inside with some jelly. They're only supposed to give them to married women but of course if you know the right people –

And of course Igor does know the right people, I said.

Well, she said, just as well. That bit was pretty odd, I mean of course I'm used to taking my clothes off and waving my legs around but having the nurse teach me that and then the doctor checking it didn't move around when he – well, anyway, that's what we did. She sat up, arched her back. Bloody hell, this baby, do you want to feel it again? I didn't, much, but I let her take my hand and put it on her belly, where I could indeed feel the baby – you – bumbling around. So it didn't work, I said, obviously.

Oh no, she said, it worked. It works. Get yourself one, if you can, you don't want to end up like me. No, I thought, I don't, I'm not losing my Oxford place for any man nor child, these legs stay closed until I've got my degree.

It works as long as you put it in, she said, and there was one night, New Year – we had quite a lot to drink, more than usual, I mean, or at least I did, I don't think he was particularly drunk, but it was the last night of the fucking Nutcracker, people always go a bit wild, you've no idea how much everyone hates that show. I did, I'd been hearing about it for years, and we both knew that she chose every time to dance the fucking Nutcracker rather than coming back to the farm for Christmas, especially when Maman wasn't there which was mostly, Maman was particularly good at not being there in winter. We went for dinner, she said, there's this Hungarian place in Soho he particularly likes and the food just kept coming, course after course though to be honest I don't think I remember the pudding, and a new wine each time and then a dessert wine I do remember, if you ever get the chance to have Hungarian dessert wine –

Enough, I thought, about my chances, I'd take my chances over yours any day of the year.

We went on to the bar at the Gorman, she said, a group of us, Igor and a friend of his, a violinist, I'd always wondered a bit about them, the pair of them, and I think Mariane was still there with her boyfriend but sort of trying to make Igor jealous, and a few of the others but no one else from the corps, no one would have been able to afford it. There were cocktails. If you ever get the chance— Yes, I said, if someone ever offers to buy me cocktails at the Gorman, I'll remember your advice, thank you. Well, she said, you never know, though I agree sometimes you can guess. They had sparklers in them, some of them, and those paper umbrellas Maman used to give us sometimes, I suppose people were buying her cocktails, somewhere. Like mother like daughter, I said, Paris, Monte Carlo, Venice, which was not fair, Maman had better taste than Monte Carlo. Anyway, said Lydia, people were dancing and at first we didn't, we were all tired from the show and we'd eaten well, and then someone saw Olivier tapping his feet and said come on, Grandpa, let's see what you can do, and you know what Olivier's like about his age – I didn't; I thought Olivier was one of Lydia's ballet teachers but I hadn't met him – so he took to the floor and of course everyone stood back to watch and then he called us all on, and you know actually often ballet dancers aren't much good at casual dancing, we need steps and sequences, but I suppose we'd all had enough to drink and then Igor took his shoes off and did some of his jumps and the whole place went wild and he was flying about pretty much literally hanging from the chandeliers but you can imagine the hotel people loved it, there were passers-by staring in through the windows. Lèche-vitrine, I said; the French for window-shopping is window-licking. And Mariane had left by then, said Lydia, so I went on and I knew the Nutcracker pas de deux, more or less, from watching her so we did that, with Igor's friend on the piano and honestly, Edie, I know fun isn't your thing but even you would have liked it. It was silly but glorious. She trailed off, remembering, resting her hand on her belly where I could see the baby – you – moving, through her nightdress.

They'll put that on your tombstone, Lyd, I said, silly but glorious. Better that, she said, than fun wasn't her thing. (We didn't, by the way, put that on her tombstone, and I don't care what anyone puts on mine but I think, I like to think, that Pat likes me too much, that he and I have had too much fun, for Fun Wasn't Her Thing.)

I remember the dancing, anyway, she said, and then we were in a taxi and I remember trying not to be sick, which I must have managed because the rest wouldn't have happened otherwise. We went back to Igor's flat, me and the pianist whose name by the way is Emil, and the sun was coming up all red over London and then I don't remember any more until the next morning, I mean later the same morning, well, it was afternoon by then, getting dark again and at first I didn't know if it was the same day, I thought I might have slept all the way round, you know what it's like in winter when you wake up in the dark and don't know.

I did not know.

She looked so sad. I leant forward to brush the hair from her face. Don't tell me, I thought, don't tell me the next bit. Leave me with the flying through the chandeliers.

And when I woke up, she said, when I woke up I was in Igor's bed, which is what I expected of course, but Emil was there too, I was lying between them. And – are you sure you want to hear this, I probably shouldn't tell you this, maiden aunt – they were both naked and at first I thought I was still dressed but under the dress I wasn't. And I wriggled out at the bottom of the bed, not to wake them, and there were my knickers on the floor by the door and the dress was all torn and then I had to be sick and afterwards I ran myself a bath – you can imagine, Edie, the bathrooms in those flats, huge baths – and – well, obviously I'd, someone had – and I was a bit bruised and sore, there was some blood – I hadn't –

I knelt up and put my arms around her. Don't, Lyd, I said, you don't have to tell, you don't have to go through it all again, you poor love, don't. I felt her stiffen, brace, and thought for a moment that it was the baby, that the strain of telling had started it off, but it wasn't that, it was my sister steeling herself, controlling herself, and she didn't weep, she patted my back and said there, don't you take on now, so I didn't, neither of us took on.

We sat up. She finished her drink and poured another. The house lay still silent around us, but in the window behind the sofa the outline of the mountains was beginning to show to the east.

And so you see, maiden aunt, the lesson there is to put your Dutch cap up your snatch before you go out drinking. I had it in my handbag, in case, it comes in a rather smart plastic case almost too easily confused with a powder compact you might take out on a train, but as we have proved they don't work so well in a handbag.

Lyd, I said, that's not the lesson, you know that. But I didn't, in those days, know what or whose the lesson might be. She'd been having an affair with Igor for weeks, she'd gone out drinking with him, she'd gone back to his flat while drunk, no one in that time would have told her that it wasn't her fault or that she wasn't responsible for the consequences. What else had she expected, what else would any red-blooded man, the man on the Clapham omnibus whose ideas of reason lie at the base of English justice, expect? And now the chickens had come home to roost, and she was lucky Igor had put her up in his Italian villa and backed up the farradiddle of her knee injury instead of letting the company sack her, being only corps de ballet and easily replaced. Well, she said, that's the lesson for you, anyway. And I meant it, about not telling anyone, do you understand? On pain of death, I said, I understand. And I kept that promise until today, or maybe until you read this, if you read this, since unread writing is hardly betrayal.

Good, she said, see that you do. I'm going to go to bed for a bit, if I can get off this sofa. I unfolded my legs, put her glass and my own on the table. Come on, I said, I'll give you a hand, and to my surprise she accepted it. Lyd, I said, when she was on her feet, hands to her lower back the way Granny used to stand on wash day, Lyd, just one more thing. What, she said. Why did you keep it, I said, the baby? Why didn't you sort things out, go back to that doctor? Did you realize too late? She drooped her head forward and rubbed the back of her neck. No, she said, of course not, I realized pretty quickly, I know my own body and the timing was exactly wrong, I almost knew by the next week. Well then – I said. Oh, Edie, she said, because it's Jewish, obviously. Because the baby's Jewish, isn't it? Maman is so I am so it is. What kind of niece and granddaughter would I be if I got rid of a Jewish baby? There's been enough of that, wouldn't you say? I think even Maman saw that, though I wasn't sure she would, that's why I waited to tell her. Once it was too late. Because she's a pragmatist, Maman, whatever else she does or doesn't do, I knew she wouldn't fuss.

Oh, I said, yes, I suppose so, I understand, but I didn't really understand. It would take me years to recognize what she'd meant, or maybe to invent my own meaning for it since we never spoke of her decision again. I remembered that night when we decided to move from London to Ireland and Mike said he wanted Pat baptized, that it would just be easier and better for him to be a Catholic child in a Catholic country, to fit in, which wasn't wrong, it was easier, especially when we needed to get him into the Catholic school where it was just easier and better for him to take his First Communion with everyone else. I remembered, unreasonably, the stories of Jewish mothers who smothered the baby so its cries didn't betray the whole family to the police; I remembered the problem of all the Jewish children who'd spent the war sheltered in French convents, converted, surviving; outrageous, I was, to consider this in the same breath as Pat's First Communion, with which I went along, which I attended in the right sort of South Dublin mauve dress and motherly pink lipstick. Jewish survival skills: know when to keep quiet. Show the right passport to the right uniform on the right day. Lydia gave you what she had, which was life and silence.

I'll stop there, for now. That's probably enough for you, in one go. I wish I had wise words for you and I hope you have someone close at hand who does. By modern ideas, you're the child of rape, although at the time it wasn't, exactly, certainly no jury would have convicted which doesn't matter because no policeman would have charged which doesn't matter because no woman would have reported it. Your father is Igor or Emil but we'll never know, they're both dead now, and I'm not sure why you'd want to know, what difference it would make. Neither of them, so far as I know, had or anyway acknowledged other children. And you're Jewish, at least according to Jewish law, whichever of them is your father, Judaism being matrilineal which is popularly, unpleasantly, said to be because Jewish women have been raped so often over the centuries by men who hated them that there was often doubt about paternity. I was going to say, you always know who the mother is, tactless of me. Well, you do now. You're Jewish enough for Hitler and therefore also, if you were wanting an extra passport, you have the paperwork and your politics can accommodate it, for the state of Israel. Welcome to the family. Mazel tov.

your enemy

She doesn't often go to Gunter's house. He regards cleaning, doubtless rightly, as a bourgeois preoccupation, though as she has pointed out the preoccupations of the bourgeoisie invariably relate to their own comfort and there is nothing, is there, innately wrong with being comfortable. But you sleep with me, he said, because I'm a rebel, because I'm the opposite of Mike the solicitor and my house is the opposite of the Marital Home. You like it when I hold you down on my dirty sheets, you are turned on by la boue. No, she said, I prefer it at my house, I prefer, since we're talking about the bourgeoisie, my very expensive mattress, my shower whose glass is cleaned with a rubber blade after every use, my linen sheets even if they are a bugger to dry in this climate. But sometimes, he said, kneeling up, parting her knees, you like it here.

She leaves her car in the lay-by. She can coax it up to the house but after all the rain it's not worth the risk of getting stuck on the track. She should probably think about a four-wheel-drive, since she seems to have settled here, since she's not going to sell the cottage for a small – very small – apartment in Paris or London as she said after the divorce. Who would have thought that she'd live out her days here? Maybe anyone who'd seen where she grew up. Limestone landscape, big sky, only here you get the sea as well, and the changeable light of it, here at the edge of the continent, with another calling from over the horizon.

He is expecting her, he invited her, but he's not in the kitchen, where the washing-up hasn't been done and there's some bean thing, some lentil soup he'll insist on calling dhal, simmering on the stove. Come with me to London some time, she's said, to Birmingham, taste at least the diasporic real thing, but she may not mean it. She's not sure she'd like him as much somewhere else. He's never in the sitting room, no one is, and he doesn't answer her call up the stairs. Studio, then.

His garden is loved. Herb and vegetable beds are bordered by the stones from the land, the meadow lawn now florid, pots squatting between outbursts of lavender and broom. It's barely raining, misting her face and hair, and the long grass catches around her ankles. Yes, the light's on in the studio, and there he is, standing at his bench, everything stone and wood and clay but the white metal kiln with its red eye. Grüß Gott, she says, a private joke, he's not Bavarian. Ah, he says, sorry, only this glaze, ten minutes I promise you. It's all right, she says, will I watch or wait for you at the house? She likes watching him work. Quite apart from the joy of watching anyone make anything – glass blowing, she thinks, is probably her favourite, melted sand and heat and human breath – there's anticipation in seeing his hands on the clay, seeing a new form under his fingers, knowing that later they will go, will make – He's doing something fiddly, some brush-work and scraping, doesn't look to be his usual plain style. As you like, he says, then, stay. Sit down, I think it's clean.

She's wearing her old jeans, sits on the corkscrew wooden stool shaped to a human behind, though not quite to hers. He's working on a piece bigger than he usually makes, a vase – maybe vessel is a better word, not the kind of thing for a bunch of flowers, more like the burnt bones of your enemy, the ashes of your best hunting dog – the height of his forearm. Rain patters. It's warm in here, the heat from the kiln. It smells dry, woody, and she can almost feel her skin tightening the way it does on planes, recalls the softening of the first breaths of Irish air as she comes down the mobile stairs even in the smog of the airport. We're half-aquatic here, she thinks again, our lungs and skin, our surfaces, adapted to the rain. Amphibious.

Can I talk, she asks, or are you concentrating? He looks up, smiles. Both, he says, talk to me. How is your day? Damp, she says. He's painting wavy lines diagonally across the vessel's curve, leaning sideways. All glazes seem to be shades of white until they come out of the kiln. Glazing is an act of faith. We defy augury. I meant to swim but I didn't, she says, mostly I've been reading, and thinking about whether to go to Italy with Cassie and Priya, Cassie wrote to me today. A girls' holiday, it would be, although the girls are in their seventies. Cassie's found some place in Tuscany she's excited about, a farm-stay thing, she says. Nowhere near the lake and the villa, Edith hasn't been and won't go back. You can't go back, or home. Keep moving, forwards, sometimes one sorry foot, one sorry minute, in front of the other.

Onward. To be practical, she's not sure there's any sense in going anywhere hotter than Ireland, remembers last summer and the summer before and the summer before that when the rest of Europe dried out and burnt down. It's not that it's not coming here too, but we can pretend a little longer. Keep driving our cars and burning our peat, flying to Italy. London friends, he says. Cassie's an Oxford friend, she says. Fifty years ago, and then I met Priya through Cassie in London when Pat was a baby, her twins were the same age. And now Priya lives with one of the twins, in a specially-built annexe. Works for everyone, Priya says, I'm on hand for the grandchildren now and if the boot's on the other foot in a few years they won't be driving up and down the country taking me to doctors' appointments and opening jars and I've told them, if it gets beyond that I want a one-way ticket to Switzerland. They all say that, this generation who've nursed or refused to nurse their own parents through the decades of discomfort and indignity that seem to be the fruit of medical research and European public healthcare. Not that you'd rather go without, and not, actually, that the one-way ticket to Switzerland is as readily come by as her friends make it sound in these conversations. He glances up. What are you thinking, he asks. It still surprises her, to hear a man ask that question of a woman. It still makes her soften. What an absurd luxury dilemma it is, she says, whether to go to Italy, how ridiculous of me to be thinking maybe I won't because it will be unpleasantly hot rather than because my flying there will make everything hotter for everyone everywhere. Take the train, he says, you have the time, it's fun. Mm, she says. It's not her idea of fun, the ferry to Wales and the train to London and the

Eurostar to Paris, both now infrequent and overcrowded, before a better train from Paris to Milan, Milan to Florence, Florence to wherever. I just think, she says, it's all very well people who live in Amsterdam or Berlin or Paris or even London telling you to take the train, maybe people living on islands off islands are allowed to go on flying a bit longer.

He sits back, turns the pot on its wooden stand. There, he says, genug. Enough. So fly, if you prefer. Or stay here. I know, she says, I'm being ridiculous, I am ridiculous. She's about to be petulant, she can feel it like a weather front in her mind, she's about to say she knows perfectly well that to most people her whole life is a holiday, was her house not a holiday cottage, does she not spend her days almost exactly as she likes in this place that she chose, is she not the native of an oppressor nation and the epitome of the oppressor generation, does that not mean she's not allowed to mention any problem of any description ever, not that she said or thought that whether to go to Italy with Priya and Cassie was a problem, only a question that regardless of its socio-economic dimensions requires an answer one way or the other? He stands up. It is convenient, he says, that I know how to stop you being ridiculous. I was going to take you upstairs, I had in fact made up the bed in your honour, but we can just as easily do it here.

traces, trails, passage

I'd have slept longer the next morning. Sunlight on my face woke me, and it was already past ten which meant I had missed breakfast, and Signora Pilone and the village girl would be at the door any minute, trying to dust and make the bed even though I always did both myself. I stood up, pulled off the bedding to air while I bumbled to the bathroom, where the village girl stopped cleaning the bath and scrambled away apologizing in a way I could not imagine as sincere. I looked at my face in the mirror, half-expecting a change, an overnight maturity, but I just looked dozy and puffy. I washed my face and neck thoroughly in cold water, brushed my hair vigorously, helped myself to one squirt of Eau Folle.

Downstairs, there was still a coffee pot in a quilted jacket on the sideboard, and a napkin over a plate on the table, under which I found two bread rolls with butter, a dish of jam and an egg, probably, I thought, for Lydia, but coffee wasn't supposed to be good for babies and anyway she could spare me a small cup. I had begun to like coffee. I didn't bother with a saucer, had never seen the point, harder to carry and another thing to wash up.

Tom was on one of the chaises longues outside, lying back with his hat tipped over his eyes so I thought he was asleep until he said good morning. Bad night, he asked, not like you to oversleep. Too much dissipation, I said, rich food and late hours. Too much wine, he said, more like, how do you feel now? Fine, I said, and I was about to ask if he'd seen Lydia, if I should take her breakfast in bed, when he took the hat off his face and said your sister's in the pool, by the way. I put my coffee down. There she was. I hadn't noticed because she wasn't moving, had been still so long the water had settled around her. She stood by the ladder, copper hair shining in the sun, her arms floating and her distended body now only a flickering shape. Leave her be, he said, I would, it probably feels nice, being waterborne, she's really beginning to lumber on dry land. I picked up the coffee again. Is she all right, I asked. He craned his head up to look at her. Probably, he said, at least for a dancer who's eight months pregnant with no father in sight. I presume it's Igor, by the way? I shrugged. So do I, I said. And she has a plan, doesn't she, he said, she's not thinking she'll come back to London with a recovered knee and an infant? She must, I thought, have said nothing to anyone, which from what school and village life had taught me about most people's ability or willingness to keep secrets was probably sensible. We have a plan, yes, I said, Lydie and my mother and me, the baby's going to be adopted. And then Lydie will go home and dance the Nutcracker. Leaving the baby in Italy, he asked. Leaving the baby, I said, to grow up in a safe and loving home. Which was probably true, likely to be true. Maman wasn't a monster. Maman had reason to know the value of a human life.

I was thinking I'd go change into my swimming costume and join Lydie, try to cheer her up, when the door opened and Signora Pilone came out carrying a tray. She brought it to me. Your breakfast, she said in English, you sit and eat. Isn't it for my sister, I said. Tua sorella ha fatto colazione, she said, your sister has had breakfast. Sit and eat. Oh, I said. I sat at the foot of the other chaise longue and let her set out the food on the table beside me. There, she said, buon appetito. Oh, I said again, grazie. Grazie mille. Di niente, she said, but her care didn't seem like nothing. It was nice to be treated like a child.

I buttered a roll and watched Lydie. The water was moving around her now, though her head and arms stayed still. One hand rested on the poolside. Wait, I said, is she dancing? Tom looked up again. Maybe, he said, bit of barre, yes, it's probably a good idea, actually, with the water supporting her. Oh, I said again. Nonplussed, I thought, it is a morning for being nonplussed. I tapped my egg on the table. Do you want both those rolls, Tom said, only I was up early to practise. You can have half, I said, there's plenty of fruit on the trees if you can't wait for lunch, I'm hungry too. And a bit of that jam, he said.

He sat up and we ate. Lydie turned to rest the other hand on the poolside, and her foot appeared above the water, shoulder height. I imagined the baby tunnelling, burrowing, wondered if it might come out more easily for her strength and flexibility. Igor, I thought, was at least small and slight for a man, so if things worked along the same lines as the breeding of horses and cows the baby shouldn't be too big. Emil I had not seen.

The foot cut through the water, shark's fin, and then her arabesque dipped her face. I put my bread down. Do you think – I said. I think she's fine, he said, I think she's a dancer dancing. What are you going to do today? A walk, I said, surprising myself, I'm going to go for a long walk, because soon I won't want to leave Lydie a whole day. I'm going to take a picnic – I'm going to ask Signora Pilone for a picnic – and I'm going to take it up the mountain. Yes, I thought, yes, a day out, a day away, a day off. A mountain day. We didn't exactly have mountains, at home. High ground, hills, but the tops rolled for miles, you could spend a whole day high up without ever being able to say you were on a summit. I liked the idea of climbing to the top of a thing, a destination, and I didn't especially want Tom or anyone else to come too. What are you going to do, I asked. He crossed his legs, eyes on Lydia. Rest, he said, eat, swim. Another practice with Katja. You know we're leaving next week, don't you, me and Ed and the girls? Oh, I said. I had not known. No one had said. No one had told me anything, though if I had thought I would have realized that their holiday could not be long. Dancers' careers are too short for long holidays, they lose enough time to injury; retire, with luck, in their thirties. I wondered how it would be, me and Lydie and la signora. And then someone else, you. So all the more reason, Tom said, for you to have adventures while we're here.

I finished my breakfast and felt better. Lydie was in the middle of the pool now, the water swirling around her shoulders and waist as her arms danced in the sunlit air. She did a step that ended with a jump, lifting the bump out of the water and sending waves over the edge of the pool. I stacked my dishes neatly and went to talk to her on my way to returning them to the kitchen. She was trying to spin. You can dance distress.

I put the dishes down and squatted at the poolside. It's beautiful, I said, your water dancing. She was breathless, resisting, turning more like a paddle, like oars, than like a nymph. Shut up, she said. I waited, watched. She must tire, must fall, but Tom was right that when she did, the water would hold her. Lyd, I said, Lyd, about last night, about— Shut up, she said. Shut up, shut up, we're not talking about it. OK, I said. I stood up, stepped out of my shoes, did not glance back at Tom before I pulled off my dress and stepped off the poolside. It was warmer than a few days ago, all that sun. She stepped away from me and revolved faster, doing that ballet thing with her head and her fixed smile. They can smile while they pirouette on broken toes. I didn't try to speak to her again. I took a step towards her, into the orbit of her spinning arms, stretched out my own arms and began to spin too, a cog in her wheel, holding her speed, churning the water to her rhythm. After a while I felt dizzy but I kept going, turning churning, intersecting, until I felt sick and stumbled, and then she was there holding me, wet skin on wet skin, bodies formed in the same body, and I felt you turning too in the water on the other side of that skin. I knew then not to speak. As my dizziness eased she stepped away, submerged, came up at the other end of the pool, as far from me as she could be in that water, and I recognized another move in the dance, stood there, let her retreat, return, retreat, and I wondered if you were dancing to your own tune or hers, under the skin.

*

Afterwards, having seen my sister again settled in her chair with Katja beside her, I steeled myself and knocked at the kitchen door. Signora Pilone called from inside but I couldn't hear words and didn't want to go in if I hadn't been asked. I waited and heard another call, so I eased the door open and peered around. She was up to the elbows in a bowl of flour, moving more energetically than for pastry. Bread, maybe, but I didn't think the bread we'd been eating was home-made. Sì, she said. It was obviously a bad moment to ask her to do something else. Could I, I asked, would it perhaps be possible, permissible, to take some food up the mountain? Could I make myself a packed lunch, I wanted to say, but even though I had the grammar and most of the vocabulary – *packed*? – lined up, I wasn't confident about tone, or that 'make myself lunch' worked in Italian as it does in French. It was important that she should understand that I wasn't expecting her to prepare a picnic for me. Up the mountain, she asked, where, up there? She gestured up the hill behind the villa. Sì, I said, above the church. I had seen where the track led on from the hillside chapel, winding upwards. She went on kneading or squeezing the dough in the bowl. My family live up there, she said. My brother and his wife. I was a child there. A farm, I asked. Just a few cows, she said, and some goats. Chickens. In summer, up there, in winter, here in the village. Perhaps like your farm, at home? We keep sheep, I said. I paused, watched her hands work the flour, building the sentence. We live in the same house winter and summer, I said. It is close to the village. But you have snow, she said, in winter. Yes, I said, probably less than here. The sheep are hardy, I wanted to say, hardier than cows, but probably Alpine cows are bred for Alpine seasons and I didn't know *hardy* in Italian. You will take them a parcel, she said, a gift, my brother at the farm? Of course, I said, trying to imagine myself knocking on the door of a farmhouse where I wasn't expected and might have trouble explaining why I was there, hoping Italian farm dogs might be more relaxed about visitors than some of our neighbours' dogs at home. The whole point, I thought, was to get away, to be off the clock and invisible for a few hours, I was going to take a book and maybe just sit somewhere nice and read, the way I did on summer days at home. I always ask, she said, if someone is going up. So maybe they would be used to it. In a quarter of an hour, she said, you come back, everything will be ready. I hesitated. Let me help, I said, tell me what I can do. She looked up at me. Very well, she said, you can cut some bread for yourself, it's in the box there. Cheese in the dispensa. She gestured to a door leading towards the dining room. I crossed the room – the furthest I'd been into the kitchen – and opened it. Larder, I thought, dispensa, dispensary. There was a stone floor and marble shelves, a high window so small I hadn't noticed it from the outside. We had a cold cupboard at home and Granny still liked to keep the cheese there because she said the fridge was too cold for it. I carefully picked up the cheese stand, a glass edifice with a glass dome, a way of displaying cheese I'd remember when I encountered Dutch still life paintings in the Ashmolean a year later. I kept my eyes on the job as I carried it to the tiled kitchen counter. What are you making, I asked her. Pasta, of course, she said. Yes, I said, of course, sorry. You don't have pasta, she said, in England? Yes, I said, in London, it's not English food. My grandmother does not cook it. I sliced cheese, trying not to take too much. What then, she asked, only potatoes? Often, I said, with meat and vegetables, yes, or bread. And your English puddings, she said, every day. The usual range, I thought, and we baked a couple of times a week and made it last, fruit crumbles and pies are perfectly good cold, generally Gran and I were good at leftovers, but we'd never eaten the same dish twice at the villa and it all seemed far too complicated to explain. Mostly, I said, yes, our English puddings.

I thought then and I was right that I would always remember that afternoon. From below, the mountain looked steep, as if it might be difficult or even dangerous to climb, but there was a good broad path all the way. For the first time, there was a note of autumn on the air, a coolness lifting my hair and fanning my neck as I walked. I heard the cuckoo again, near and then further in the trees, and as I came out above the woods the sounds changed, shifted into harmony, like hearing an orchestra from the right distance. A cockerel in the valley below, church bells, wind in the trees, bells around the necks of goats or cows on the hillside, a dog barking. I am in the gods, I told myself, thinking of the Opera House. I was carrying my lunch and a woollen jersey Tom had insisted on lending me in Dad's knapsack, and I thought about what Dad would notice here. We had never kept goats, no one local did, and he would have been curious. They must have been for milk, the cheese in my bag, and I supposed they could graze terrain impossible for cows though it seemed unlikely that they would present themselves daily and stand peaceably to be milked. I should write to Dad about it. I'd sent only a postcard since I arrived. And I should write Gran a separate letter, though they'd read them together, tell her that Lydie was still energetic and that Signora Pilone was feeding her well, and about the orange and lemon trees and the tomatoes and peppers growing in the kitchen garden. I could feel homesickness gathering itself, which was ridiculous, there I was strong and free in the sunshine with an elegant villa behind me and a small adventure under foot. I bent down to rub mountain thyme between my fingers, and sniffed it as I walked on.

I'd wondered how I would recognize Signora Pilone's brother's house, but there was only one, a solid stone building in the dip between two hilltops, built in the shelter of the col and surrounded by pine trees taller than the house. I almost recognized it from Heidi, which was among the books Nancy and I had reread and played out the summer we were eight. There was a well-fenced henhouse to the side, and a small barn with a newly painted door. Dad always said you could tell a good farmer by the state of the barn. I stopped to pick up a big stick, but the dog that came out was only curious and allowed me to pat it before I called out. It's much easier to shout hello than buon giorno. A woman appeared, much younger, or younger-looking, than Signora Pilone and to my astonishment wearing trousers. Buon giorno, I said again, I come from the villa below. Signora Pilone – I paused to line up the grammar of direct and indirect objects – gave me something for you. Sì, she said, grazie, benvenuto. Come in, please, let me offer you a drink after your climb. Grazie, I said, grazie mille.

Dad and Gran would have loved to see the house. It was stone-flagged, but the hall and the sitting–dining room were panelled in dark wood. The furniture was just benches built along the walls, a table and carved chairs that could have been hundreds of years old, and a square thing tiled in blue and white with a metal chimney going up the wall that must have been some kind of stove but seemed to have no door. Benvenuto, she said, I am Lucia. Dita, I said, experimenting. We nodded and smiled at each other, and then I remembered and rummaged in the knapsack. I had a soft brown paper parcel for her, and a jar of plum jam that was still slightly warm, as if asleep. Grazie mille, she said, please, sit down. I sat on one of the chairs, which was heavy to move. She left the room. I wanted to ask her proper questions, is that a stove and how does it work; how much of the year do you spend up here; what is it like at night, so high and alone; is it wolves or foxes from which you're protecting the hens; what do you do in the evenings; what do you do if someone needs the doctor; do you always wear trousers or is it just a summer mountain freedom; do you like being here? Do you miss your friends in the village or is it good to be away? The windows looked down over the meadow and valley, but the glass was wavy and they were so small that the room was dim. The only decoration was a small crucifix, a metal Christ on a polished wooden cross. I settled Dad's knapsack beside my chair and rolled my shoulders, felt a sudden pulse of worry about Lydia. What if she went into labour while I was gallivanting around up here? For the matter of that, what when she went into labour anyway? It wasn't as if I would know what to do. She and Maman must have made a plan, probably with Signora Pilone, who must know the local midwife and doctor. They couldn't be expecting me to do more than boil water, whatever that was for, and bring towels, whatever they were for, and come to think of it, it wasn't particularly likely that Signora Pilone would want me hefting her pans around her kitchen or rummaging her linen cupboards either. Probably I would just call the number Maman had given me, which I'd written out a couple of times in case I lost the letter, and then do whatever the sisterly equivalent of pacing the library smoking cigars might be. Reading, probably, trying not to hear the noises, the cries of agony—

The door opened and Lucia came around it, a tray in her hands. Oh, I said, let me – di niente, she said, please. On a white cloth embroidered with blue flowers was a glass jug of something pale yellow, two glass tumblers and a glass bowl of blue-blooming plums. Please excuse me, she said, we have little today, I have not been down to the village. Not at all, I said, I am only thirsty but your plums look delicious. I paused, hoped that in Italian I could use the same word for plant and human growing. They do not grow where I live, I said, and saw in her face that what I had said made no sense. I do not have trees of plums at home, I tried. She poured our drinks, I hoped not wine or God forbid spirits, I'd never make it back to the villa. In England, she asked. I was on safer ground. In the north of England, I said, a farm in the hills. Like us here, she said. We keep sheep, I said, I think you have goats? The drink didn't taste alcoholic, sweet, aromatic, very nice. Also cows, she said, for the milk. I can do this, I thought, I can manage this conversation, here in a stranger's farm up a hill in Italy, I can do anything.

Lucia set me on the path leading across her meadow. It was full of flowers I couldn't name and grazed by small pale cows with dramatic eyelashes, who watched me with mild curiosity. The day was warmer now, but still I caught the season's turn on the air like Maman's perfume after she had left a room. As the path rose, I looked straight over the lake to the more serious peaks on the other side, where patches of snow lay between rocks and clouds tangled around cliffs. I had never in my life been so high up, never seen water from so far away. I stopped to listen: wind, birds, faint goat bells. I could tell where there were boats on the lake from the lines of their wakes and the folding of the water, traces, trails, passage.

On, up, until there was nothing behind the hill rising in front of me, until I came out on the top and could see in every direction, across a sea of summits, over the other lake into Switzerland, hill calling to hill, a new country at altitude. I turned slowly, delighted to be me, delighted to be there in that hour. I found a rock and sat on it, turned to the call of a bird and saw some great hawk, something that could have been an eagle, turning and passing below me. To see from above a bird in flight, to see the sunlight on its dappled back, to see the spread of its wings above the earth!

where he comes from

It's light, these days, by the time she wakes up. She'll probably get up at dawn on midsummer's day, there's a casual and recently invented local tradition of a swim, the yin to the midwinter yang in which she considers herself not masochistic enough to participate. Until then, she thinks, sunrise can happen without her, though she knows she'll go on sleeping opposite the uncurtained window exactly so the first light falls on her face, exactly so she wakes with the morning. Up now, anyway, she wants to get to Bríd's before Méabh, maybe have Méabh's coffee waiting for her, token of care. Cappuccino, sugar – though Méabh doesn't really like coffee at all. She had messaged late last night: Breakfast tomorrow? Not an apology, plainly, but then for what, really, should she apologize? Méabh has done no harm to Edith and aren't they too old to end a friendship over politics? Though where would you stop, and isn't it easy enough, to overlook political difference when for you the politics aren't personal? She's heard of friends of friends whose grandchildren stopped speaking to them over Brexit, but that was personal for the grandchildren, whole unlived lives of study and work and relationships taken away. She pushes back the covers, stands up. Left her yoga mat out the night before to make the next step easy. Didn't Pat break up with a girlfriend over her parents' homophobia, or at least because he wouldn't tolerate the girlfriend's acceptance of their homophobia? What is it they say, what you're willing to overlook is what you're willing to tolerate. Darling Pat, she got some things right, or he did, along the way, though she does wonder, now, as he gets older and seems to have no permanent attachment, no one to whom she's been introduced, is it her fault, hers and Mike's, did they show him that love doesn't last, that marriage is no great shakes, autonomy preferable to belonging, and if so, was that wrong, could he not still, like Gunter, achieve happiness? He has friends, plenty of friends, she must have shown him that at least. How far would Méabh have to go, if Méabh had said what Eilidh said about Africa, would she still – Start in child's pose, not as easy first thing in the morning as it used to be. Gently now, ease in. Breathe.

She's following the Paddywagon along the main road, and there's another company's bus taking up half the car park at the Parish Hall, doors open, disgorging people disconcertingly like herself though she would never take a coach tour. What are they thinking, these people who appear to conduct professional adult lives in Amsterdam, Frankfurt, Rome, when they wait in their hotel lobbies for a bus to come and take them for a day out under the care of an undergraduate paid by the hour to perform Irishness? Maybe it's nice, to hand over responsibility to someone else for a few hours. Or maybe they're scared to drive the roads, which wouldn't be entirely stupid though it doesn't seem to cross the minds of Americans driving the Wild Atlantic Way – whoever thought of renaming the N67 deserves either a life-changing bonus or pushing off the Cliffs of Moher, depending on your point of view – that there might be challenges involved in navigating a narrow coastal road in variable weather on the unaccustomed side. And stop it, she thinks, with the national stereotyping, it's not as if she doesn't – didn't – stride around Paris in Birkenstocks and no make-up, because it's still sometimes necessary to piss off your dead mother.

She inserts her tiny car in what wouldn't be a parking space for anyone else and shimmies out of the door held millimetres from the shiny black SUV beside it. Ukrainian plates, every time she sees them she thinks about the drive across Europe, pets and kids in the back, Poland, Germany, Belgium, France, a few days for the journey that took her family two generations. What would you take, she remembers her neighbours wondering in the shop when the first cars arrived, but she knew exactly what you should take, what was in the bag Maman kept half-packed, at least in her head. Passports, as many as possible; jewellery, under your clothes; cash, several currencies, keep it in your bra, not to say they won't go looking but they won't see if they don't; certificates, to help you start again. A few photos if you must, but no need these days, phones and laptops. No more than you can carry, though that's different, of course, if you're packing the car. Even so, know what to abandon if you have to. Know what to keep until they take it from your hands. Oh, stop it, this isn't all about you. Or about Maman, or Maman's mother or the other Lydia. She remembers again standing on the pavement below the apartment in the Marais, the sun through her English clothes, Maman's bizarre panic at the sight of the old woman going through the front door, the only time she remembers seeing Maman in disarray – funny how these things come back now, after decades of not thinking about them, as if there's a need to tell, to remember –

It's the market today, the tourists herded towards it which is good, money straight into local pockets, or in some cases blow-in pockets, Hannah-Jane's cakes which she decorates with edible flowers and sells by the slice, Tony's goats' milk soap which is worth what he charges if that's how you want to spend your money. She checks her watch and stops to buy a box – two boxes, one for Méabh – of Sean's duck eggs, because he's not going to sell those to the tourists and you can see him being pleased for Hannah-Jane, whose Californian cheerfulness is audible across the square. And some asparagus to go with them from Mary whom she thinks of as Mary the blonde to avoid calling her Kevin's Mary as everyone else does, asparagus and duck eggs, she'll maybe ask Gunter over to dinner, in which case also some of your lovely Guinness bread, please, and isn't it nice that rain passed over in the night, we'll maybe have a dry morning of it. She knows the friendliness isn't friendship, she knows she'll never be local anywhere now, but isn't it better to live with people whose default is friendliness, in a country where kindness, the performance of kindness, is a way of life whether people actually feel like it or not? She remembers the protest. Personal kindness, maybe. If you introduced any of the people on that road to any of the people in that hotel, sat them together at a table over pints or tea, they'd be courteous. Probably. She hopes.

The café's busy, warm enough with bodies and loud enough with talk that last year's worry flickers in her body. It's still around, of course, the virus, she has friends in England who still haven't emerged, will probably now die without ever going to a theatre or party or restaurant again. She shrugs to herself. Chacun à son goût. Here she is. Morning, Bríd, she says, you're busy enough now, is there a corner for me and Méabh to have breakfast? Always, Bríd says, give me a minute, and in not many minutes somehow their preferred window table is free.

She stands up to hug Méabh as she comes in, the air shifting around her hair and scarves and perfume. Start as you mean to go on. I've missed you, she says, I'm glad to see you again. Ah sure, it was only a few days, says Méabh, taking off her coat, moving the chair, no eye contact. Edith understands that the protest, the refugees, her accusation, are among the things of which we do not speak, that there will be no airing, no reconciliation. Or alternatively, that this breakfast, this breaking of bread, is the reconciliation. Even after a few days, she says, I'm glad. How are things? Méabh sits down, looks at her folded hands. Not much new, she says, Aoibhinn driving John out to the pub every night and fighting with her brothers, Caoimhe moving things around my kitchen, all very petty I know, and yourself? Oh, hot sex and holidays in Italy, she wants to say, all the way. Much the same, she says, I heard from Pat, the other day, he's thinking of coming over, in the summer. And I might go to London, there's a theatre festival. Méabh looks up. Good, she says, that will be nice for you.

Nadia comes neatly through the tables and pushed-back chairs. She knows, Edith thinks, exactly how much space she fills, knows the kinesphere of waiting. Of various kinds of waiting. An espresso, please, Edith says, and the granola. Scrambled eggs on toast for Méabh, tea, though when Nadia's gone Méabh says I do resent paying three euro for a teabag that barely costs three cents and a kettle they're boiling anyway, maybe I should have said a cappuccino but you know I don't think I really like coffee all that much. I know, says Edith, have what you want, that's what you're really paying for, to have someone bring you what you feel like because that's their job so you don't have to be grateful or offset it against whatever irritating thing they did last, you don't get your money's worth by making them froth milk for a coffee you don't actually want. Méabh, she says, what's up, really, are you coming to the end of the road with Caoimhe and the kids in your house? I can't, can I, says Méabh, there isn't an alternative, but anyway, no, that's not it. She waits, doesn't say well what is it then. At the next table, a pair of plump, well-scrubbed Americans are arguing with disproportionate venom about which of two conflicting weather apps should determine their day's plans. Too long on holiday together, she diagnoses, or not enough practice at being on holiday together, and also this is the west coast and there will be rain before bedtime whatever the apps say.

Méabh pushes her hair about. It's — you won't tell anyone, will you? No, says Edith. I had a letter, Méabh says. I mean an actual letter, in the post like, it's a mercy I was the one who picked it up. Yes, says Edith.

It was from — says Méabh, you really won't say anything? No, says Edith, I won't.

From a person, Méabh says. A man. Yes, says Edith.

Nadia brings the tea and the coffee. Milk jug, sugar bowl, Gunter's mugs. Thank you. The American couple have retreated into their phones, which won't, Edith thinks, improve their holiday. She and Mike took separate holidays from very early on, Pat usually with her, they had some good adventures together, mother and son, Mike's absence from those trips probably one of the reasons the marriage lasted as long as it did.

Méabh adds milk to her tea, two teaspoons of sugar. Her fingertips on the spoon are white. I'm telling you, she says, because I have to tell someone, and because I might need you to come somewhere with me. Yes, says Edith, I'm not local, Méabh, I don't know anyone here as well as I know you. I can keep a secret.

Méabh looks around. The Americans might hear, if they are listening. Come and sit next to me, Edith says, or wait and we'll take a walk after breakfast. It's OK, I have all morning, there's no rush. Yes, says Méabh, but I don't, and I gave myself until today, I said I'd write back, or call the number, today. She stands up, flurry of chairs and coats, and Edith slides along the bench. Rose perfume again, almost touching, Méabh's hair on her shoulder.

He says he's my brother, Méabh says. Our brother. Our half-brother. He says Mam gave him away, before she had us. He says he just found out, and he didn't want to wait, in case – in case he was in time. To meet Mam.

Edith puts her hand on Méabh's clenched fist. Yes, she says.

And I don't know, Méabh says, I don't know if it's true, if it can be true. I mean, you wouldn't invent it, would you, something like that, you wouldn't just pick on some woman in another country and write to say you're her brother if you weren't, would you?

No, says Edith, probably not. But you can check it out, you know, the DNA test, that'll be how he knows. There are ways to be sure.

Nadia brings their food. Edith lets go of Méabh's hand, does the smiling and thanking for both of them.

Méabh looks up. A tear falls. I've hardly eaten, she says, everything tastes like porridge. Yes, Edith says, have some of your eggs while they're hot, you'll feel better.

She sips her coffee, starts her granola. Stewed apples, cinnamon, good yogurt. Méabh prepares a forkful, puts it down.

I just can't imagine it, Méabh says, except that I can, sort of. It's not impossible. You know Mam was – she had –

Yes, says Edith. Méabh's mother died fifteen years ago, before they met, but in the way of mothers she's always there.

It's not a complete shock, is what I mean, Méabh says, only it is. That there might have been a secret, all families have them, don't they, no one tells their children everything. Only the thought of him growing up over there, in America – and in the photo he looks just like Dermot, twins almost, only the beard, but I haven't said, I haven't told anyone –

Yes, says Edith. Eat something, Méabh, take a minute.

Méabh eats. Her hands are shaky. Can I put another sugar in your tea, asks Edith, and Méabh nods.

And then earlier this week, Méabh says, Monday, the letter came. I mean, out of the blue, I suppose these things always are, it's not as if a letter's going to come gradually or preceded by warnings, is it.

No, says Edith.

He says he wanted to write rather than social media, he wanted me to have time to think about it. But he can't be the only one who knows, he found me through some genetics website, Seamus did it last year, the boys gave him one of those kits for Christmas. I told them at the time, I said you think it's just for the craic but you don't know what can of worms you're after opening, it's who might find you as well as who you'll find, not that I suspected Mam but you hear enough stories, crimes and old secrets. I get that part but I don't see how my brother's DNA gives him my address.

No, says Edith, nor do I.

They didn't tell him he was adopted, his American parents. He says he always felt strange, disconnected. But they were good people, he says he was happy. He has a degree and you know none of us could do that, he wouldn't have got that kind of education from Mam and Dad, and he was a teacher, a high school teacher, maths. Divorced, he says, they do that all the time there, don't they.

Yes, says Edith. Also here, she does not point out; Méabh had been married almost twenty years when divorce became legal in Ireland. Even in Dublin, Edith knows no other divorced woman of her generation.

And kids, he has three kids, grown up now of course, kids of their own. I suppose they're my nephews and nieces, aren't they? And grand-nephews and nieces?

Yes, says Edith, genetically they are. Remember your breakfast, your eggs are going cold.

Méabh takes an uncharacteristically obedient mouthful.

I suppose he wants to meet you, Edith asks.

He says he'd like to. Me and the others. He says he wants to see where he comes from. But he won't if we don't want him to.

Where he comes from, Edith thinks. He, who has never set foot in this place, comes from here, and she, who yearly seeks the invisible flower with her own feet and hands and eyes, remains a stranger.

You can think about that, she says, there's no rush. You can take your time.

Méabh eats some more. Her hands are calmer. I know, she says, but it's taken so long already, he's older than me of course, pushing seventy. None of us is getting younger.

Will you tell the others, then, she asks, your brothers?

I suppose so, says Méabh, I better had, hadn't I? If you think it's real. All those years.

Méabh, Edith says, I don't know what's real, don't take my word for it.

brightest star

We had a party for their last night. A gala performance.

The evenings were cooler now, the snow line morning by morning a little lower on the mountains at the end of the lake. I should have brought more clothes, wondered as I crossed the grounds towards the barn if I might borrow money from Lydia and take the boat back to Como for some shopping. If finished clothes were too expensive I could buy some wool, knit myself a jumper, though I wasn't sure that even with so little to do I would knit a jumper faster than the season turned, and then the thought of knitting reminded me of the baby. Should I make a matinee jacket, as we'd been taught in Domestic Science? A bonnet? It seemed suddenly sad, that no one was knitting for this baby. For you.

They had invited Signora Pilone, who had surprisingly accepted, and the village girl who turned out to be called Giovanna and had asked if she could bring her friend and then her friend asked if her mother could come and the friend's mother wanted to bring her own mother and in the end we had to gather most of the chairs in the house for what seemed like most of the women in the village, men being apparently uninterested. We'll be traditional, Louise said, no point shocking them with Balanchine. I didn't say that I thought she was overestimating their discernment in relation to ballet traditions, that I didn't think Giovanna and her friends were likely to see the difference between Petipa and Ashton. Will you watch, I'd asked my sister, because she didn't usually go to the barn. No, she said, I'll dance. Lyd – I said. Not en pointe, she said, no jumps, it's still dancing, isn't it, if you stay on the ground. Yes, I thought, Petipa's famous solo for the ballerina about to give birth, but I said yes, I'm sure, only what will you wear because I don't think Lombardy is ready for a heavily pregnant woman in tights and a leotard. I'll find something, she said, why don't you worry about what you're going to wear.

Ed, Tom, Giovanna and I spent half the afternoon carrying chairs about. Is it easier or harder than carrying dancers, I asked, and Tom set down his chair on the grass, put his hands around my waist and almost stifled his grunt as he lifted me above his head. I held myself up, as if I might weigh less that way. Fly me, I wanted to say, but I said put me down, do, you want to save your strength. Lydie and the girls were doing something in Louise's room, something that produced laughter and raised voices. Ed and Tom moved the gramophone from the villa into the barn, and of course Igor's record collection, even in a villa he hardly visited, included all the big ballet numbers. I swept and Giovanna mopped the barn's floor, and then Giovanna returned to the kitchen from which a herb and meat smell came and I looked again along the bookshelves in the drawing room.

They were full but, apart from a whole run of George Eliot and Dickens and Shakespeare which was keeping me going, mostly of nineteenth-century books mostly in Italian. There was, at least, a complete Dante, which I kept intending to start and then reading more Dickens instead. I suspected Igor had bought them with the house. I took Bleak House, bound in blue leather, showing no sign of ever having been opened before, and went to sit on the terrace but it was too cold, a brisk wind coming off the lake. I wandered back into the drawing room and sat on the sofa, where I felt somehow silly, distractingly out of place, so I went back up to my room which was dark with the balcony doors closed and cold with them open. I thought of getting into bed, mostly to imagine Granny's face at the very idea, and then it occurred to me that there was nothing to stop me taking a bath even if it was the middle of the afternoon, a purely recreational hot bath about which no one would ever know or care. But baths are boring without a book and you can't hold someone else's leather-bound volume over water hot enough to make a decent bath. I wandered onto the balcony and leant over the parapet, rough on my bare arms. The poplar leaves were beginning to turn, the trellised roses to darken and droop, and the sky had lost the uncanny brightness of Alpine summer. At home, the days would be noticeably shortening now, Dad up before dawn, Granny checking our winter coats for moth and, every year I could remember, sighing over my outgrown school uniform while Lydie, whose ballet school kit was elaborate and far more expensive, obligingly wore the same sizes for years. It was time for moving on, summer's end, time to resume routines, time for the simultaneous return and renewal of the new school year, and without it, without a new number by my name and without the anticipation of new learning, I felt adrift. Next year, I thought, next year I will be going to Oxford, but that wasn't much help now. I thought of Nancy, about to start French and German at Edinburgh, and Sheila who would be training as a nurse though really she wanted to do music, and Tim from the grammar school who would be doing Law in London and seemed much more interested in London than Law, and here was I, marking time, marking my sister's time, on an Italian hillside. When Lydia returns to London, Maman had said, you can go to Marcel in Paris, won't it be nice not to have to spend the winter on the farm? I like winter on the farm, I'd said, but she was right when she said nonsense, you'll be eighteen, go to Paris, you should be wanting to see the world at your age, it will do you good. And wrong when she added, maybe you'll decide against Oxford after all.

The wind moved over the hillside, through the trees, ruffled the lake like velvet stroked the wrong way. Tomorrow, I thought, the house will be so quiet we will be like ghosts, it will be as if we have disappeared from the world, which was of course Lydia's plan, to disappear. I felt as if I were being buried with her, like the servant of a Pharaoh, which was so idiotic I went down to the kitchen to ask if I could help with the preparations for dinner.

Sì, said Signora Pilone, of course you can help, do you know how to cut vegetables? The kitchen smelt of olive oil and garlic, exotic. Yes, I said, and she gave me an apron, ironed blue linen, and a knife heavier and sharper than I was used to. Giovanna scrubbed the carrots in the deep marble sink while I chopped onions, enjoying the weight of the knife and the length of the blade. It brought extra dignity to the task. Smaller than that, said Signora Pilone. Giovanna sent me a quick smile. Have you seen ballet before, I asked. She glanced to Signora Pilone. Permission to chat, I thought, granted with a nod. No, she said, there is a theatre in Como, I have seen a play there but no dancing. Do you go often to Como, I asked. Not often, she said, sometimes. So you go to school here, I asked. The carrots were big, so I cut them lengthways first and was rewarded by a nod from la signora. I finished school, said Giovanna, last spring. So did I, I said, how does it feel? She shrugged. Now I must work, she said. Shame flickered. She wasn't, I thought, going to ask anything in return, I was just being nosy. I tipped the carrots into the bowl with the onions. And you, asked Signora Pilone, you will work? University, I said, next year. After my sister— Sì, she said, capisco. And you will study? Literature, I said. They both nodded, eyebrows raised, whether surprised or impressed I couldn't tell. And – may I ask, I said, you, signora, you grew up on the mountain? School in the winter, she said, until I was ten. Since then, work! You are fortunate, signorina, to study so long. Yes, I said, I know. I had heard it, of course, at home, in the village, where my Oxford place in some ways compounded the offence of Maman's French delinquency and Lydia's notions of herself. Ideas above our station, all three. Like mother, like daughter, what a shame there wasn't a son to carry on the farm, not that Dad hadn't brought it on himself, marrying the way he did. Well now, Edith, aren't you a lucky girl? I heard they liked you, then, at Oxford, what a chance for you, you and your sister both away down south! But you know there'll be plenty of clever folk there, don't you, you won't be a big fish in that pond. Yes, I said, I know, I'm very lucky, of course it's exciting but I'm worried I won't keep up. I wasn't worried about any such thing, couldn't wait for the company of 'clever folk' and the sumptuous libraries and the banquets of lectures. I would work hard enough to keep up, that was all. I wondered if they were saying the same things to the doctor's son, off to Cambridge for Medicine. Pay no heed, said Gran, it's just their way, and also, love, remember this is a small pond, there'll be folk from everywhere there, you can't always be the brightest star. Fools rush in, she meant, don't show off.

When did you begin to work here, I asked Signora Pilone, at the villa? After the war, she said, my husband was injured and his commanding officer bought the house. He lived in Milan with his family and he wanted a housekeeper and uomo tuttofare. I knew how to keep house and my husband could do the outdoor work, and so. She shrugged. Uomo tuttofare, literally a man who does everything, handyman, I thought, adding it to my vocabulary. And then my husband died, she said, and then the owner died and the house was sold but the next owner also wanted a cook, and the next and now Signor Igor. So she was, almost as much as Dad, part of a house, except that Dad owned our farm. I wondered what she would do if Igor sacked her, or sold the house to someone who didn't want a housekeeper or already had one. I wondered what I would have done if I'd left school at ten. And you, I wanted to ask Giovanna, where will you work, what are your dreams, who will you be and where will you go, but I said to Signora Pilone, and the mushrooms, shall I slice them too?

I thought about all the women in the village, getting the dinner on early so they could come to the dance, all their hands holding knives and wooden spoons, all they were remembering and hoping as they chopped and stirred, and for a moment I thought I understood what my English teacher had meant when he said it was inevitable but a pity that adolescents don't understand Middlemarch, which I'd resented at the time because I did understand it, as a novel about a beautiful girl conned into marriage and denied education, but I didn't like it because the narrative voice was unnecessarily preachy, much less fun than Wuthering Heights or Jane Eyre. *If we had a keen vision and feeling of all ordinary human life, it would be like hearing the grass grow and the squirrel's heart beat, and we should die of that roar which lies on the other side of silence.* Impossible to hold in one's head, in one's seventeen-year-old head, the idea that all the women in the village, all the humans in the bowl of the mountains, along the boot of Italy, across the continent of Europe – never mind the grass and the squirrels – have their own reality, are the central characters in their own worlds, that there are as many tragedies and comedies as entries in the census; I had not, of course, yet learnt that tragedy and comedy, plot and endings, are merely the tools of fiction, fairy tale. Ripeness, not readiness, is all. Life has no form, you don't get to choose. I shivered.

The sun went behind the mountain early in the evening now, but there was still light in the sky as I joined the village women in the studio, and we kept the barn doors open for the sunset glow reflecting off the hills across the lake. It was hard to tell age, but half the women wore black, and the others were in dull colours, long skirts, hats, the Sunday dress of middle-aged women in my childhood that was now, at home, tempered by new fabrics and rising hemlines. There was some murmuring as I slipped in. Fallen women and dancers; mostly I quite liked the idea of being disreputable, if only by association, but their disapproval seemed palpable, though on the other hand, here they were, curious at least. Squirrels' beating hearts, I thought, every human soul a central character. I pulled at the hem of my dress, wondering if I'd grown or if it just seemed shorter in this company, thought again that I would have to do something about my clothes. I sat at the back of our assemblage of chairs, on a stool I'd set aside for myself earlier, inconspicuous. No one spoke to me and I spoke to no one.

There was no curtain, no wings. I'd thought probably one of the men would come on and start the gramophone, but instead Giovanna's friend, who was sitting by the open door, exclaimed and pointed. We all turned. They came dancing across the daisied grass, Louise and Katja, Tom and Ed, no Lydia, all four shimmering, as one and then spacing out, a leap moving along their line, and as they reached the gravel the step changed, wings outspread, a wave or gust beginning in Ed's fingers and passing over his arm, shoulder, arm, Louise's fingers, arm, shoulder, arm, Tom, Katja, and then they were here and the music began. Not Tchaikovsky, not Petipa, some wild angular thing and they all began to fly across the barn, swallow-swift, criss-cross, and I remembered Ed saying you have to know what the dancer behind you is doing, you have to be able to feel where people are when you can't look at them, and not just where they are but where they're about to be, no dancer is an island, not even Igor. The dance dances the dancer, he'd said; I had not read Yeats then and I doubt now that he had either. Lord of the dance, I thought, but in Ed's account the dance was the lord and to dance was to follow. I had the feeling this idea was related to the one about Middlemarch but I couldn't see how, and while I was trying to think about that the music changed, soft and slow but not without menace and the small back door opened and my sister stepped slowly across the wooden floor, carrying her hands crossed as if there were a bird sitting in them. As she danced, she lifted her hands, opened her arms high, and the others came in around her, weaving and twisting and then Ed and Tom began to spin Louise and Katja, hands on their waists in a way that made me suddenly ache, suddenly want someone – a man – to touch me, guard my balance, lift me as Ed and Tom were now lifting the girls, flying them around Lydia's orbit. Queenly, I thought, she is imperial, imperious, in her gravity, she is the axis. I would not have thought such small movements as she made could command so much space.

most loving thing

She thinks of Méabh for the rest of the day, as she goes to yoga, makes a batch of soup, cleans the house, sits in her rocking chair reading and drinking tea. She should volunteer for something, really, the way she used to, the way she always did, making herself useful, showing Pat that privilege should be put to use, proving that she wasn't, or wasn't only, a housewife, but it turns out now that maybe much of the motivation was to get away from her husband and son and even her friends, to set herself in places where people didn't think they knew all about her, where she had potential. And now she lives alone, unwatched, uncontested, the urge to put privilege to work is much diminished. She never claimed to be a nice person, and she never thought volunteers – or anyone ever – acted from pure altruism. People have reasons for their altruism, debts to pay or penance to perform, only now apparently she doesn't have a reason. She could teach English to Ukrainians, she's even qualified assuming TEFL courses don't lapse after a decade or two, but mostly they seem to speak good enough English and there are plenty of people queueing up to help. It crosses her mind to accuse herself of absurd, unforgivable envy, of a fantasy that it might be worth being hunted across Europe to be accepted in the new place. After all these years, could her need be so craven, so immature? She could volunteer for the Samaritans again, did that for years, but in the end the angry men and the sex callers got her down, left her feeling that they phoned up to empty their lust and rage into her and she had to digest it for days. Snake-like, she thinks, weeks and months in your system, half-life. You wouldn't, of course, phone the Samaritans to rant or wank if you didn't have a problem, as the volunteers always told each other the ranters and wankers also needed help, but after a while her readiness wore out. Rape Crisis, then, though probably angry men phone them too, probably angry men phone everyone.

Rape crisis. Méabh's mother, and all the others, even her own generation in the Homes and laundries, Magdalens while Edith and her friends were bed-hopping in Oxford and then London, post-pill, pre-Aids. It sometimes seems as if her Irish friends grew up in a different era from her, even those who are ten years younger, though of course by British standards also Maman and Lydia made sure that Edith was unusually liberated unusually early, especially for a country girl. Nancy, she remembers, was shocked when her first university boyfriend expected her to have sex with him. Nancy had come from Edinburgh to visit Edith in Paris that year, Nancy's first time abroad, her parents wanting a postcard to say that she'd arrived, as if the journey was the day of possibilities. I thought he knew I'm not that kind of girl, she'd said, sitting on a bench in the pretty park near the bookshop in the Marais. Why aren't you, Edith had said, that kind of girl, which was, maybe, in retrospect, the beginning of the end of that friendship, because Nancy married the next boyfriend, who presumably knew she wasn't that kind of girl, and he didn't like Edith and didn't bother to pretend, and while you can be friends with someone whose husband dislikes you it requires effort neither of them made. She puts down her tea and reaches for her phone: Hope the day's going as well as can be expected, I'm around if you want to talk. Méabh writes back immediately: OK, thanks. Fancy a wet walk tomorrow? Monks' Hill? Irresistible, obviously, she replies, just say what time.

They meet at the church. Modern building, architecturally dull. She knows whose fault it is – among greater evils, the English didn't exactly spend eight centuries encouraging the building of beautiful Irish churches – but she's still always taken aback by the mundanity of church buildings, designs given about as much attention as petrol stations or supermarkets, but maybe it makes sense, maybe it's a sign of greater faith, to consider the site of holiness in the same terms as fuel for your car and your body. It is raining. Just a fresh rain, Méabh will say, as if there were a stale kind that would be less pleasant. She wriggles over to the passenger seat to pull on her waterproof trousers but has to step out to lace up her boots. She can hear Méabh's car coming.

Hello, says Méabh, you're very kind to come out in this, are you sure you don't mind now, we can go for a coffee if you prefer. Not now I've put my rain gear on, Edith says, you know I don't mind, but will you be comfortable? Méabh is wearing leggings, trainers, a skirt sticking out from under a jacket that was once waterproof, a cotton scarf wrapped over her hair, horrible, Edith thinks, once it gets properly wet. Ah sure, she says, it's only a fresh rain and I don't think it's set in.

They set off, up the lane past the big houses, Galway commuters who've invested in their fences and gates. Rain patters, potholes brim. Under the beech and chestnut trees there's a green underwater dimness. How are you, she asks Méabh, how are you feeling? She peers around the blinkers of her hood, but Méabh's face is behind hair getting wilder in the rain. Her waterproof trousers scissor. Rain patters. I don't know, Méabh says, excited, a bit, and scared, I want to meet him and I don't, and I still wonder if it's all true, how it could have happened and Mam never said, not even at the end. I was thinking about the dates, Mam would have been barely sixteen, it's no wonder, really, in those days, she couldn't have kept him. No, says Edith, I know.

Rain, extra drips from the trees, but when she looks up Méabh might be right, the sky's maybe clearer to the north, a paler grey. You don't seem surprised, Méabh says, you're not shocked. She shrugs. I'm past shock, she thinks, an obviously hubristic thought. I don't think it's very unusual, she says, I have two friends in Dublin with similar stories. And a sister, she does not say, with a different one. They have a shape and a form, those tales, she thinks, our stories tell us, not the other way around, and perhaps especially the stories that run in our veins, though if you follow that line biology becomes destiny which is not true either. Children are never lost in stories, because we keep them in stories, even or especially when they are lost to us. Hansel and Gretel are lost in the woods but we know exactly where they are, in the middle, protagonists.

She pushes her hood back. So you're going to meet him, she

asks. What's his name, by the way? Henry, says Méabh, Henry like the kings, and they both laugh. Not, for obvious reasons, an Irish name. Do you think, Edith asks, your aunts knew? Your grandmother, surely?

Under her raincoat, Méabh shrugs. No idea, she says, probably? The house was small enough, they were sharing beds, but then I've seen it myself, some girls stay very small when it's a secret, there were two I remember at school – well, you know yourself how it is.

Yes, says Edith, I think I do.

She has measured her integration by that phrase. *You know yourself how it is.* At first, thirty years ago, she actually said a couple of times no, I'm sorry, I'm an immigrant, I don't know how it is, please could you explain? She winces at the memory. And then for a while it meant a version of what her grandmother used to say, them as asks no questions won't be told no lies; if you don't know, there's no point trying to explain, and then she did know, usually, often something innocuous, a shorthand handshake, and then she heard herself use it one day, calming a tricky meeting of the Parent–Teacher Association at Pat's school. And in this case, surely she does know something of how it is, how it was.

Your poor mother, she says, imagine it, Aoibhinn's age.

Yes, says Méabh, well. I hope Caoimhe's spoken to her, it's not my place.

They come out of the trees and the road becomes a track, an old green lane following the line of the hill from the village towards the town at the head of the inlet. Sheep despondently crop the grass between limestone slabs. The birds have taken shelter, flustering in the hedges. She's afraid she's hurting Méabh with her questions but also thinks that Méabh has chosen to tell her partly because, not being Irish, she will ask questions. Sometimes people want to be asked what they can't tell, and sometimes that's the foreigner's job, to be the fool who rushes in. And some people, she thinks, are fools and foreigners everywhere, are always lost in the woods and holding on at the centre of the story.

He doesn't remember, Méabh says, he says in his letter, I mean, of course he doesn't, he was six weeks old, only he says he always wondered, he didn't look the same. He has a sister and a brother there, you see, younger, you wonder if the parents found once they'd adopted they could have their own, often seems to happen. He's grey now but he says he was a proper Irish redhead, no hiding it, and the parents, the adoptive parents, were both dark. And I keep thinking all those years we didn't know, and Mam going to her grave, and I wonder did they ever speak of it, her and her sisters, but probably not, you know, probably nothing was said, they thought it was for the best then, but she must have thought of him, mustn't she, birthdays at least, Christmas, she must have wondered – Oh love, says Edith. No, says Méabh, don't be nice to me, I'll cry. So what, says Edith, cry, it doesn't hurt. She can see Méabh's shoulder rise, the breath held. I don't want to cry, she says, give me a minute.

The light on the sea is changing, brightening, which doesn't mean the rain will stop, exactly, but things might be a bit drier in a while.

They were nice, she says, his parents, they were good people.

He says that. A happy childhood, and that's what you need, isn't it, a good start, even if there's a secret, that's what makes the difference?

The rain's easing enough for her to push her hood back. It's almost like going outside over again: light, wind, sound. Yes, she says, I think so, to be loved, to feel loved, I don't know how much it matters, who it is who loves a child. Maman, she's thinking, did Maman love her daughters, did Maman's mostly benign feelings, experienced mostly across a continent, qualify as love? Was Maman loved? Probably. Who's to say what qualifies as love, how would you measure it? Maman's parents sent her away, didn't they, and that was the most loving thing, under the circumstances. Sometimes it is the most loving thing, to give up, hand over, your child, to neighbours or traffickers or social workers. Or a French nun. There'll be good blackberries along here, she says, in a few weeks, and we must remember that apple tree.

On their last walk, they found a gravid apple tree by the gate of a ruined cottage. They share a mental foragers' map: hazel groves, blackberry hedges, damsons and sloes. Méabh can make nettle soup, Edith's one attempt made her and Gunter ill.

I think I'll tell them, Méabh says, the others. I think I should.

Edith squeezes her waterproofed arm. It's hard to know, she says, isn't it? But I can't see why not, I can't see why you should have to carry this.

No, says Méabh, only I know and they don't, so it is my choice now, to carry on the secret or not. He said it was my address he found, goodness only knows how, but I wonder – I remember hearing someone on the radio in a similar situation saying he'd been told to approach the arty sister first. Apparently arty sisters are the weak point.

Méabh, she says, are you a bit scared of him?

Méabh looks up through rain and hair. Well, she says, a complete stranger approaches me out of the blue and he knows my name and address and who my parents were and all sorts, and all I know is what he's told me.

Yes, says Edith, I see that. You could get Aoibhinn onto it, have her do some research for you? Everyone's online these days, it'd be almost more suspicious if he wasn't.

Maybe, Méabh says, once I've told them. Or maybe once I've met him, made my own judgement. I mean, he's not going to stab me and throw me in a bog if we have a coffee, is he?

Unlikely, says Edith, it would be a complicated way of organizing things. She hesitates, for Méabh and for herself. I'll come with you, she says, if you like, I can be a human shield.

Would you, says Méabh, I didn't like to ask, I know you like – well, I wouldn't impose.

No imposition, says Edith, two judgements might be better than one, of course I will, just tell me when and where.

Only, she thinks, I might be on holiday in Italy. And what was it Méabh was going to say, what is it that she knows Edith likes?

There's sunlight, now, lying in pools on the shook-foil surface of the sea, though rain still falls.

Only I don't know where, says Méabh, he says he wants to come here, he says this is where he's from, but then everyone would know.

So go somewhere else, Edith says, Galway, Dublin, London if you want. Paris or Rome or Edinburgh, where do you fancy?

I can't just go off, says Méabh, I'm not like you, I can't just book a flight and go, I'd have to ask and explain and tell stories and I can't, I don't want to. And anyway he wants to come here.

Sorry, says Edith, I know. It's always been her immigrant's advantage, even when Pat was little. Her Dublin friends paid for their parents' help with the kids and the DIY projects by constant attendance at lunches, birthdays, First Communions, baptisms and weddings and funerals; weekends and holidays spent working at least as hard on maintaining community and family bonds as weekdays were on earning money. She sometimes envied the on-demand childcare, but the demands went both ways. Once Pat was in secondary school, she could always say, I'm planning to go see Dad next month, or, Sandrine's inviting me to her birthday, you don't mind if I go to Lyons for a few days? It would have been easy enough, to meet someone somewhere, not to mention it, and she would have done, no real compunction because that side of the marriage never recovered from Pat's birth and it wasn't as if Mike hadn't himself had a spate of business trips, started to come home with flowers and the wrong sort of perfume. Only it never arose, so to speak, the men in whom she might have been interested showed no signs of interest. Years, decades, of dutiful married love, she deserves Gunter, deserves this late-life discovery of what she perhaps wanted all along. And perhaps, since she can, since she's paid the price all these years, she will go to Italy with Cassie and Priya, because it would be fun.

The rain is finer than it was, the light on the sea sharper, though already she can see the next band coming over the inland plain. Further west, sometimes, you can see the shape of Ireland's weather, watch the cloud following the shape of the land from the very edge, almost out to sea.

You think, she says, where you'd feel as safe and comfortable as possible, meeting him, and I'll help you arrange it.

Mm, Méabh says. Edith, I know you'll say no if you want to, I'm trusting you to be frank –

Trusting you to be a foreigner, Edith thinks, but it has its uses. Yes, she says.

Could we maybe, I mean, could we think about if we met at your house? Only everyone's used to you having visitors from all over, no one would think much about it, you could say he was a friend of Pat or one of your English relatives or anything, and I'm often over.

He'd have to be an American relative, Edith says, if you think he's going to go into the shop or Bríd's, they'll hear his accent, but yes, sure, why not, he can come for lunch.

Oh, says Méabh, do you think he would, go to the shop or Bríd's? Maybe better somewhere else, only you never know who's going to be having a day in Galway and I'd have to explain if I went to Dublin, you know I never do, almost never, I'd hardly know where to go.

There are places in between, Edith says, but if you feel you can ask him to come to my house and not stop in the village, do.

I don't know, Méabh says, I don't want him to think I'm ashamed of him.

But you are, Edith doesn't say. I'm sure he'll understand, she says, he sounds nice, I expect he's read the books and seen the films too, I expect he's thought quite a lot about it.

starlings on telephone wires

On my way down the stairs the next morning I saw four suitcases waiting in the hall like dogs expecting a walk. Eight o'clock and even Lydia was there, helping herself to sponge cake and fruit though she was still in her nightdress worryingly lifted at the front and the dressing gown that no longer closed. There was a bowl of brassy dimpled pears, the first apples of the season, a cascade of grapes whose purple skin showed through their powder. The others sat at the dining room table, indoors although it wasn't raining, as if already pulled towards the front door. I took a pear, knew now to look for the grape scissors.

Nobody was talking. Tom nodded to me and passed the coffee pot. They all seemed to be dressed differently, though I didn't think anyone was wearing anything new. I thought of the day ahead of them: boat, train, lunch in Milan, dinner in Paris, London the next day. Back to low grey cloud, puddles, privet hedges, starlings on telephone wires. Who wouldn't rather be under Italian skies, watching autumn come down the mountains but still swimming in a sun-warmed pool? Me, I thought; in that moment I would have given a great deal to shirk what was ahead and go home. I helped myself lavishly to cream and sugar, stirred my coffee until it made a vortex one way and then the other. Are you looking forward to going home, I asked.

Sort of, said Ed. Looking forward to the new season, not so much going back to my digs, distinct lack of marble and trompe l'oeil not to mention the plumbing. And the food. It's always nice to go home, said Louise. She lived with her parents, who were musicians, and a brother studying art, in what sounded like a big house in Hampstead, a life I had enjoyed trying to imagine. Enviable, said Tom, what about you, Katja? She shrugged. London is not my home, she said, but looking forward to my work, yes. I'll be back in a few weeks, said Lydia, I'll be dancing again. I sliced my pear, Ed buttered a roll. I will, she said. Yes, said Louise, so you will, back to normal.

Lydia and I waved them off from the front door. They were already in coats and hats, dressed for English weather, each carrying a suitcase and slightly curved to the right. Look after Lydie for us, said Louise. You'll write, won't you, said Katja to Lydie, you'll let us know? Lydie shrugged. I'll be back soon, she said, there won't exactly be news, you know and I know what's going to happen. Good luck, said Tom, Edith, stay in touch, won't you, maybe I'll come and see you in Oxford one day, we'll go punting or you can take me to dinner in hall or whatever it is people do there. Yes, I said, that would be lovely, and I was grateful to him for conjuring a future in which I would know what people did and would do it.

Their footsteps crunched gravel. Ed and Louise waved, Tom tipped his hat. They were gone.

Right, said Lydia, I'm going back to bed for a bit, I'm tired after last night, could you ask la signora to bring me a cup of tea? I'll bring you one myself, I said, but first I'm going up the hill to watch their boat go, I'll be back in twenty minutes. Suit yourself, she said. I'll suit you, I thought in half an hour, and then for several weeks, but right now I'm not ready to go back into a villa without dancers. Not that she wasn't a dancer, but mostly she was my sister, in trouble and no more gracious than usual.

I hurried past the barn, where most of the villa's chairs awaited my attention, across the orchard's dewy grass, up through the wood to the chapel path. At the first bend there was a rock where I sat down. There was a similar big rock in our beck field at home, from which I could see the road to the village, and I used to climb up and sit there and wait when Maman was expected, or to catch a last glimpse of her when Dad drove her to the station. I used to wave so hard I nearly fell off, though she was too far away for me to see if she was waving back and I never asked her if she noticed me there.

The lake was already busy, fishing boats at ease in the middle, small craft scurrying along the edges, ferries ploughing their rough lines. The village pontoon was behind the trees but I saw the ferry coming towards it. Sunlight flickered over the water. There was some high pale cloud, not much, the beginning of another warm September day. Tomorrow and tomorrow, I thought, and then to Paris, home for Christmas, and Lydia's baby gone wherever it is going, embarked. The ferry passed under the hill. They would be boarding now, along with the women going to Como for their shopping, a few people setting off on longer journeys, students for the high school up the lake. They would be looking back at the villa, pink and plush above its turquoise pool in its setting of dark trees, at the white chapel above. They would be, perhaps, relieved to leave the drama of Lydia and the fruit of her womb before it reached the inevitable finale, glad not to have to hear screaming and hurry with towels and hot water, or to witness – the ferry nosed out again, sharp white against the moving water, and I found myself waving so hard I had to guard my balance, though I knew they couldn't see me.

I watched the ferry until it went out of sight down the lake, delaying Lydia's tea, but after a while the rock was too hard and it was time to go. I walked slowly down the hill, back to the house, went straight to the kitchen. La signora was alone there. Good morning, I said, did you enjoy the dancing, though I had looked at her during the performance and noticed her withdrawn manner as she served dinner afterwards, back to her demeanour when I first arrived. Here in Italy, she said, women do not show themselves like that. I expect they do, I thought, at the Milan Opera House but I said yes, I was also a little surprised the first few times I saw it, it is the same in my village at home, but you know this is art, it is professional theatre. And your mother, she said, your grandmother, they like this, for your sister? My mother, I said, enjoys the company of musicians and artists and dancers, my grandmother – well, she does not say so, but I think she would understand what you think. Signora, may I take some tea to my sister, she has gone to rest? I could see her choosing not to say what she thought about Lydie, her dancing last night and resting this morning, her requirements and her situation. Prego, she said, you know where the things are.

I picked a couple of roses for Lydie's tea tray, added a few grapes and some of the dry Italian biscuits she liked, carried it all carefully up the stairs. I'm not good at trays, you want a ballerina for that. I couldn't knock at her door so I just pushed the handle with my elbow and went in. Oh, Lyd, I said. She was sitting up in bed, propped against the pillows, crying. I hadn't seen her cry for years, couldn't remember the last time. Long ago, little girls. Don't, she said, it's just hormones or something, it's stupid. Even then, I could see nothing in the least stupid about someone crying when she was about to have a baby she didn't want, attended by her ignorant teenage sister and presumably some people who didn't speak her language, having just watched her friends leave to return to lives and jobs that had once been hers and, whatever she said, might not be hers again. It's not stupid, I said, cry if you feel like it. No, she said, I'll have to stop some time and then it will be worse. She was still crying. Well then, I said, stop now and have some tea and smell a rose and then it will be better. I perched beside her, offered the tray. She sniffed, bit her lip. I'd give you a clean hanky, I said, if I had one. S'all right, she said. She wiped her nose and eyes on her sleeve. Edie, she said, what are we going to do now, how will we pass the days, how do we not die of boredom? Tea and roses first, I said, sleep if you can, lunch. Walk in the garden, read, play the gramophone if you like, swimming if you like. Afternoon tea, rest, maybe write letters or something. Dinner, bath, bed. Only you'll have to talk to me and I see I'm not that interesting, but we'll have to manage. I don't think the books are your kind of thing though there's all of Dickens and Shakespeare both of whom are meant to have a pretty broad appeal. Not that broad, said Lydie. I tried and failed to imagine what it might be like to prefer abject boredom to uncongenial reading. I'm the mind and you're the body, I thought, brains and beauty, only just now your body is about its own business. Drink your tea, I said, passing her the cup and saucer. It's not for long now, is it? Beginning of October, Maman had said. It might be late, Lydie said, Maman sent me a book that said first babies are often ten days or two weeks late. I can't do another month, I can't bear it, I won't. One day at a time, I said, and heard myself in time to find it entirely reasonable when she said Edie, if you say that again I'll throw the teapot at you.

I took her tray back to the kitchen, leaving the roses on her bedside table, and when I went up again to check that she wasn't crying she was asleep, draped over an elaborate arrangement of pillows and snoring a little. Air stirred from the window, but the room smelt of Lydie's musky perfume, stale coffee, unwashed socks. It was messy, as Lydia's rooms had always been despite Gran's irritation and la signora's passive-aggressive tidying; like Maman, she was immune or oblivious to sulking and sighs. Last night's clothes lay where they had fallen on the floor, knickers in shameless rings, stockings like shed snakeskin. There was a glass that smelt of strong drink on the marble-topped dressing table and a scatter of pink powder on the solemn grey stone. She'd left the top off her lipstick, her hairbrush matted with bright hair. The curtains were half-open, as she always kept them. That way, she'd once said to Gran, leaving her briefly speechless, you don't have to be forever opening and closing them. On the writing table, a faded copy of the Dancing Times served as a coaster for what I could now identify as an espresso cup, half-empty with a rainbow scum on the top, and a plate for half a biscuit and a scattering of crumbs. If I hadn't known Lydia's remarkable capacity for conjuring chaos out of order, I'd have thought no one had cleaned her room for days. I picked up the cup, tipped the crumbs out of the open window where I stood eating the biscuit and looking out at the lake. The others would be at the station now, maybe on the train to Milan, none of them reading, but napping or gossiping, probably about Lydia and what would become of her. The woods were changing colour, even the midday light softer than it had been, and I supposed soon the mountain farmers would be moving down the valley. And the baby would come.

Lydia slept with her hand on her belly. There was a puffy blue vein behind her knee, which I hoped she didn't know about, and she hadn't shaved the backs of her legs. Maybe I should have offered to help. We weren't accustomed to such intimacy, though it was she who taught me to shave my legs the summer I was thirteen. You can't go around like that, she said, not anymore, though no one else had suggested there was anything amiss. And you need deodorant, she said, and the weekly hair-wash isn't enough now and this is just the beginning, welcome to womanhood, sister. And a few days later she went back to London and I shaved off half an inch of the skin above my ankle. It bled so much I had to tell Gran about it and she was properly angry, which was rare. Nonsense, making loose women out of little girls, giving razors to children, though I'd been using the kitchen knives for years. Not on your own skin, you haven't, she said, and at least peeling veg is useful, it's a good thing for your sister she's back in London, that's all I'll say. Lydie farted and stirred. I shouldn't be there, I thought, watching her, it's mean to watch someone sleep, but I didn't move. If her baby were a girl, and if she'd been going to bring it up herself, she'd have taught it all that and more, how to flick eyeliner at the corners and how to stop a ladder in stockings with nail polish and how to make hair stay up, but then what if the baby had been like me, uninterested, waiting to go outside or read? I tried to imagine a female version of Igor but from the little I knew, his personality wasn't separable from what I then thought of as manhood and would now call masculinity. I couldn't see how any girl in any world I knew, including prima ballerinas, would reach adulthood, much less succeed in any endeavour, behaving like Igor. Even Maman had wiles and evasions to do what she wanted.

I knew I should go, who would want to wake up and find someone watching, but as I crossed the room I saw a book under a cast-off bra. Paperback, new. Your Pregnancy and Birth, a line-drawing of a woman in the kind of smock Lydia wouldn't touch smiling up at a man in a suit. The artist had bothered to draw the ring on the woman's left hand, as if to reassure readers of the book's respectability. I picked it up and took it into the garden: knowledge, at last. I knew how to learn from a book.

I see that you might be interested in the days that followed, but they're hard to write about. Almost nothing happened. I felt as if I were pulling my sister up the minutes, straining at the rope of a sledge, trying to ration the number of times I looked at my watch. Thirty years later, nursing Dad through his final days, I would remember that time, waiting for a momentous event which might take place now or not for days, a nauseating combination of readiness and tedium. I'm sure it was worse for Lydia, who must have been thinking about what would follow the birth, your birth. I was worrying about the event itself, about what might be required of me, and I'd almost forgotten that when it was over we would have a baby to care for.

We fell into a sketchy routine, as people do in all circumstances. I woke early, went to my balcony to assess the weather and plan the day, then down to the kitchen where Signora Pilone had a pot of coffee on the stove but allowed me to assemble my own breakfast, boil an egg to go with two rolls, a slice of butter more generous than Gran would have countenanced and a spoonful of la signora's home-made jam. I liked to eat it on the terrace, even if I had to put on the waxed jacket I'd found in the hall cupboard, far too big for me and smelling of sweat, rain and a spicy cologne. I'd discovered that most of our food was delivered to the back door early in the morning, that the baker's van came daily from the town five miles down the lake and the butcher twice weekly from the next village up, a boy – la signora's nephew or cousin – carried milk in a metal churn from the farm up the road, and a man came from the village to look after the kitchen garden. But Giovanna had stopped coming when the dancers left, so I was allowed to feed the chickens and collect the eggs, and sometimes to run down to the village shop for things that didn't need choosing, coffee or sugar or soap, not trusted for cheese or fish. I liked these errands, spun them out stopping to watch the ferry come or go, walking the long way around up the hillside and down the narrow back lanes, sitting sometimes a while on the stone parapet watching the water and the birds, until the ducks and moorhens forgot I was there and passed right below my feet. After a while I got cold – I didn't have the nerve to wear the smelly jacket in the village – and anyway Lydie would be getting up and la signora waiting for the messages.

The first couple of days, I tried to give Lydie breakfast in bed but she didn't like it. I know you think I'm a slattern, she said, but I do actually like to get up and wash before I eat. Whether because of the colder weather or because the others were not around to countenance her leisurely mornings, she also put on one of the two dresses that more or less fitted, covered with a fluffy cross-over cardigan that she fastened above her belly, pulling in the dresses that were cut, as was then considered necessary, to draw a veil over her situation. Signora Pilone prepared her breakfast, including a glass of milk that Lydie never drank, and I carried it on a tray into the dining room, where she drooped at the head of the table, looking down the gleaming expanse of teak to the gardens, the lake and the hills. Sit up straight, I kept wanting to say, because it upset me to see her soft and hunched, she who had carried an invisible book on her head for as long as I could remember.

Breakfast over, we had four hours to cross to reach the island of lunch. Although she'd barely set foot in the barn when the other dancers were flying and spinning there, she went to practise every day now. I went too because I imagined that my presence might stop her trying jumps and pointe work. Stop looking at me, she said, I don't know why you insist on following me, you must be frightfully bored if this is your idea of a good time, and I said I liked to watch and anyway what if she fell, surely it was always a good idea to have someone within calling distance, and she said she wasn't doing anything that could possibly make a person fall and I said a person could fall walking across a room and she said no normal person and certainly not a trained dancer. It does not, I hope you understand, fill me with pride to recall many of these conversations. I had all the certainty of adolescence and I was a prude and I hope and believe I would have had kinder and better instincts even a year or two later. In the way of siblings, she and I were stuck with ourselves and each other. I kept accompanying her and after a couple of days she stopped protesting. I took a book and sat in the hayloft, but it was Dickens and mostly I watched her: barre, pliés, floor. Some of it looked alarming because her belly was so big and her body so small, but I could see that she was making accommodations, not stretching as far or balancing as delicately as she had even a few weeks ago, not jumping or spinning. Her movement had lost the spring and coil I'd last seen at the final performance. She was going through the motions.

There was still time to fill before lunch. Sometimes she took a bath – no, Edie, for God's sake I do not need your help, the slipperiness of a wet marble floor is not your unique insight, I have just a teeny bit of experience in not falling over – sometimes we sat on the terrace, where I tried to make conversation and then read and she sighed and fidgeted. I tried to get her to stroll in the garden, to come and see the ripening fruit and look at the hens, but she said she was tired after practising and anyway she was familiar, thank you, with fruit and hens. That,

I think, was the hardest hour, at least once we were into the afternoon we were on the day's descent. Lunch, served at the dining table by la signora, during which I tried to craft amusing anecdotes from my morning outing and Lydia snapped at me, and then she went to rest and I helped in the kitchen because it felt wrong to go gallivanting while someone else washed up, and then I put on the jacket and went out to walk along the shore or up the hill. I tried the pool a couple of times but it was really too cold now and reminded me too sadly of Tom and Ed. I was allowed to take Lydie a cup of tea at four o'clock, and then we had another three hours before dinner. You get the idea. I'd thought I'd been bored in the first week at the villa, but among other lessons these waiting days taught me to regret the past, to wish for earlier days to come again. How could I have been bored, with the corps de ballet? No, this was the first time I'd known real tedium, the first time I'd had to manufacture activity out of nothing day after day. Day after day, past the loosest definition of 'early October', towards the midpoint. The Devil finds work for idle hands, Gran had often said, usually meaning stop reading fiction and do some housework, but he wasn't finding much for us.

think in movement

Gunter comes over after dinner on Thursdays unless one of them changes the plan. Easier that way, she doesn't want to be always unsure, to be sniffing at her phone like a teenager, will he or won't he, has he something better to do, and he hardly looks at his own phone, leaves it in the car or behind the kettle for days at a time. Which is fine, of course, his choice, it just means it would be a younger or more foolish woman who hoped for contact between meetings, who confused emotional intimacy with friendly sex. She finds the whisky her Inverness friend Alison brought last time she visited, the two expensive crystal glasses she kept from the sets in the Marital Home. The relief of breaking up sets, of divorcing silver and china! No more matching, never again. Isn't there something Fascist in needing your saucers to wear the same uniform as your dinner plates? She pops ice out of the tray for her own fizzy water, whisky no longer being worth the morning after and also the sex is just fine sober. If you used your phone more, she's said to him, you could make plans with people, you could meet Tony, say, or

Morris, for a coffee or a swim. Leave me alone, he said, leave them alone, say hi to Méabh for me, and Brigid and Mary, the yoga girls and the swimming girls and the book-group girls and whoever else it is this week. Women, she said, women, we are every one of us over eighteen and in fact over forty and mostly over fifty. You'll die alone, she wants to say, at this rate, but maybe that's what he wants, or at least what he thinks he wants and who is she, to tell the difference?

She whisks around her room, though she knows it's tidy, picks out a drooping flower from the vase of narcissus by the bed, checks herself for metaphor but the narcissus, she thinks, is there for the smell, that's all, and because she likes the deckled edges of their orange yolks against the white kid petals. A rose by any other name. She'd used to think, in Dublin, in the Marital Home, that middle-class men of a certain age relied on their wives for social contact the way they relied on them for meals and laundry, mysteriously finding status in the apparent inability to meet their own most basic needs, but since observing some of the single men here in the west she thinks it wasn't dependence but lack of interest, perhaps in relation to the meals and laundry as well as the friends. Maybe some men like being alone, unwashed, living on fried things and bread. Maybe some women do, or would given the chance. She should ask her friends, her suburban married friends, next time she's in Dublin, what would you do if no one was watching, how would you live an unwitnessed life? If she and Gunter are representative, with daily showers still, with clean underwear and fresh vegetables. When she first moved here, she'd thought it might be the beginning of indolence and greed, that with even the light surveillance of city living removed she might spend days in bed reading novels and living on tea and biscuits, but it turns out that she actually likes early mornings, brisk walks, social interaction. Good to know. She pulls out the neck of her top to smell herself but there's only laundry soap, cucumber deodorant, her default leathery cinnamon perfume. I'll miss your smell, Mike said, right at the end, papers signed, sets unsettled, house all but sold, and she said good, I'll miss you too, it would be worse, wouldn't it, if after forty years there was nothing to miss?

It can't be the case that so many men her age simply don't want friends, there must be some profound cultural damage preventing them from forming social relationships with each other. Afraid of being thought to be gay, or just raised to value independence over connection. Oh yes, she thinks, spare a thought for the patriarchs hurt by patriarchy, for their unvoiced fears and emotional deficits, the rest of us are just collateral damage, only she still, obviously, finds them attractive, men, patriarchs. Wouldn't it be so much easier, she and her married friends have been saying to each other for decades, checking through lowered lashes, imagining it, if we were all lesbian, isn't it a nuisance, fancying men? (It would not have been easier, not in twentieth-century Ireland.) And several of her English friends discovered that they were or wanted to be in love with women, and for some of them it was easier, once the divorces were out of the way and the children told. It shouldn't be surprising, Alison said to her once, that a woman knows what to do with a woman's body, only we're all so conditioned to think it's all about the phallus. But for herself she thinks, it was, really, all about the phallus – about receiving, opening, being done to, right from that first time with her tutor in Oxford. She is, has always been, a woman who likes men. It wouldn't be allowed now, the likes of her deflowering, though how you stop consenting adults, which in theory she was, nineteen and eager – Sometimes, he'd said, as she gathered her papers after a Middle English tutorial, sometimes I teach girls other things, if you'd be interested. Some girls like to have a few lessons, so they know what to do with a man, if you understand me, if you'd like to meet for a drink perhaps tomorrow? Perfectly straightforward, she'd thought then and still thinks, no pretence of a relationship, sex education and very useful it was too, unlike any other source in those years he was interested, encouraged her to be interested, in her own pleasure. He was comely enough, in a well-scrubbed English way. Tweed jacket, brogues. Matthew, she thinks, Matthew or maybe James, that sort of name. Matthew, Mark, Luke and John, bless the bed – Take off your clothes, he said, and come and stand with me before the mirror, see how lovely you are? And she watched, in the mirror of his mullioned college room, his tanned hands on her skin in places the sun had never seen, rose-white, narcissus-white. It will help, he said, if you can tell a man what you like, see, takes the guesswork away, means he doesn't have to spend so long on trial and error. Will you come over to the bed now? Lovely, is that nice? Part your knees, let me touch. How's this for you? And this? Hmm, there you go, see? Yes, I thought so, good girl. I have a condom, see, we don't want any little surprises, do we, and now you won't mind if I – That's right, that's it, first time perhaps? Now if you dip your hips that feels nicer for me, do you see? You have lovely thighs, men will like them. Can you open your legs a bit more, how's this? Some girls, he said on the second occasion, enjoy some other things, shall we try, do you think you might like that? He was right, that tutor, about what she desired, what completed her, though there must have been others about whom he was wrong and it was of course outrageous, the whole arrangement, though was it, really, was she not freely consenting, in fact grateful, and is that experience of consent and gratitude truly invalidated by later cultural change, is she obliged to deny her younger self, to correct memory and claim a victimhood she did not feel? It did not seem like a transaction, much less an act of domination, at the time, no more than any other exchange of pleasure, of carnal knowledge. Was almost every woman of her generation a victim, almost every man a rapist, or were there unvoiced forms of consent, performances of resistance, that most people most of the time knew how to read? No, she thinks, no, it was a joy, men are a joy. She remembers the boys at the Grammar School, what's-his-name who went off to do Medicine, lovely earnest young man with beautiful pale hair, angelically chilly, may I as he unbuttoned her school shirt, may I as he ran his cold fingers down her bra strap, and this, as his hand cupped and new circuits connected in her own body. Oh, so this is it, more. Boys at Oxford, beneficiaries of those lessons, men in London who taught her a few more. She was, until Mike, until she fell for the idea of borrowed or proxy security and belonging, absolutely that kind of girl.

Dusk, already, headlights along the lane, here he is. She pushes her hair back, tugs her top straight, as if he'd notice or care.

*

Afterwards, when he wants to go to sleep, she finds she wants to tell Gunter about Méabh's brother, a surprising instinct. She lies back with her head in the hollow of his shoulder, moves his hand from her belly – which is fine, considering, but who wants to consider – to the muscle between her ribs, in which she has confidence. She wants, she thinks, another immigrant to agree with her that national identity isn't genetic, that blood doesn't give you rights of ownership, whatever the passport rules say. Méabh's brother can't just come here and call it home, say he belongs, when nothing she or the Ukrainians do will ever entitle them to say such things, when the lads at the hotel aren't even allowed the air they breathe and the water they drink, when this island makes no space for their smallest kinespheres. It's all blood and soil, all nativism, this confusion of biology and citizenship. Bodies don't own land, land doesn't own bodies. Home is where you are. But not here, where the national papers publish unselfconscious articles about 'pure-blooded Irish' writers and musicians and sportspeople, actors who have 'Irish bones' even if they have French passports. Yes, Dearbhla said last time she commented – Dearbhla writes for that paper – ethnic purity is one thing for settlers and another for colonized people, that's not news. But how many humans divide so neatly between innocence and guilt, perpetrators and victims? She strokes his arm, the woolly hair on the outside and the softness inside his wrist. She has always liked these contrasts in the male body, the rough and the smooth, muscle and hollow. Bodies and land, no body without land, no being without body. Easy to argue about the meaning of land ownership, no doubt, if you're English, which she supposes she is, more or less, push come to shove, if you grew up on a farm your father owned and his father before him. Not that two of her passports don't come down that hereditary route, visas in the bloodline, but she's not claiming to be truly Israeli or truly French, whatever such a thing might mean, they're just emergency exits, and despite Dad's lineage no one in the village ever counted her and Lydia as local or belonging.

Gunter, she says, are you still awake? More or less, he says, that was very nice. Yes, she says, it was, Gunter, do you feel Irish? His body shifts under her. Do I feel what? Irish, she says, do you feel as if you belong here? Of course, he says, I've been here fifty years, you know that. I certainly don't belong anywhere else. OK, she says, but are you German or Irish, first answer, whatever comes to mind. German, he says, but if I think about it I want to qualify that. German-Irish. A bit Irish. I vote here, pay tax. Passport, she asks. German, he says, no reason to change. OK, she says, and if Germany's playing Ireland in a sports game? He moves again. I don't care, he says, you know that, I'm not interested. She lifts her head. Heads are heavy and he won't complain when it becomes uncomfortable. I think that makes you German, she says. He turns onto his side and she rolls to face him, rearranges her pillow. His hand on her hip. Do you think in English, she asks. Mostly, he says, I hardly speak German now. She's not sure he speaks much at all, most days, and the workings of other people's minds are always mysterious, the patterns of words and images and however people express themselves to themselves surprisingly hard to imagine. For herself, words, sentences, paragraphs, language – a specific language, with a grammar and a lexicon – the precondition of consciousness, no thought without words, but she has learnt that others work in other ways. And to that extent, George Eliot was wrong about the scratched mirror; the roar on the other side of silence is more mysterious than she allowed, though perhaps in the days before moving images people thought differently, perhaps the forms of art shape the forms of cognition. We imagine ourselves in films, novels, paintings, but only the films and novels and paintings we have seen, in their forms and structures. Even so, who is to say what happens in the other head on their pillow, much less in the mind or heart of a squirrel? Do dancers think in movement, musicians in sound? Mike's friend Phineas in Dublin is a sound engineer, hears whole orchestras of weather, traffic, birds that for her are only ambient noise. Sound and signal, she thinks, meaning in every atom and cell if you remember to look and listen. And Dennis the chef, eyes half-closed as he attends to his tongue, names each herb and the provenance of the oil in a salad, and the perfumery up the hill here, every note in a scent, they say, music the metaphor for smell, all of everything, everywhere.

Why do you ask, says Gunter, his voice sleepy. Oh, she says, Méabh and I were talking, you know, Americans who find a surprise Irish granny and come here thinking they own the place, or the place owns them, suddenly say oh yes, I always did like potatoes and the colour green, must be my Irish blood, I'd better learn the dancing. You sound envious, he says, isn't that what most people want, to feel that they belong somewhere? It's a choice, isn't it, between belonging and autonomy, and you and I choose autonomy, we have no family and we do what we like. I do have family, she wants to say, I have Pat, but Pat is all she has now, everyone else lost to death or divorce, and she's not sure one person, one person over the water, counts as family. And you know, he adds, the Irish granny was probably forced to leave. She rolls away, wants to say don't you dare tell me about being forced to leave, what were your grandparents doing when mine were boarding the cattle trucks, but she says I know, eight centuries of oppression, never mind. Only spare a thought, she thinks, for the Native Americans who were dispossessed when Irish immigrants reached America, each wave of refugees breaking on someone else's soil. Is innocence the product of oppression? Her Icelandic friend claims hereditary innocence, but if you believe the stereotypes of Vikings, all that raiding and pillaging, you could argue about that, and the argument would make reference to Celtic slaves but then the Celtic slaves turn out to provide pretty much all Icelandic mitochondrial DNA so are Icelanders half-oppressors and half-oppressed and if so, guilty or innocent, Russian or Ukrainian, English or Irish? Are some Icelanders more oppressed than others? A Marxist professor once told her that Bhutan is ideologically pure. There is no health in us, she murmurs. She's going to have to find a way to rise above it, this tribalism. She spent the best part of her life trying to belong and it didn't work, these late years are for other purposes such as friendship and sex. Gunter is asleep.

the most obvious thing

Ludicrous to begin, Lydia's baby came at last.
 Your life began.
 You are here.

I still slept with the balcony doors open, and a towel now on the floor for when the night rain blew in; I knew perfectly well what la signora would say to a wet parquet floor and she kept telling me I would catch a cold. I'd been waking later as the nights lengthened, taking longer to prise myself from under the blankets into the fresh air, but this morning it was still dim outside, the mountaintop across the lake only faintly outlined, trees heard but hardly seen. There had been rain and wind in the night and the branches and eaves were restless. The lake, I thought, would be choppy. I liked the days when waves broke, movement and action, and though it seemed increasingly unwise to leave Lydia longer than I had to, I still stole time to sit on the parapet and watch the water leap at my feet.

 I got up to hang the towel and close the doors before Signora

Pilone could see that I'd slept again with them open, and then the morning called me out onto the balcony in my pyjamas. Wind, an early bird, and then a sound between a sigh and a moan. If there were ghosts, I'd have met them by now. I peered over the balustrade. There was a light on downstairs, and the French window open. Lydie, I called, Lydia? She was on the terrace. I think it's starting, she said, a while ago, I didn't want to wake you. Stay there, I said, as if she would go anywhere, I'm coming.

I ran down barefoot, almost slipped on the stairs, caught myself painfully on the banister. There was a hollow on the drawing-room sofa, a blanket thrown off and a half-empty cup of tea. She was leaning on the stone table outside, exhaling loudly. Oh, Lyd, I said, what do I do? Is it horrible? She leant forward, swallowed. No, she said, not yet. It's not that often, I don't think we need to do anything. I touched her back. I'll call that number, I said, just to be sure. I meant, I don't want to be alone with you, I don't know what to do, I want an adult to be in charge. I just told you, she said, not yet, it could be hours. I don't know how long it will take for someone to come, I said, do you even know who it is that we're calling? She stood straight. I'm fine, she said, go back to bed, it might not be the real thing, people get practice contractions at this stage. Braxton Hicks, I said, I know, but people also have babies at this stage, seeing as how we're already a week late. We, she said, what the hell do you mean, we? Calm down, I said, I'm sure it's not good for you, getting worked up. Fuck off, she said. That phrase was shocking then in a way that no words are now, and I fucked off back up to my room to wash and dress.

When I came down she was walking slowly along the terrace, swaying her hips as if dancing an elephant. I stood on the step, said nothing. The sky was beginning to brighten over the mountain. Snow had come further down in the night. Sorry, she said, only don't tell me to calm down, it doesn't help, actually don't ever tell anyone to calm down. All right, I said, sorry, I'm a bit nervous. She turned and came back towards me. That makes two of us, sunshine, she said. So – er – can I call that number, I asked. It was light enough for me to see her expression. I'll tell you, she said, when it's time – oh, another one, wait. I watched. She stopped by the tiled table, braced her arms on it, arched her back as she breathed slowly. I wanted to help, somehow, with something, to make something better or at least further on. She circled her hips, stood up again, walked on. Lyd, I said, Lyd, sorry, tell me to shut up – I will, she said, shut up – but is it a good idea to be walking about, won't you tire yourself out? Shut up, she said, you can more or less assume that if I think a thing is a bad idea I won't be doing it, OK? OK, I said, sorry.

The book said that women could become irritable as labour progressed but in Lydia's case I didn't think that would tell us much. Cup of tea, I suggested. Shut up, she said, and then, actually, yes, and could there be toast and honey? Rolls, probably, I said, see what I can do, but before going to the kitchen I went upstairs and found the telephone number. I wasn't about to call, not yet, but I felt better with the slip of paper in my pocket.

La signora arrived while I was preparing Lydia's tray. What are you doing, she said, that's yesterday's bread. I know, I said, my sister wants it. I hesitated, had even less vocabulary for these matters in Italian than English. The baby is coming, I said. She dropped her basket and the scarf she'd untied on the kitchen table. Mother of God, why did you not tell me. I did, I said, just now.

I had not seen la signora hurry before. She rounded the kitchen table and crossed the hall, heading for the stairs. She's outside, I called, on the terrace. There can be something very calming about another person's agitation. I heated a cast-iron frying pan and cut two rolls into thin slices. I didn't see why foreign traditions should deprive my sister of toast with her tea in the hour of need, but before I'd filled a milk jug and found a honey-spoon I heard raised voices and went out. The sun was still behind the mountain but the sky was pale now, colour coming down the valley, and the birds sang. Birthday, I thought. Lydia was still swaying up and down the terrace, a surreal guard-keeper, and Signora Pilone stood in her way, hands on hips. Tell her to go to bed, said la signora, tell her she must not be outdoors. Tell her to leave me alone and get out of my way, said Lydie. Please, I said, signora, I need your advice, would you come to the kitchen? When your sister goes to her room, she said. Lyd, I said, you wouldn't like to be inside a bit, would you, only it's warmer in there. Shut up, she said. She stopped walking and leant on the table again. Signora Pilone looked at her watch. Please, I said to her, just a moment. She sighed and shook her head but followed me back inside.

The toast in the pan was still warm. Is that what you do, she said, where you come from, you scorch the stale bread? Yes, I said, and usually we eat it with salted butter and bitter marmalade and we drink Indian tea with milk, but my father prefers to eat – oats, no idea, avoine in French, avena? – grains boiled in milk with salt. I could see her not saying you are barbarians. Did my mother, I asked her, give you a telephone number, for when the baby comes? She filled the milk jug and handed it to me. For afterwards, she said, you are to call, Signor Igor said, the lady's sister will have instructions. For now, we call the nurse. I buttered the toast in the pan, to keep it warm as long as possible. Do you call the nurse, I asked, do you have the number? She shrugged. Everyone knows the nurse, she said, I will tell Beppo when he comes, I think we have plenty of time. But make her come indoors, she should not be out there, it is not correct. I looked up and caught her eye. Nothing about this, we were both thinking, is correct. I will ask her, I said, but you know my sister is – she has – her disposition is not – and she is my older sister. My big sister, I thought, though only metaphorically, only with regard to her disposition and her kinesphere, for some years now. La signora sniffed. Women are not animals, she said, we do not calve in the fields. I've helped, I said, with cows.

It was a bright blue day, your birthday, one of those October days that makes everyone say autumn is after all their favourite season. The two big beech trees on the lawn were gleaming copper, plenty of leaves still to whisper on the wind, and poplar leaves spun and whirled towards the pool. Light glinted off the lake, but softer now than in the summer. Lydia laboured, worked, outside most of the morning, up and down the terrace, leaning on the table, up and down. She took an occasional bite of her cold toast, didn't want me to take it away, and sipped at the tea long after it was scummy. I'll make another pot, I said, and she said no, and the next time she came past, don't bother, I don't want hot things. I wondered should we take her temperature, is that a thing you're supposed to check, but the book said nothing about it and she didn't want to stop walking, didn't want to be touched, seemed almost like a sleepwalker or sleep-worker, swaying and breathing. I sat on the step, intermittently reading and bearing witness, timing the intervals between contractions with my little wristwatch which had no numbers on the dial and no second hand; the nurse had sent word that she would come after her morning round unless the pains began to come more than every five minutes, in which case we should call the doctor.

The sun was overhead and the shadows of the trees on the lawn dense and short when I saw a woman pushing a bicycle up the drive. Lydie, I said, Lydie, look, the nurse is here, I think you'll need to go in so she can examine you. You will have internal examinations, the book said, every hour to check your progress. They can be uncomfortable but they are important for your and your baby's safety, so make sure you relax and do as the doctor tells you. Mm, she said, I know, oh, another one. She braced herself again as the nurse came up, feet and wheels crunching on the gravel. A youngish woman, even to my teenage eyes. Navy skirt, white blouse, navy cardigan and hat, clumpy shoes, reassuringly like the district nurses at home. She nodded to me and stood holding her bicycle, watching Lydie. Bene, she said. She looked at me. I hear you speak Italian? A little, I said, I studied it at school. But not your sister, she said. No, I said. We both watched. Lydie sighed, straightened up. Good morning, the nurse said to her in English, I am Nurse Rosetti and I will help you today. You speak English, I said, what a relief. Very little, she said in Italian, I will need your help and your sister will need mine and together we will manage very well for her. I'm Lydia, said Lydie, standing still but swaying. I could see that she needed to keep walking. Signora Pilone came out, drying her hands on a cloth. Elena, she said, good morning, we have told her she must go indoors, you tell her. Good morning, signora, said Nurse Rosetti, the room is all prepared?

Nurse Rosetti and I coaxed Lydie indoors and up the stairs, where she had to stop and grip the banisters. I saw the nurse checking her watch. Good, she said, good girl, Lydia. Signora Pilone had tidied and cleaned Lydie's room, taken away the blankets and pillows and made up the bed over something stiff and crackly. All her make-up and pots were gone from the dresser, which was covered in a white sheet on which sat a pile of folded white towels. The scene was set. Lydia walked her swaying gait to the window, back across the room. Tell your sister, said the nurse, that after the next pain I would like her to lie on the bed. I told her, she nodded, returned to the window and gripped the sill.

The examination was nothing like I'd feared. Nurse Rosetti set a chair for me at Lydie's head, facing the wall behind her, and draped a sheet over Lydie's waist and raised knees. Tell her to tell me if there is a pain coming, she said, and I will stop, but now ask her please to put her feet together and open her knees. There'll be a ballet word for that, I thought, a choreography of midwifery, but I passed on the instruction and Lydia complied. She was gripping the sheet so I put my hand tentatively over hers and was surprised when she grasped it. She held my eyes as the nurse moved. It's all right, Lyd, I said, it's all fine, she's just checking, it'll be over in a minute. Mm, she said, ow. Her grip tightened and I gripped back. There, said the nurse, thank you, Lydia. Lydie straightened her legs and I helped her sit up. Six fingers, said the nurse, you're doing very well. She bears her pain very well, she said to me, it is her first time? Yes, I said, she's a dancer, a ballerina, she is accustomed to bearing pain. Ah, said Nurse Rosetti, she is a strong young woman, that will help her now. She says, I said to Lydie, that your dancing will help. Tell her to let me move then, said Lydie, tell her she can't stop me. She pushed off the bed and stood up again, and then turned, eyes widening, grabbed my shoulders as another pain came. I followed my instinct to rest my own hands on her shoulders and felt the spasm pass through her body. She breathed again. She needs to walk about, I said to the nurse, she is a dancer, it helps her to move. She nodded. For a little while, she said, but she should rest, she will need her strength later.

Another hour Lydie paced and braced, and a sunny breeze came in from the open window. Outside, the world went incongruously about its business, the boats on the lake and the cars on the road, a flurry of excitement from the hens which must mean that la signora had realized I hadn't fed them that morning. Lydie began to sink into a deep squat when the pains came, using the windowsill or the foot of the bed as a barre. The nurse nodded, as if satisfied, but said tell her soon it will be time to rest, I will examine her again after the next one and then we will tell her she must rest. I waited for her to stand up again and then touched her shoulder, because I wasn't sure she was hearing or even seeing the room around her. Lyd, I said, Lyd, you're doing brilliantly, in a minute she needs to have another look, OK, but before we could arrange her on the bed again she said, Edie, I'm going to be sick, quick – and the nurse was there with a metal bowl. I held Lydie's hair, which had come loose. Is she ill, I asked, but Nurse Rosetti shook her head. È normale, è buono. Signora Pilone came in with a canister of hot water, as if she'd been listening at the door, and I wiped Lydie's face. Sorry, she said. It's normal, I said, it's fine, don't worry.

Nurse Rosetti helped her to the bathroom, managing somehow without translation. I went and stood by the window, taking big breaths of autumn air, wishing I could just go for a walk and come back when it was all over, but at the same time excited. I realized I was hungry, and that my hunger would have to wait. I turned back and noticed for the first time a basket on a white towel beside the wardrobe, understood for the first time that very soon there would be another person in the room, that three of us had entered and four of us would leave, and I thought of the number I would call. Four of us would leave, and then we would part, and go our ways, and some of us would meet again and some of us would not, and some of us would remember this day and one of us would not.

They were coming back along the hall. Lydie was – was not entirely Lydie, was in a state or kind of being I had never seen before, and I wanted to go away. Her gaze was glassy, and as Nurse Rosetti helped her towards the bed she began to make a sound so much like a cow that it was uncanny, absurd. It's all right, said the nurse, it's perfectly natural, and it took me a moment to realize that she was reassuring me rather than my sister. Lydie climbed onto the bed, but instead of lying down she crawled up to the headboard and knelt up, gripping it, bawling, and as she fell silent collapsed forward over her belly and the bed, still gripping, folding. I need to sleep, she said, go away, I'm too tired, and she slid down onto her side, pillowed her face on her folded hands and seemed to go to sleep. It's all right, said Nurse Rosetti again, Edith, don't be afraid, this is natural, she will rest a few minutes and then the baby will start to be born, and then I will need you to translate, yes? Don't be afraid, I am here. I don't like it, I said. I could feel myself welling up, infantile, failing in the moment of need. I'm scared. All is well, she said, the doctor is waiting at home if we need him, but she is strong and healthy, your sister, all is well. I watched Lydie's face, softer than usual, strangely peaceful. What if she's dying, I thought, what if this is the end? What if I have to tell Dad – Edith, said the nurse, we need you. Your sister is well and soon her baby will be born. You will tell her what I am saying while the baby comes. Yes, I said, yes, of course, if I can.

Lydie stirred, but settled again. The nurse sat on the small bedroom chair, hands folded in her lap, almost as much at rest as my sister, and then Signora Pilone knocked softly and peered around the door. Uno spuntino, she said, a snack, and she brought in a tray with two cups of coffee and some fruit and slices of the plain lemon cake she often made, and Nurse Rosetti and I made a strange picnic as we watched over Lydie.

I had eaten my cake but drunk only half the coffee when Lydie stirred, groaned, opened her eyes and scrabbled back to the top of the bed. It's coming, she said, it's pushing. Nurse Rosetti was immediate, no more picnic. Tell her deep slow breathing, she said, tell her to go gently. Lydie was quiet, present as she had not been before she slept. My back, she said. Hurts. I translated, and rested my hand tentatively on her lower back.

I could feel the muscle ripple and grip. Yes, she said, press. The nurse nodded, so I put a knee on the bed behind Lydie and pressed a hand either side of her sacrum. Yes, she said, and then another pain came. I kept pressing, as if I were working too. Deep breaths, said the nurse, and I started to regulate my own breathing before I remembered, not me. Lydie swayed kneeling, circled her hips, and then leant forward and softened as the pain passed. Well done, said the nurse, good girl, Lydia. She put a towel under Lydia's behind. Another came, a pause and another. You're doing very well, I translated, soon the baby will be here. Baby, I thought, another person, a baby will be here with us, and then the baby will set out on his or her journey.

Nurse Rosetti gestured to me to move and she took over pressing Lydie's back, and then flattened herself to peer up under her nightdress. She can see the head, I told Lydie, not long now, but I didn't think she was hearing us. Going back up, Lydie reported after the next surge, can't do it, but she sounded factual. I translated. No, the nurse said, you are doing it, you are doing wonderfully, and then fluid came out and splashed onto me as well as over the towel. I remembered the book: the baby's water just broke, I told Lydie, it's nearly here, and she nodded. Tell her small breaths, the nurse said, small breaths, blow out a candle, no pushing now. She tapped Lydie's shoulder and demonstrated and Lydie, of course, accustomed to the direction of movement, complied. Cows and sheep, I thought, had it so much easier, though perhaps it was as hard for them and we did not know. The nurse peered under, tucked up Lydie's nightdress, did something, and then I glanced down and saw a human head protruding from my sister, a second head at the other end of her spine and for a moment it was horrible, monstrous. Tell her she can touch her baby, said the nurse, but when I translated Lydie shook her head. Everything stopped. Do something, I thought, don't leave her, leave them, like this, how can the baby survive? The head wasn't moving, didn't seem alive. I felt sick. Lydia grabbed the bed again, made a terrible sound and the nurse held the child as it slithered onto the towel in a gush of blood and mess. It was red, alien, not a person, a thick blue rope pulsing from its belly. Lydia was still kneeling upright and the nurse, hands full, had to prompt me. It's here, I said, you've done it, it's over, but I was watching as one might watch an animal killing prey as the nurse rubbed the slimy red thing that had come from inside my sister. Its arms moved, its alien face gaped and there was a bleat, and caw.

Sorry, that's you I'm describing, I remember. I was perhaps too young for the scene, too naive and fearful. You were a baby, that's all. You were born.

Lydie sat back onto her heels, started to pivot. Wait, one moment, said Nurse Rosetti, and she tied the cord and cut it with a horrible sheering sound. The room smelt of blood. Nurse Rosetti wrapped the baby – wrapped you – in a clean towel and cradled it, which made it seem more human. It bleated again. I mean, you cried. As babies do. Lydie turned around and sat back, legs extended. The nightdress was still caught around her waist and she tugged it down, wriggled her toes. There were tears on her reddened face. I dipped a corner of a towel in the now-cool water and wiped it. Thanks, she said. Bloody hell, I'm never doing that again. Your baby, said the nurse, it's a boy, but she shook her head and looked away. Tell her I don't want to see it, she said, tell her it's someone else's baby. I said nothing, wiped her face again. That's enough, she said. There was blood on the towel under her. I looked at it and at the nurse, who seemed undismayed. It's normal, she said, not too much. A little blood, I remembered Gran saying, goes a very long way, and though she meant that one's impression of bleeding was usually excitable, another reading was that the supply is limited. Nurse Rosetti was doing things with the baby. I stroked Lydie's hair, which was a mess. You were very brave, I said, it looked – it looked a lot. It was a lot, she said, oh God, Edie, it's starting again. Afterbirth, I said, much easier. I saw that she couldn't get up again, was too tired. I helped her lie down, held her hand for the last pain and the placenta came out, looking exactly like a cow's or sheep's. Hold the baby, said Nurse Rosetti, and before I could answer she put you in my arms. Take it away, said Lyd.

I'm sorry, but that's what happened, that was how it was.

I carried you over to the window, which was now closed. I could feel your quick breathing and your warmth. You looked at me. I looked at you. Hello, I said, welcome to the world, here it is. I touched your head, still damp and sticky. You had black hair and blue eyes – they say babies' eyes darken in the first weeks, but Pat's stayed blue so I wouldn't know. You were curled, unoriented, not quite human. This is air, I said, this is daylight, it's afternoon now. This is a bedroom, inside a house. That, I wanted to say, is your mother, because your need for a mother was the most obvious thing. You weren't crying, just looking surprised, as well you might be. Your arm wavered inside the towel in which you were loosely wrapped. Hello, I said again, hello, baby. I angled you up a little. Sky, I said, trees, hills and sun, but your gaze was fastened on my face.

I looked back towards the bed. Lydia's knees were still wide, splayed, and the nurse was looking between them. There was a little more blood but she was right, not much, and some paler fluids. You bleated again and Nurse Rosetti glanced up at me. Tell her it will heal, she said, it will be sore but I don't need to stitch. I translated. Good, said Lyd, no scarring, I can get everything back to normal. I felt the weight of you, looked at her, at the impossibility of the whole event, a new human being coming out of an older one, a whole person being curled up inside and pushed out of someone smaller than me. And scarring, it had not occurred to me – I felt my own parts tighten, protective. And normal, what could normal be, after this?

cats and custard

She has to remind herself to have charity for the people who rush into the studio late, or even at the last minute. The policy is that if you're not there fifteen minutes early they'll give your place to someone on the waiting list, which everyone knows is nonsense, there is no waiting list and Áine's not even there to unlock the door fifteen minutes early, same as everyone knows it's nonsense that you must be freshly showered and have eaten nothing for the last four hours. How likely is that, at 6 p.m.? In Ireland it doesn't much matter what you say the rules are because everyone – everyone who knows – knows that everyone will do what makes sense anyway, which is one of the reasons she likes it here, though of course making sense is culturally specific and sometimes takes time to learn. If you were happy in Switzerland or Singapore, somewhere where the written rules apply, you probably wouldn't settle easily here. Indian common sense, to generalize wildly but in the light of her friend Seema's experience, is not Irish common sense. Many kinds of American common sense are not Irish common sense. Maybe eventually the immigrants will force the Irish to write down the real rules, stop them signing boreens as 90 kilometres an hour and pretending none of the GPs are taking on new patients. It's a maximum, not a recommendation, eejit. It depends who you know, sure my sister-in-law's young one is the receptionist there, will I give her a call?

Edith arrives in time to take her favourite spot, end of the middle row, nice view out over heath and rock, plenty of sky, wall to touch if she wobbles in some of the balances, better view of the teacher than at the back and not as visible as at the front. We have not evolved, she thinks, to concentrate when there are people looking at us from behind. Rubbish, what would she know about evolution? Incense drifts, odour of sanctity. Hi, Edith, hi, Áine, isn't it lovely to see the sun today? She unrolls her mat, lines it up along the floorboards. Oh good, here's Mary, she won't be the only over-fifty, not that it matters. How are ye, hope you've been outside this afternoon, wouldn't you think it was summer almost? Svetlana, can't help herself wondering if those boobs are real and if so, what genes! Hello, how are you? In her Dublin class, you kept silence once you'd crossed the threshold of the studio, took up mildly competitive crossed-leg poses with sometimes ostentatious heavy breathing though she'd always found it worthwhile, the performances of Orientalism, for the strength and flexibility. Easy for her to say. Ma, you should try weightlifting, Pat used to say, you wouldn't have to pretend to be all about the inner light. I'm not pretending, she didn't say, you can actually achieve inner peace by breathing, at least as long as you have shelter and food and clothes, access to clean water, healthcare and education and I do so there we go.

Cormac, good lad, mostly enjoys it that she can hold a side plank longer than he can. Old-lady grit, he says, no offence intended. None taken, especially while she can also lift the top leg when he falls over, and also, unlike most older men in yoga classes, he doesn't bark and grunt like a hippopotamus all the way through. You wonder sometimes, darling much-missed Clare said, do they really not know they're doing it, is it possible they think the rest of us don't groan like constipated gorillas because our little pink voice boxes just aren't built that way or is it that they have to roar to show they're still men even in a yoga studio? Inner peace, however. How are ye, how are ye. Dublin greeting spread west. Sore head still, he says, good session last night, this'll sort me out or kill me so it will. We'll see about that, says Áine, welcome everyone, once you're settled we'll be starting in child's pose, and of course that's when Deirdre rushes in, sorry, work, kids, traffic, bang the door, drop a water bottle, what is it with the under-fifties and water, really, love, we all used to go hours without water, lunch until dinner, did no harm at all and this is yoga you know, not exactly high-intensity. Stop it now, salute her for making it here at all, with the work and the kids and the traffic, salute her for stepping free.

Edith kneels, opens her knees, big toes touching, folds her ribcage between her spread thighs. She's remembering for some reason a circus performance she saw in Lyons once, years ago, with Leon who is now dead and Rosa whose mind has wandered, how the young man braced his sculptured arms and legs against a wheel, like the Leonardo da Vinci cartoon, and danced in it and with it, how he wheeled and spun; how a fairy girl with arms and nerves of steel flew from and caught her trapeze, all the things the body can do, could do, could have done. Lydia, dancing – Take a deep breath in through the nose now, says Áine, fill up your lungs. Hold it. Lion's breath out through the mouth, and they all have the manners to sigh quietly. Does it matter, that none of them has ever seen a lion, barring zoos? Does it matter that when Áine says lion's breath she remembers the lion that used to roar at the beginning of films, back in the day, one of the Hollywood studios? She can hear the jingle now, remember the excitement, a beginning, two hours in a new world, didn't change between her childhood and Pat's but she's not seen it in years now, did the studio close or did it just become old-fashioned, that kind of thing? Well, it was old-fashioned, wasn't it, even then. One more big breath, says Áine, fill up your lungs from the bottom, feel the air coming up your spine. Anatomical nonsense, she's fairly sure, you probably don't control where the air goes in your lungs, it's not like piping custard into a doughnut, but it makes sense in her body. And hold at the top and one more lion's breath. Superspreader events, surely, all this breathing. She thinks again of the English friends who still haven't come out, Trisha and John, who shut themselves up obediently three years ago and forgot how or why to be in a room, in an audience or a congregation or a queue, entombed themselves, funny that it seems to be more her English friends than the Irish or French but maybe the English are right to be scared of each other, whole place lost its mind you'd think looking at it from here. Push up into tabletop, says Áine, shoulders over wrists, hips over knees, now we're going to flow through cat and cow. Let the movement ripple along your spine. Can we think or speak of our bodies without metaphor, without cats and custard, cows and tables, waves, are there words for what it is like?

innocent abroad

I did not know what to do with you. It felt wrong to put you down in the basket, you who had never known air on your skin, never seen colour and shape. You should not be left alone, abandoned to strange sensation, but also I had needed the loo for a while and the bedroom was in a state requiring the work of more than one person. Lydia was propped up against clean pillows, eating a bowl of rice pudding that Signora Pilone said was always given to new mothers, not looking at you and me. Nurse Rosetti had taken the placenta and some other things away and not yet come back, presumably attending to her own urgent needs. As she examined you, you'd cried a bit, the first time we heard your voice, but you stopped when she wrapped you tightly in a towel and you were just there, being present, breathing and looking. There was still blood in your hair and I thought that I would have to bath you, that someone would have to show me how, because surely you would be with us at least that long, long enough to be cleaned and dressed, to begin your humanity. Lyd, I said, Lyd, you are going to feed him? Did we have a bottle, had la signora procured what was necessary? You squirmed and frowned and I thought that I had betrayed you, that I could at least have made sure we could give you milk. Shut up, she said, Edie, can you not take it away?

I'm sorry. I can imagine this is hard to read. It's not particularly easy to write, some of it. Remembering your birth does make me wonder, if it helps — why would it help? — about my own birth and especially Lydia's. Maman must have had to labour and deliver in English, probably without a translator, must have thought about her own murdered mother as she became a mother herself, because the birth of the first baby is always also the birth of the mother. And perhaps Maman greeted her firstborn with little more joy than Lydia found for you. I don't think Maman much wanted a baby. She wanted to go looking for her first family. None of us turned out maternal. It really is very likely that the mother you found, the woman who chose to be your mother, served you better than the mother you lost. I hope so. And I think even if it hurts, even though it hurts, you might rather know. I think I should set down what I remember, while there's still time. Maybe I'm doing this for me as much as for you, reckoning, summing up. Making my confession.

I'll stay here for now, I said, I think it's a bit early to leave you alone. Even horses and cows, I thought, have care for a few hours afterwards. One body becoming two takes time, and no time. She finished her pudding, leant out to put down the bowl. I saw her wince. In my arms, you stuttered into sound, as if you'd felt her pain. I rocked you a little, but where the towel brushed your cheek your mouth turned desperately. Lyd, I said, I know — I didn't know. I knew nothing. Lyd, would you — Nurse

Rosetti came back in. I think the baby is hungry, I said. Yes, she said, good, tell your sister he needs her milk now even if he has a bottle later. Your voice was rising. I don't think we have a bottle, I said. Sì, she said, there are bottles downstairs. But first he needs his mother's milk.

Lydie, I said, she says he needs your milk first. She says there are bottles but it's important that he has your first milk. Colostrum, the book had said, different from what comes later and different from formula. Shut up, she said, fuck off, take it away. I'm tired.

I looked at Nurse Rosetti and saw that she had understood. I looked at you, settling into your hunger song, and saw that you had not. Maybe later, she said, I will go prepare a bottle.

Edie, said Lydia, I mean it, take it away, I can't bear the noise. You are not, I thought, supposed to bear the noise, that is the point of the noise, it is like the lamb's call and the calf's bawl, completed in the response, but I carried you out into the stone-floored corridor where your puny cries reverberated and echoed. Shh, I said, poor baby, milk's coming, shh. I was afraid to carry you on the stairs, though the rugs downstairs would have absorbed some of your dismay and the proximity of the nurse would have reassured me. How could Lydia not hear, not listen? I understand better now; it is not, of course, your fault, but the only element of this sorry situation that was her choice was your departure, and she was not old enough and perhaps not of a nature to accept what she had not chosen. Acceptance is not a characteristic of elite artists or athletes, and dancers are both. How could a dancer fly, if she did not believe in control, in agency, if she humbly received gravity?

I paced the corridor and you reddened and wailed until Nurse Rosetti hurried up the stairs and took you. She brushed your cheek with the rubber teat and you opened your mouth like a fish and began to suckle. There, she said, what a good strong boy! I watched milk becoming baby. It wasn't exactly surprising, that you knew what to do, I'd seen enough lambs and calves come into the world to recognize that portal between not-here and here, to understand that being born like dying teaches us that life and death are not the opposite they appear when we are not actively involved in either process. There is a spectrum, a grey area, between living and dying; are we not all always doing both? You were there, you had arrived, and you were before my eyes becoming human, taking your small place in the world. You'll have to teach me, I said, how to make up his milk. How to do everything, I thought, because surely you would stay that long, wouldn't you? There is food for you, she said, in the kitchen, go wash your hands and eat.

I did not look at the telephone as I passed it.

I did not look at the telephone as I came back, having for the first time sat at the kitchen table to eat my soup and bread.

Already it was getting dark again, trees fading against a reddening sky, dusk softening the bushes and flowers in the garden below the landing window. I thought that we would not see winter here, that we would be gone before snow reached the valley and perhaps never come back, the villa in all its intimate detail fading and softening in memory. Lydie would forget as much and as fast as possible, would soon say that she couldn't remember the shape of the pool or the colour of the roses on the terrace, that she had never known Giovanna's name and had no recollection of eating figs still warm from the tree, but I, I thought, would not forget, not the flesh of plump oranges nor the lover's bite of the night-chilled pool, not the deep windows of Signora Pilone's childhood home nor the scent of those heavy roses, their dark petals soft as thighs and surprisingly cool to the touch.

I went quietly into Lydia's room. You were asleep in your basket, swaddled now in a white waffle blanket with only your squashed pink face and a wisp of dark hair visible. At first I thought Lydie also slept, curled away from the door with damp hair coiling across the pillow, but something about the angle of her shoulders and the rhythm of their rise and fall betrayed or announced her mind's work. Lyd, I said quietly, Lyd, can I bring you anything, is there anything you'd like? She moved and looked back over her shoulder. I know it sounds odd, she said, but would you mind bringing my perfume, the Bois d'Automne? It's put away, top drawer. Of course, I said.

Her dresser drawer was a mess, what Gran would have called a rammel of underwear, stockings tangled around bra straps, elastic hair-ties knotted with bright hair, a couple of used cotton hankies. Under it all, a square glass flask with a plain gold lid and a cream label. I was still learning that the most expensive things are simple. Here, I said, will I squirt your wrists? If I can give birth, she said, I can probably squirt my own wrists, though I saw her wince as she rolled over and sat up. Is it very sore, I said. Bit, she said, it'll mend, don't fuss. I passed her the perfume. She looked well, the habitual remoteness that had ebbed as she pushed out the baby restored to her. She bared a wrist, sprayed Bois d'Automne, rubbed it against her neck. I wondered if it was only because I knew the name that I smelt blackberries, fig leaves and something darker, mushroom or leather, overripening. From Igor, I said. She shrugged. Where bleeding else, she said, you don't imagine I could afford it myself. No, I said, and I couldn't help wondering what perfume I might one day wear, who might buy it for me, what I might afford myself. You snuffled and I looked towards your basket, wanting to hold you again and also wanting you to stay asleep, to give her a little longer before she had to reject you again. Whatever you're going to say, she said, don't. OK, I said, shall I put that back in the drawer for you? I'll keep it here, she said, I like the smell. You might open the window, before you go, I'm not having this Italian paranoia about fresh air. Got it, I said.

I stood on the landing, fingering the slip of paper in my pocket. I could see that the longer I left it, the more I saw of you, the more unnatural the next step would seem. And after all Lydia was quite right, she was in no position to bring up a child and why should she, it wasn't as if she'd wanted to be pregnant. It was Igor, I thought, who should be dealing with this, who should be suffering, at least witnessing what had happened and was about to happen, what I was about to do.

I took out the paper and smoothed it against my arm, and then I went downstairs and learnt how to put through a call from Lombardy to what turned out to be a convent outside Paris. My mother, I said in French, had asked me to call, Rachel Braithwaite or perhaps to you she is Rachel Cohen. She said you would be expecting my call in the first half of the month. I waited, unnerved, wondering what on earth I would do if the sisters said sorry, who, what, no idea what you're talking about.

Take you and flee, I thought ridiculously, I'd want you if no one else did, as if Oxford might take me with a baby, as if Gran and Dad could just rear you on the farm along with the calves. As if Lydia would allow any such thing. Ah yes, said the woman who answered the telephone – a Telephone Sister? – one moment, you must speak to the Mother Superior. Another new experience, Derbyshire not being well-endowed in the way of Superior Mothers, or indeed nuns of any rank. Nancy, listen to this! Bonsoir, she said, deep-voiced, ici Mère Pauline. Good evening, I said, I am the daughter of Rachel Braithwaite or perhaps Cohen, the younger daughter, I am calling about my sister, Lydia. Yes, she said, of course. The child has arrived? L'enfant est arrivé, as if you'd got off a train. Yes, I said, the baby was born this afternoon. I will not, I thought, collude in euphemism, it is not in my nature or culture to pretend that what is happening is other than it is, because in those days it still seemed to me that directness was truth and indirectness lying, that there was only one way to be honest. And all is well, she said, with mother and child? I wished for a better obstetric vocabulary in French, but of course all my farm work had been in English, with Dad. All is well, I said. My mother told me I should call you, after the birth. She said that you would make the necessary arrangements. Of course, she said, everything is prepared. You may expect Soeur Mathilde to collect the child on Friday. Five days. It seemed both brutally short and brutally long, because I could already see that every time I held you it would be harder to give you up but also that Lydia had little time to welcome and part from you. So soon, I said. It is better that way, she said, do not worry, we are very experienced, there is a good family waiting. The child will want for nothing. L'enfant. The distinction between un enfant and un bébé is not the same as between a child and a baby, but even so I wanted to push her, to make her name the reality of what we were about. Le nourisson, I said, the nursling, seems so new, so very small, to make such a long journey. It is better this way, she said again, we are very experienced in these matters. You should expect Soeur Mathilde on Friday afternoon. Goodnight, my child, God bless you. I waited until we'd hung up to say, that won't be necessary, thank you.

I went outside for a bit before going to tell Lydie. The moon was rising over the mountain, full, the sky clear. The birds had settled and Signora Pilone must have shut in the hens for the night. From up the valley, a dog barked, and a boat puttered along the lake. There was barely a breeze; a couple of leaves swayed leisurely to the gravel at my feet. I breathed in: bracken from the hillside, jasmine from the pot by the front door, dying leaves. Colline d'automne, I thought, goodnight.

You were crying. I hurried up the stairs, not that I knew what to do, and was greatly relieved to find Nurse Rosetti coming out of Lydie's room with you in her arms. I will stay here, she said, just this one night, to care for the baby so your sister can sleep, but I will show you what to do. Yes, I said, thank you very much. She turned you against her shoulder and patted you. Come with me, she said, I will show you how to prepare the bottle. Lydia still won't feed him, I asked. She shook her head. Your sister will not look at the baby, she said. She will not see or hear him. I followed her down the stairs. He's being collected, I said, the baby. On Friday. My mother arranged it, with some nuns. Yes, she said, I understand. I will teach you to take care of him until then. We went into the kitchen and she handed you to me. But if I may, she said, some advice. Please, I said. In my experience, she said, it will be better if your sister can hold her child, before he goes.

In her experience, I thought, the nuns who have a great deal of experience. I am an innocent abroad, an idiot, but of course I was only, barely, less each passing hour, a child.

hot December days

He wants to come next week, Méabh says. The flights must cost a fortune, short notice, I asked him would you not wait for the summer and he said he's waited years already and he has plenty of airmiles, I suppose they do fly a lot more, over there. Big country and not many trains, says Edith, anyway you let him worry about that. Does next week feel too soon? You know you can say you're not ready.

They're sitting on the sea wall, waiting for the tide to rise a little further, nursing thrifty flasks of tea though Edith knows she should save it for after the swim. It's the first day it's almost or just warm enough to sit outside and you learn, in these parts, to take your chances. Sunlight spangles over the water at their feet, though further out there are clouds on the move. Something about this water at high tide excites the seabirds, a twice-daily banquet, and they're gathering bright white and sociable along the shore where waves surge over the limestone flags and it's never safe for human swimmers.

I know, Méabh says, but sure he's the flights booked and I

don't know when I would be ready, I don't know what would need to change. And maybe he's a great man, my brother. My half-brother.

He's your half-brother for sure, then, asks Edith. Different dads? The waves are almost spraying her dangling feet and the sun won't last, you can feel it on the wind.

He just said we have the same mother, I'm assuming that means half-brother. It would make sense, my parents always said they'd met at a dance when she was twenty-one. So there must have been someone else. Before.

She glances at Méabh, who looks away. They both know what that might mean, how likely it is that a fifteen-year-old girl in rural Ireland was in any way consenting –

You know he wasn't from here, my dad. Up Roundstone way. They met when he was visiting friends. They used to meet in Galway, courting.

Roundstone is maybe thirty kilometres round the coast, but not a quick journey even now. You'd still probably meet in Galway, courting.

Is it true, she asks, that the priests used to go to the dances? As morality police?

Méabh shrugs. They went everywhere, she says, not that they were all bad men, some of them were very kind, people forget that now. Still are, your man over in Gort, they'd never have got the women's refuge without him.

They all tolerated bad men, Edith says, which is more than she usually allows herself. Still do, look at my ex-husband's posh school up in Dublin, protecting its own, she does not allow herself. Not her fight. Not for an English person, a Jewish English person, to criticize Irish Catholicism. Not for an ex-wife to ask her ex-husband what was done to him, what he witnessed, sixty years ago, what recollections the age of reckoning awakens in him. She's just glad she held out, didn't let Mike send Pat there, not because she'd thought the teachers would deliberately harm him but because by then she'd met enough men, Oxford and London, who'd gone to schools where they learnt that they were better than people who didn't go to those schools, and she didn't want her gentle Pat to think that way. And don't we all tolerate, turn a blind eye or perhaps the other cheek, to the unconscionable, is it reasonable to expect more of men in holy orders? You can still blame the English, plenty of people do, for the way Irish people didn't or couldn't resist the power of the Church once independence came. Assertiveness could be fatal under English rule and it takes generations to forget those lessons.

So, she says, next week?

He was saying Thursday or Friday maybe, or the weekend if I prefer but sure it's better in the week with the kids at school and John out of the house. Méabh frowns out to sea, the wind lifting her hair, fiddles with her scarf.

You know you don't have to, Edith says again, you know you owe him nothing, if it's going to be painful or distressing or even just uncomfortable, you can cancel or postpone, there's no obligation, nothing has to change for you.

Ah Edith, she says, I think it's already changed, I think the knowledge changes things. Mam wasn't quite what I thought she was. Maybe I'm not quite who I thought I was. And poor Henry, so much harder for him, all those years, a whole life believing what wasn't true, would it not rock your faith in everything, finding out that you don't even know who you are? No, there's the obligation of one decent being to another quite apart from the blood.

That all depends, Edith wants to say, on what you think makes you, on whether you think it's your action and your memories, what you do and make and feel and think, what you believe, who you love, or the codes in your blood and bones, and of course it's both, we all know that, nature nurture, done to death. Henry's parents still loved him, didn't they, he still had a good childhood, he's still American, still an accountant or a lawyer or whatever it was, still divorced and the father of his children, he just formed in a different womb before he knew anything about anything. And then she remembers the baby in Italy, his need for his mother the most obvious thing, a wound beyond healing. The calf's bawl and the lamb's call, call and response, incomplete.

So, she says, will you meet at my house? Thursday or Friday, I don't mind, I've to go out on Thursday evening but it can be late. I know, says Méabh, Gunter's night, I'd need to be home by then anyway, I have to put the dinner on the table. You don't, Edith wants to say, there are three adults in your house and three young people of more than capable age, but she says I can always postpone or cancel if you'd like me around in the evening, even for debriefing, why don't you stay for dinner anyway? You're very kind, says Méabh, but no, I'll get home once he's gone, a cup of tea maybe. Stiff drink, more like, says Edith, and just say if you want me to stay or go or stay and then go or come in later or whatever, no need to decide now. Do you think the tide's about right?

Her body has stiffened, sitting on the stone wall, and she has to make an ungainly turn, knees on rock, before she can stand up. Jesus Christ, says Méabh, that was a mistake, give me a hand up. She braces, leans, pulls, Méabh's hands cool and dry. For a moment it's not going to work, for another moment they're both going over and then they're upright and laughing and she's remembering all those years ago with Nancy, how they used to sit half the afternoon on the rock by the stream, feet dangling, how a little sunburn was just summer, how they ate hard-boiled eggs kept cool in the water but the butter had always melted into the bread, how in July they browsed the bilberries like sheep, but it can't have been that often, can it, the weather was like that and they were together? She should have stayed in touch with Nancy, even just Christmas cards. Nancy, after all, had braved her parents' disapproval of Maman and Lydia and the arrangements on the farm for years, even if she let go when her husband expressed similar dissatisfaction. Was it intolerable to most people, who Edith used to be, how bold and sure she was, before her Oxford notions and Jewish blood were veiled, muffled, by Mike's suburban ways, before she came to live among people for whom Oxford and Judaism were at best barely visible and at worst pretentious? Was it necessary, salutary, for marriage and emigration to cut her down to size, to limit her kinesphere? And if so, who is she now, what room is now required, late in the day, for the action of being Edith? Her cottage, she thinks, her cottage, these hills, this sea, a yoga mat and a bed that is sometimes shared, a seat to break bread at Bríd's table and a place to walk at Méabh's side.

She should know if Nancy is alive. It used to be that the

grannies remembered summers that could never have been, longer and sunnier, more golden and more blue, and soon, she thinks, soon if not already, it will be the winters passing into folklore, the years when puddles froze and you had to scrape your car in the morning, she'll tell her grandchildren how she used to see her breath, though the northern winter will always be dark, won't it, we won't ever accidentally or on purpose straighten our planet's lovely tilt? Will it be a relief, she wonders, to Aoibhinn and her children, the long nights a blessed cooling of hot December days?

Méabh is stripping off April layers, coat and cardigan, leggings under a long skirt. Do you think, Edith says, do you think eventually winters will get so hot people welcome the long nights? Not here, Méabh says, isn't it meant to get colder when the Gulf Stream dies, aren't we going to be seeing more snow and ice, us with our shite insulation and gas-fired power? And we should make the most of the swimming, even you won't be going in then, among the ice floes. Edith has her fleece-lined coat over her togs, no battle with damp elastane for her. I might, she says, I expect people do in – I don't know, what's on our latitude in America, Connecticut, Massachusetts? No ice floes, anyway. Méabh's down to her togs at last, matronly, practical. Try Canada, she says, try Newfoundland, that's what we're talking about. Surely not, Edith says. Come on, says Méabh, enjoy it while you can, I'll show you later on my phone. She turns around and climbs down the ladder. Edith jumps, while she can.

understudy

I've slowed right down, I'm aware of that. But you did leave that Friday, and I thought you'd want everything I could remember of the time you had with my sister, or at least in her vicinity. I'm wondering if you'd rather I told you a fairy tale, if it would help you to believe something other than the truth since you'll remember none of this anyway and I'm the only surviving witness, the history is in my hands. Would you like me to say, when I woke the next morning I found Lydia nursing you, that the two of you made a pietà as the rising sun gilded her copper hair and your softer-than-soft skin? Would you like me to say that she cradled you and held you close as the day took hold of the valley outside the window of the room where you were born? That she could not, did not, stop stroking the feathers of dark hair on your head still shaped by its passage through her bones, that she marvelled as parents do over the whorls of your ears and the dimpling of your knuckles? Stop here, then. Stabat mater.

The walls of the villa were thick and I was young and tired. I slept deeply that night, though when I woke and stepped barefoot onto the balcony the gardens and lake were storm-worn, wet lawns thick with leaves and broken branches, the washed sky pale through trees denuded overnight, the water still tossing though the wind had fallen. I leant on wet stone, let its roughness mark my arms as my feet chilled. The snow had come halfway down the mountain, below the level of my walks. I had a childish desire to hike up to it, go make footprints and a snowman. Babies slept, didn't they, I could take a few hours if I wanted to?

I put a cardigan Louise had left in her laundry hamper over my summer dress, but I would still have been glad of warmer things, of the thermal underwear I'd joyfully left in my bureau at home. As I washed my face and brushed my hair a sudden wave of homesickness rose, for the lumpy glass of my bedroom window at the farm, the creaky floor, the smell of toast coming up the stairs in the morning, Gran in her apron and Dad in darned wool socks, mucky boots left at the door. Why couldn't Lydia have gone there, or they come here, to be the grown-ups?

Signora Pilone was coming out of the kitchen with a tray. For my sister, I said, I can take it if you like. Prego, she said, buon giorno, Edith. Edit, I thought, Edita, Dita. Dita Braithwaite? And for you, she asked. I'll come down, I said, after I've given this to Lydia.

I almost dropped the tray while opening the door, so at first I didn't realize what she was doing. Out of bed, the blankets thrown back to show bloody patches on a towel spread over the sheet, over by the window – Lydie, I said, don't be so silly, what are you thinking? She was doing pliés, feet in second position, one hand graceful on the windowsill. The room smelt mostly of lavender and powder, but beneath those still a note of blood, of viscera. Starting as I mean to go on, she said, dipping again. Didn't you tear, I said, how can you heal if you do things like that, also doesn't it hurt? Do dance teachers know, I wondered, how much harm they do when they teach dancers to ignore pain? It's hardly a survival skill, the opposite of a survival skill, and not just for the dancers themselves, there's collateral damage. A bit, she said, but I expect things will hurt for a bit. Go back to bed, I said, I've brought your breakfast, and I knew when she obeyed me that she was hurting herself more than a little. She sat on the stained towel, lifted her legs together onto the bed, back straight as ever, and pulled up the blankets. Wait, I said, let me arrange your pillows, and she allowed me to shake them and arrange them at her back. I passed her the tray: a pot of coffee, rolls, two eggs, butter and jam. Good, she said, I'm hungry. Not surprised, I said, I realized yesterday why it's called labour. Yes, she said, tearing open a roll, actually I don't want to talk about that, OK? I was still standing at the bedside, as if awaiting further orders. I pulled forward one of the little chairs and sat on it, visiting not attending. About what, I said, giving birth? Any of it, she said, as far as I'm concerned it's over, it's as if I'd had an operation, a cancer operation, there was something there that couldn't stay and it's gone and as soon as I'm well enough I'll go back to the company and there'll be no need to speak of it ever again. She took a large bite. From several rooms away, you began to cry. But Lyd, I said, it wasn't an operation, you didn't have cancer, there's a— I know what there is, she said, I said *as if*, didn't I? And in a few days it will be somewhere else and that will be the end of that. That, I thought, will be the beginning of that, my girl, but I'd known her powers of denial and assertion all my life. If Lydia said she would pass an exam or be given a part or indeed a place at the Royal Ballet School or in the company, that was what happened. Even when what she wanted was a dress or a trip, events tended to fall into place, and though I was quieter about my desires and intentions I cannot say I was much different myself. We were both allowed to go unusually far in life before learning that we were not after all the main character, and I know some would say even now I am paying only lip service to the notion. I have, by and large, prevailed. Lucky me then, no? Lucky me and poor you, primally wounded. And poor Lydia, or not?

Lydie, I said, you should see him, the baby, you should say goodbye. Shut up, she said, I don't have to say goodbye, I never said hello. I don't want to see it and I don't want to hear about it and I don't want to know, and if you keep talking about it I don't want to see you either, is that clear? Let me pour your coffee, I said, you'll spill it. I'll pour it all over the bed if I like, she said, I'll throw it at the window, do you understand what I just told you?

I lifted the tray from her lap. Yes, I said, you were clear, I understand.

Your crying was louder, coming down the hall.

Wet circles bloomed on the white cotton over Lydia's breasts.

My poor darling brave sister, Giselle.

I put the tray on my chair and went out to stop the nurse bringing you to your mother.

*

Don't, I said, she doesn't want to see him, I'll take him.

Nurse Rosetti was carrying you upright, her hand cupping your head on her shoulder. You were red-faced, agape. He's hungry, she said, your sister should feed him. She won't, I said, she doesn't want to, you'll have to show me what to do with his bottle. Your cries rose. You gobbled at her neck, desperate, and she plugged you with a bent finger. For her also, she said, it would be good to feed him, she will have milk today. I think she does, I said, and I think you'll have to make it stop. There must be ways, mustn't there, I thought, better than we have for sheep and cows, though mostly in those cases there's a calf or lamb who needs a new mother and mostly you can persuade them to accept each other. Dad used to flay a stillborn lamb and tie its skin over an orphan, so the ewe would recognize the smell, though it always seemed to me that if she could tell her own lamb by scent she could probably also scent the flaying. Nurse Rosetti shook her head. First we feed the baby, she said. And we feed me, I thought. He's surprisingly loud, I said, as we went down the stairs, for someone so small.

It was not much different from feeding the runt lambs we sometimes reared in the farm kitchen for a few weeks, to see if they could put on, only you had to be more careful about sterilization. New babies get sick very easily, she said, especially without the mother's milk, you must take care. Yes, said Signora Pilone, and Edith, remember, if he is sick he will not be able to travel, you understand? Sì, I said, capisco.

I liked the warm weight of you, parcelled in a cotton blanket, on my arm, and the way we could hear milk becoming baby. You gazed intently at something, or nothing, a few inches above the bottle. He's very dark, I said, his hair and eyes. The hair may change, said Nurse Rosetti, but perhaps his father? I shrugged. I haven't met him, I said, I don't know. They were exchanging glances, the two women. I looked back at you, wondered who you thought was your mother, whose skin and smell you were learning. I will take Signora Lydia's tray, said Signora Pilone, I will clean her room if she will permit.

Nurse Rosetti showed me how to tip you upright and rub and pat your back. Often they cry, she said, for wind. Fare il ruttino, a new phrase, not, in Italian, the same word as the wind in the trees. It hurts them, she said, so we do this. Yes, like that. I wondered how she knew, how anyone knew why babies cry. Maybe we teach them why. And you can walk with him, she said, only one becomes tired. It's just for a few days, I said, I rather think I'm going to be tired anyway. I will visit, she said, once or twice a day, but it seems that you will need to care for him when I am not here. Aye, I said, it does that an' all. Sì, I said, capisco. You squirmed and mewed against my shoulder. I found myself bobbing on my toes, a small baby-dance. Shh, I said, shh, you're fine, I'm here. It was far from clear that my being there meant you were fine. Perhaps, I said, you can show me how to change his – his napkins? I gestured. A-level Italian did not include nappies, which was on reflection interesting when I recalled that it did include 'sabre-rattling' and 'nuclear deterrent'. It had already occurred to me that it would have been a kindness among our teachers and examiners to give the outward-bound adolescent girl a vocabulary for menstruation; perhaps they felt that the words for pregnancy and babies would only encourage us. Yes, she said, of course, come with me. And then if you have no further questions I must go home. Yes, I said, of course, I understand, you must be very tired. I have other work, she said, other patients. Come now.

We went into the room I still thought of as Katja's, stately, full of morning light that showed no dust on polished wood or sun-striped air. I had learnt, I realized, how to carry you, how to hold you so we both knew you were safe. Nurse Rosetti took a folded white towel from the wooden rail beside the washstand and spread it on the bed. Now, she said, put him down carefully on his back, remember to support his head. It did not seem possible to forget to support your head, because I could feel in my hands as well as knowing in my mind that you could not do it yourself. I lowered you carefully, but even wrapped as you were we could see you startle and flail. Air and gravity are surprises that take time to wear off. And unwrap him, she said, he can't fall now. You began to stutter into sound, agitation rising to a sustained note. Don't worry, she said, of course he doesn't like it, but if we don't change him he will have – an eruption? An irritation, she qualified, an irritation of the skin. A rash, I murmured, Sì, capisco. And that will hurt him, she said, now he just tells us he doesn't like it. Sì, I said, capisco. She directed me to unroll your blanket, unfasten the ties and buttons of your comically tiny clothes, unpin the white towelling bundle swathing you from the uncanny stalk of your navel to your knees. Don't touch the cord, she said, we will bathe it tonight and soon it will come away. Now, unfasten the pin. There was a safety pin almost the size of your hand securing the whole affair. Put it in your dress, she said, that way you know where it is and it won't hurt the baby.

Undressed, you didn't look ready to be among us. Your legs reminded me of a tadpole's, vestigial or provisional, and your arms wavered like antennae over the twin bulges of head and belly, limbs an afterthought to thinking and digestion. I wanted to put you back into your eggshell or pouch, pack you up safely until you were ready for the world, but remembering your birth it was obvious that you had run out of time in the womb. You were wailing again, and I murmured and then sang to you, afraid to touch your new skin and weak flesh, while Nurse Rosetti went for water and a clean napkin. I went to gather blaeberries, blaeberries, blaeberries, I went to gather blaeberries, I lost my darling baby-o. Perhaps not. What do you sing to babies? Lully lulla, thou little tiny child, by by, lully lullay. What, I wondered, had been sung to me, perhaps by Maman and probably in French? It was hard to imagine, Maman holding and rocking, comforting, though I did remember that once when I had chickenpox and my hands were covered in lotion, she sat on my bed and spooned custard for me. She wasn't callous, Maman, it wasn't that she didn't care, she just couldn't stay. O sisters too, how may we do, for to preserve this day, this poor youngling, for whom we do sing. How indeed? My singing didn't seem to be helping, or at least not helping you. I stroked your head but that didn't help either, and then Nurse Rosetti came back and taught me to lift your red bird-feet – so undignified, sorry, but we've all been there and some of us will be cursed to go there again, Lord have mercy – and sponge you where we all need sponging, dust you with powder which would only later be found to be carcinogenic and certainly smelt nice, repackage you in your white layers. Put your hand there, she said, that way you feel the pin before the baby does. Keep the ties away from his neck and mouth, make sure they are inside the blanket. It had seemed perhaps cruel, certainly strange, to keep your arms and legs swaddled tight, but as I fastened up the parcel of you for the third time your crying ceased, and when I picked you up I bounced only a few times before the weight of you changed. Asleep, said Nurse Rosetti. Do you want to try to put him down? I wanted you not to cry again. I wanted you to stay asleep, so it wasn't an emergency. No, I said, it's fine, I'll hold him. Have you had breakfast, she asked. I'll do it later, I said, when he wakes up, though I could already see that when you woke up I would have to feed you and then probably change you again, this time alone and without direction, and that you would cry on both these occasions. All right, she said, I must go now, I'll be back later. Unless you have any questions?

Bathing, I said, I don't know how to bathe him. I don't, I thought, know how to do anything, I don't know how to keep a baby alive, don't leave me here with him, you can't go. We'll bathe him together later, she said, for now you just need to feed and change him. He will cry, babies do. She was backing towards the door. And if you can persuade your sister to hold him, you should do that. It's not easy, I said, to persuade my sister of anything, I'm not sure anyone ever has. I'll be back this afternoon, she said, probably about five o'clock, Signora Pilone is here, you'll do well. Goodbye now, Edith. Wait, I said, how do I know if he's too hot, what if he has a fever? If you and Signora Pilone think he's sick, she said, you should call the doctor, of course. But he has taken his milk and now he is well and I will be back in a few hours. Goodbye now. Sì, I said, capisco.

I listened to her footsteps going down the stairs, to you snuffling. I was understanding things I did not particularly want to understand.

I wanted my breakfast. I wanted to climb the hill. I did not want you to start crying again, because your crying filled my head with sirens and alarms.

We went along the corridor towards Lydie's room, you and I. There was silence behind her door and our nerve failed. We went carefully down the stairs, my hip brushing the stone banister, my mind showing a film of my hands or feet slipping, you plummeting, bouncing, sea-urchin skull on stone corners. We achieved the hall, with its worn Persian rugs over whose tassels a careless nurse could also trip. I leant back so your head wouldn't fall off while I used one hand to open the kitchen door, thinking that'll have to stop, keeping doors closed, I can't be forever sparing a hand just to open doors. Signora Pilone was at the sink. Shh, I said, he's asleep. She looked over. Sì, she said, do you want your breakfast now, it's late? Yes, I said, but I don't know how to eat while holding the baby. Put him down, she said. He'll cry, I said. He might cry. Conditional tense. Sì, she said, he might cry. You want bread, fruit? Yes, please, I said, anything. I bent back again, pulled out a chair. It scraped on the floor and you startled, coughed. Shh, I said, shh. I held the backbend while I sat down; of course there would be a choreography of infant care, a dance of – well, not love, was it, love wouldn't have been useful under the circumstances and anyway we'd only just met. A dance of care, the understudy of maternity.

I thought, with your ear to my chest, you might be troubled

to hear chewing and swallowing, but I suppose they were familiar sounds. You must have known Lydia's body through its noises in a way that no one else ever would, not even Lydia; your ears under her heart, between her guts. I wanted to restore you to her, reunite your bodies. I ate my breakfast, hoped she wasn't back at her improvised barre upstairs. The book didn't say much about after the birth, but the emphasis was more on the need for exercise, the inadvisability of staying in bed, than the need not to do pliés, the author's concern plainly that women might take childbirth as an excuse to rest and slack off the housework, a continuation of his anxiety that pregnancy might license laziness and self-indulgence. It was the first time I thought that I would not have children, that I would rather go to my grave without the blood-wrestling of birth and the appalling responsibility of infant care, and though if you find him you may assure Patrick – your cousin – that even in this final reckoning of secrets he has always had his mother's love, I'm not sure I was wrong. I have not been good at motherhood, certainly not in the Irish fashion. I was not a good wife. I did the correct things, mostly, but I did not give myself. I did not merge myself with my son, there was no abnegation. I remained more of a narrator than a participant. Self-centred to the end, you might be thinking. I am. I narrate. I make myself, in this late accounting, the main character. The scratches in the mirror centre around the candle of my version.

You stayed asleep, though as I finished eating, your eyelids began to flicker and from inside your cocoon I could feel fluttering. Dreaming, I supposed, perhaps mourning your lost life inside my sister, or rehearsing the shocks of air and touch. I limboed over to the sink, gave up any idea of washing my dishes, gave up any idea of peeing and brushing my teeth, gave up the idea of going out for a walk while you slept. I shifted you slightly into the crook of my arm and we went to spend the morning on the sofa reading Daniel Deronda and worrying equally about the periods of silence and the creaking of the floor in Lydia's room overhead.

Not the whole morning. Babies don't give you the whole morning. It was about eleven, the sun high and strong through bare branches and brown leaves, when you ran out of sleeping fuel. You began to cry before you opened your eyes, as if the realization of consciousness was upsetting. I closed the book, where I was in a languorous passage and aware that it would be difficult but perhaps not important to find my place again, and watched you face the world. I respected your objections; the situation was far from ideal. I carried you bawling to the kitchen where Signora Pilone held you, singing in a surprisingly deep voice while I prepared your bottle, and was taken aback by the feel of your absence from my arms, the cooling damp patch on my dress where you had been breathing and dribbling above my breast.

consider unspeakable

It's unlike her, she thinks, this fussiness. Even in the days of competitive South Dublin dinner parties, she'd won – at least in her own mind – by not playing, not putting a wreath on the front door even at Christmas, not displaying her taste in candlesticks and Nordic shoe storage, not festooning her good oak table with place-mats and bits of fabric. We like things plain, she'd said, where I come from, though in the Irish imagination all England is prosperous, white and southern, ancestral silver, damask tablecloths and candelabra, and in Blackrock and Dalkey they had no idea of where she'd come from, the moors and dark stone, the Northern respect for the unadorned, much less the mill towns where Eid and Diwali now make more mark than Christmas and Easter. She still likes things plain and keeps her house cleaner than the Marital Home was, so why is she plumping cushions and dusting, it's not as if Henry's going to be checking the toaster tray or running an accusing finger over the kitchen cupboards, it's not as if she'd care what he thought anyway. She arranges shortbread on one of Gunter's plates, sniffs the milk before pouring it into one of Gunter's jugs. No, it's not for Henry, is it, it's for Méabh, who is trusting her, who has turned to her for a place of safety. She wants Méabh to feel unimpeachable, life-jacketed in whatever wreaths and candelabra might be required. Not that she has any wreaths or candelabra. There's quite a collection of scented candles, though, kept in the cupboard with the tea towels, her friends being generally of the scented candle persuasion and generally generous. She kneels and rummages: the boxes make the absurd claims of everything intended for women. These candles will rejuvenate, relax, restore you. They will nourish and uplift and replenish, in all ways prepare you to continue to provide service and comfort uninterrupted by your own ageing or fatigue or hunger. How about actual rest, she mutters, squatting now at the open cupboard, how about a proper meal and a long walk and an afternoon with your mates, only that might inconvenience a man or child or take up resources a man or a child might want so why don't you just light a little candle and smell the pretty smell while you iron your pretty tablecloth, crone? Nothing's changed, she thinks, opening the boxes and sniffing, writing off the potential for re-gifting, nothing's fucking changed since the 1960s, which is obvious nonsense especially in Ireland where the only scented candles of the 1960s were burning on the altar and women were a generation away from owning their own bodies let alone the theoretical if not practised equalities of today. Even so, she thinks, even for Méabh, no scented candles, let's not mask the pervasive stink of patriarchy. And then, for Méabh, she chooses one that claims only to smell of bergamot and the sea – high tide, she hopes, remembering low tide in Dublin Bay when a cruise ship was in, bad enough driving past and shouldn't they be out there on the barricades protesting about the pollution instead of in here arranging biscuits – and lights it from the stove because she does have matches, what eejit doesn't keep candles and matches in this part of the world, and they're probably in the hall press with the first-aid kit and the wind-up torch and other emergency supplies but there's no emergency here, is there, nothing to get worked up about. She goes back to her room, straightens the bedside book pile, as if he's going to come in here and check, as if she'd care if he did.

Méabh's car is in the lane, old banger. She goes down the path, damp grass, spring sunshine, daffodils blowsy and lily of the valley bright white. Méabh's in battle dress, turquoise and green, the chunky silver and lapis necklace Caoimhe brought her from Turkey, hair up and secured with a silver pin you wouldn't get through airport security. Paper bag which will be full of home-made scones. You look lovely, she says, which is true. Will I change, I'll wear anything you'd like? Don't be silly, says Méabh, you always look great, it's not a blind date. Come and see the house, says Edith, make sure it's right. It's always right, says Méabh, it's always beautiful. It's usually neat, says Edith, and sure why wouldn't it be with only me in it?

They go in. It maybe does smell a bit different, Edith thinks, though whether of bergamot and the high tide she couldn't say. What will he see, the American lawyer, the lost boy found? I don't know why I'm so nervous, Méabh says, taking off her shoes. It's quite a big thing, Edith says, a new sibling at our age, at any age, he's probably nervous too. What, she thinks absurdly, if there is an emergency, what if one of their hearts or brains can't take it, a heart attack or a stroke, as if people don't survive, aren't obliged to survive, all sorts of losses and findings every day. I made scones, Méabh says, and it's not even just him, it's the way the whole story changes everything and nothing at the same time. I mean, he's still him whoever he is, I'm still me, Mam was still Mam but – a brother, all those years – and Mam must have been thinking, mustn't she, she must have wondered, and even when it all came out, the Mother and Baby Homes and the trafficking, she must have heard other women telling and finding the babies, or worse yet the bodies, she must have thought— Yes, says Edith, probably. They go into the kitchen. Would you like a cup of tea, she wants to say, but she says, did you watch any of the films with her, those documentaries about the homes and laundries, do you think she saw them? Méabh wanders over to the window. Not with me, she says, she wasn't one for the films, didn't often look at the television, we never talked about it. I suppose I thought she'd be old-fashioned, the way she was about most things, weekly Mass to the end and we got her the last rites. There was a lot we didn't talk about. I mean, it was different, wasn't it, parents and kids, you didn't question. Yes, says Edith, it does feel as if more went unsaid. But she's not sure, is it maybe like wearing fur and smoking indoors, you can't see the violence of your own moment, you can't hear what you and your friends and children consider unspeakable, you don't know what you're not saying because it hasn't occurred to you that there might be ways to say it? Would you like a cup of tea, she says. Méabh is stroking the fossil on the windowsill, one Edith shouldn't have let ten-year-old Patrick take from the shore at Lyme Regis. We should wait, Méabh says, he'll be here soon. Twenty minutes, says Edith, plenty of time. Are you wanting one, Méabh says. Edith gauges. Méabh always wants a cup of tea. Yes, she says, I think I will. Well, Méabh says, if you're putting the kettle on anyway –

She finds the tannic Irish tea she keeps for visitors, takes a cheering sniff of her own Rose Pouchong. Méabh absently watches, hands, tap, kettle. What about your mam, Méabh says, you don't often speak of her. Edith shrugs. You know she wasn't there much, she says, the war changed everything when she was no older than Aoibhinn, there's no knowing how she might have been. As soon as she could travel she was wandering Europe looking for her family and friends, away more than she was home, and once she found the kibbutz that was pretty much it, that was her home, that's where she died. My sister and I always used to tell each other that without the war we couldn't have existed, our parents could never have met. And of course that's true for half Europe. But not here, she doesn't say, not you. But did you talk, Méabh asks, could you talk to her? The kettle boils. Teapot, she thinks, for Méabh, so she can take more than one cup without the dance of offer and refusal, offer and acceptance. There's a blackbird assembling nesting material in the oak tree. Yes, she says, I think so, certainly about sex and relationships, or at least she liked talking to us about them. If anything I think she thought I was rather a prude. Not her story to tell, she thinks, let poor Lydie lie in peace, nothing to be gained by telling now. Today is for Méabh. Gran was more traditional, she says, went to church, but even she approved when they made the Pill available to unmarried women and legalized abortion, said she'd known too many lasses dead or damaged while the boys got on with their lives. The kettle boils.

Méabh's wandered over to the other window, where she picks up the round pot Edith bought in Kyoto. She'd like to go back to Japan, before it's too late, before she can't face the flight or flying becomes as socially unacceptable as it ought to be if there's to be a habitable planet for the grandchildren. I wish I knew, Méabh says, if Dad knew. I wish I knew if she had anyone to talk to. Someone must have known, surely, Edith says, someone must have helped with the arrangements. Her own mam, probably, says Méabh, her and the priest, and it was probably never spoken of afterwards. You know yourself, Edith thinks, how it is. My mother, she says, never spoke of her last weeks in Paris, not even on her deathbed. She told us stories about her childhood but not its end and she left the room if anyone mentioned the camps. I always hope she found people in Israel who could talk about it, I always hope that's one reason why she stayed.

She's spent the Dublin years not speaking of her mother, or the kibbutz, knowing when to keep silence, passing, but maybe here, now, with Méabh — They were all peace campaigners on her kibbutz, she says, back in the day, it wasn't that they didn't know or didn't think about it. But of course they were also there, in Israel, there's no way around that. Méabh puts down the bowl. They look at each other. So much pain, Méabh says, so much fucking pain, our mothers. No one is free until everyone is free, Edith thinks, and how can that ever come to be, how can those lads in the hotel and all the other lads now and always on their way over be free, and also all the young Irish people who can't have homes and can't leave home? How can there be enough for all? And since it's obvious that there is enough for all, that the problem is distribution not supply, why cannot all have enough? Partly because people like Edith have too much. Have a biscuit, she says, or a stiff drink, we mustn't get ourselves into a state, before he comes.

one is one

Nurse Rosetti returned as promised. I was sitting in the kitchen, holding you and watching Signora Pilone chop vegetables. I'd taken Lydia her lunch but not dared to ask her again about you. She was remote and beautiful once more and my memory of her bucking and sweating on a soiled bed seemed impossible, libellous. You'd cried, slept, fed, and apart from Signora Pilone holding you while I went to the bathroom you'd been in my arms the whole day, because both times I tried to put you down in your basket you howled as if I was leaving you on a hillside for the bears. È naturale, said Signora Pilone, which made sense. Lambs and calves also think it's an emergency when they can't find their mothers, not, of course, that I was – Brava, said Nurse Rosetti, you managed well, I knew you would. You see it's not so hard? The smell of outside was on her clothes and hair, wind and leaves. I had not left the house that day. It is very hard, I said, and without Signora Pilone it would be impossible. They laughed. Every mother says that, the first time. I'm not – I said. Here, said Nurse Rosetti, let me take him, have a walk around the garden and then we will bath the baby, perhaps in Signora Lydia's room? I handed you to her, a bundle that had somehow become grubby; awake and miraculously not obviously in need of anything in particular. Your gaze wavered from my face to hers. You ask her, I said, I think she'll say no. I wasn't going to ask, she said. Go on, enjoy the last of the afternoon.

The relief of stepping over the threshold was like taking off too-tight clothing. I wanted to run and jump and shout, to climb a tree and rush into the middle of the grass to spin until I fell over. Instead I walked fast up the track to the orchard, where I hung by my hands from the branch of an apple tree whose fruit was gone, whose leaves were turning. One shoulder cracked in an alarming but painless way. I tipped my head back and experimented with a quiet shout, but it felt too silly. I bent my knees and swung, jumped and landed badly in the leaf-strewn grass. There were mushrooms about which I did not know enough, and the trails of snails over pecked and rotting windfalls. I stood up, no harm done. The last pears were ripening but I was not in domestic mood, not harvesting or gathering. I ran around the trees, bits of deliquescing fruit slippery in the long grass, and then up the hill until I was breathless and stopped. I dusted myself down and went back to the house.

They were tight-lipped in the kitchen. Hello, I said, thank you, I do feel better. They had asked Lydia, I knew, or tried to take you to her, and she had said something unforgivable. It was not as if I hadn't warned them. We'll bath the baby here, said Nurse Rosetti, it's warmer for him. Yes, I said, shall I fetch a tub, where is it? I was remembering an old enamel tub we used to use as a watering trough in the barn, so small I'd always assumed it was a baby-bath. He's too small, she said, a basin will do. Another area not covered by A-level Italian, the distinction between culinary vessels. Dish, bowl, basin. I knew knife, dagger, sword.

I don't know if you've ever bathed a baby — I think I hope you have, I think even if you don't have children it might be one of those experiences like cycling in traffic and manoeuvring a wheelchair that every adult should have for purposes of empathy — but the process is elaborate and the stakes are high, if not as high as they appear to the infant in question. I'd foolishly thought you might splash and chuckle, might be comfortably reminded of the aqueous life you had so recently lost, but of course the splashing and chuckling were months in the future, for someone else's reward. You trembled and howled, red-faced. His hands are turning blue, I said in horror. Of course, said the nurse, all the blood is in his head. You weren't very good at it yet, I realized, circulation and breathing, biological multitasking, and by the time you were restored to my arms, damp and powdered and without your animal smell, we were both shaken. Darkness was falling; we retired to the big sofa in the drawing room where I put on only the table lamp while I gave you your milk. We settled. I think now, I calmed myself and in doing so, calmed you, because we were both learning survival skills.

Nurse Rosetti came in as your eyelids began to fall. Funny how babies resist sleep and adults court it, not that I've ever had much trouble sleeping and nor as far as I know did your mother, though insomnia was less fashionable then. We just got on with it, I'd like to say, but then we didn't have devices telling us we were failing to sleep, or failing to sleep adequately, and the television stopped broadcasting at bedtime though for years Radio 4 switched over to the World Service to see you through the night if you had vigil to keep. Sailing By was the national lullaby, our parents in Broadcasting House signing off for the night. Nostalgic nonsense, but it was your mother's world too, if that interests you. She spent almost all her adult life in London. Well, almost all her life, really, what with leaving for boarding school at twelve; it occurs to me that her childhood was brief. I'm going, the nurse whispered, I'll come back tomorrow. He'll sleep with you? I sighed. Yes, I said, I suppose so. Unless, I wanted to say, you can stay here again, but of course she had other work, a home of her own, and there was no medical need. Is Lydia all right, I said. I'd hardly seen her. Medically, she said, yes, she's doing well. But I still think it would be best if she would see her child. Sì, I said, capisco. He'll need milk in the night, she said, just feed him when he cries. Three nights, I told myself, two days, and I tried to imagine how it would be if you were my baby to keep, if this sudden servitude were a life sentence.

I waited until I could feel in the weight and rhythm of your body that you were deeply asleep, far out wherever babies go – stars, I always think, galaxies, or the deepest seas, cruising and wheeling wordless – and then carefully edged forward and stood up. I could cradle you now in one arm while I opened doors, but I wrapped both around you to climb the dim stone stairs. There was light under Lydia's door, no sound of movement. I tapped quietly and didn't wait to edge in backwards, my body between the bright light and your sleeping eyes, between your little face and your mother's sight. Lyd, I said, I've got the baby, I've had him all day, I won't turn round if you don't want me to, I'll take him away if you say so, but he's fast asleep and if you wanted to glimpse, to practise glimpsing, I could just turn around slowly and you could see how you feel. He's going on Friday, Lyd, you have two more days. Go away, she said, go away and take it away and don't bring it back. Now. OK, I said, but I'm going to ask again. Fuck off, Edith, she said, fuck right off and when you get there fuck off some more. Got it, I said, fucking off now.

It was the first time I'd said the word. I liked it.

The evening wore on: crying, milk, sleeping. I ate a tepid meat stew with one hand while holding you in the other arm, because even in Signora Pilone's arms you wouldn't settle. Crying, milk. Night fell. Crying. Since you were crying anyway, it seemed I wouldn't make things worse by leaving you in your basket while I had a quick bath, but you were able to cry harder, with greater desolation, in a way that showed I was making things worse. I splashed in a couple of inches of water, shivering between marble slabs, and yanked my clothes back over damp skin. Pyjamas, I wondered, but there didn't seem to be time somehow, and I wasn't sure I would be exactly going to bed. I thought of Dad at lambing time, dozing in his work clothes on the sofa sometimes when I came down in the morning. Seasonal labour, a time to be born. You stopped crying when I settled you against my shoulder and began to pace the hall, where Lydie could almost certainly hear it. I rubbed your back and sang lully lulla, thou little tiny child, by by, lully lullay. And then, in medieval mood, one is one and all alone and ever more shall be so. Not being a singer, not being interested, my repertoire turned out to be small; we had a wireless at home but no record player, none of us feeling a need for music. It was only later, everyone started to have to have taste in music, as if it were food or clothes, no opting out. In the bleak mid-winter, I heard myself sing, as if all babies were one. I would go home for Christmas, though I was not old enough to be sentimental about it. Aunt Helen would come, and would hint and carp at Maman whether she was there or away, and probably Maman wouldn't come and Dad and I wouldn't talk about betrayal or rejection, and Gran would insist on cooking complicated things and get tired and cross, especially when Dad wouldn't eat the plum pudding though he never had, not even as a boy and you'd think she'd know to expect it by now. Still, my own room, my own bed, people whose unreason and idiosyncrasy required no learning. And Lydia, I thought, would she really be in the Nutcracker in two months, staying away from us in London, pretending? Probably. If I were a shepherd, I would bring a lamb. Lydia's door opened and she peered round. Edith, she said, could you not do that somewhere else, I'm trying to sleep? She closed it again before I could approach.

We went downstairs, where for the first time there was a fire in the drawing-room fireplace. We sat on the floor and I watched its light on your face, the long shadows around the big room. Signora Pilone must have left it as her parting gift before going home to bed. After a while we moved to the sofa and read some more of the middle of Daniel Deronda, or perhaps the same of the middle of Daniel Deronda, it's not really the kind of book where it matters all that much. Crying, to the chilly kitchen for milk, more crying, back to the fireside, milk, not crying. I doubt you could see the fire very well but you seemed to be watching the flickering light, and after a while you slept. We went back upstairs – it seemed silly not to try to go to bed – but as soon as I moved you away from my body, before I'd even put you down, you cried. We paced and sang as quietly as possible, hoping you'd hear through my body and your blankets, but still you cried and I remembered about nappies. More crying, much more crying, shocked pink skin. I was surprised by what was in your nappy, greenish tar, and wondered about going out to wake Signora Pilone but then when I wrapped you up again you settled and seemed well enough. Back to the fireside and Daniel, back upstairs. I'd passed tiredness, traversing the old house in the watches of the night, the trees sentries in the dark. If someone came, if there were intruders, if the firelight was blinding me to shapes moving on the lawn – I hadn't even closed the curtains, but it wasn't worth the risk of waking you.

Later, some time, still long before the pallor of the eastern skyline, I caught myself asleep on the sofa with you in my arms. One-handed, I pulled the cushions onto the floor, put you in the middle of one and curled around you, nowhere to fall, and of course we were there, the fire burnt to ashes, when Signora Pilone came back at sunrise.

minimal sunlight at high latitudes

A car comes up the lane. They look at each other, stand up. Big shiny car, slowing. Hire car, Edith says, not his, meaning don't judge, he's not necessarily the kind of person who drives a thing like that, though he's also clearly not the kind of person who rents the cheapest one even when he'll be driving alone and up the boreens, or maybe not up the boreens since that's hardly going to fit between the hedges. Méabh clutches her as the car pulls up in the lane. Deep breaths, she says, he'll be at least as nervous as you are. She puts her arm around Méabh as the car door opens and he gets out. Not tall, heavy build like Méabh's, good in an Atlantic gale. Easy gait, ageing well. Woolly hat, cagoule, those trousers that are all pockets, fill them and you wouldn't be able to walk. Hard to see colouring at this distance. Oh, says Méabh, Jesus Mary and Joseph. Prayer or blasphemy? It's often hard to tell in Ireland. The car's lights flash and he's coming up the path, slowly, looking about. Judging, she thinks, replaces it with curious. Pretty flowers, he might say to himself, cute little place (where in America, again?). It probably all looks miniature to him, tiny and green and grey, low-hanging sky and pot-bellied hills and trees of companionable human height, low houses and small cars for small roads, little weather systems dancing through microclimates. She finds herself thinking disloyally of the pictures of the Tuscan house that Cassie's been sending her, of landscapes in silver-green and terracotta, real mountains sharp under almost frighteningly blue sky. Méabh is pulling herself together, swirling her hair into a new knot, rearranging the scarf, resetting her head and shoulders. Ready, says Edith, and she goes to the door, sees through its glass that he is also resetting, holding the hat while he smoothes cropped grey hair, unzipping his coat. She pauses, gives him a moment before he sees her but not long enough for him to knock. You must be Henry, she says, come in, I'm Edith. Méabh's just in the kitchen. If you wouldn't mind taking off your boots.

She stands in the doorway. Efface yourself. There's an animal prickle across the room, a scenting. Are you predator or prey? Méabh, she says, Henry. You're very welcome, Méabh says, welcome to Ireland. Céad mile fáilte, Edith thinks. I don't know what to say, says Henry, thank you. They look at each other. Similar enough, thinks Edith, plausible siblings but you wouldn't spot it in a crowd. Sit down, she says, I'll put the kettle on, Henry, do you prefer tea or coffee?

They don't sit. They stand, gazing. Sorry, he says, I've never met anyone who looks like me before. I always wanted – I mean, you always do. Yes, Méabh says, I mean, I don't know, I can imagine. How was your journey, did you find the place all right? The sat nav's not always the best round here, reception comes and goes, it's the limestone. Yes, he says, I mean no, it was fine,

I allowed time. You've not had the best weather, Méabh says, for your trip, it's best in May and June, with the wild flowers. More chance of a sunny day. Or at least a sunny few hours, says Edith, Henry, tea or coffee, do you take milk, sugar? Please sit down. No, thank you, he says, I mean, yes, actually, please, two spoons. If it's coffee. I can't believe I'm here. With you. Have a biscuit, Edith stops herself saying, or now you must have a scone, Méabh makes these herself.

She fills the kettle again. They're still looking at each other. Please, sit, she says, and they do, but they're gazing, not talking. When did you find out, Edith asks, about your family here, that you have siblings? Biological siblings, he says, I grew up with a brother. About a month ago. The DNA test. And of course I knew my – my birth mother probably wouldn't be alive, I'm nearly seventy, but on the other hand if she'd been a teenager then maybe— She died sixteen years ago, Méabh says, breast cancer, but you're right, she was seventy herself. In their silence, wind plays in the trees outside. Seventy plus sixteen, a lifespan and a childhood, addition and subtraction. But you knew you were adopted, Edith asks. Not as a child, he says, yes and no, it was complicated. She nods, as if she understood. Méabh sits forward. But you were happy, she says, you had a happy childhood? Their gazes meet. It's like watching magnets connect, something disconcertingly close to erotic. Ordinarily dysfunctional, he says, good enough on the grand scale, what about you? Yes, Edith thinks, what about the other childhood, the one he didn't have. Méabh laughs. I could say the same, she says, it was of its time and place, we all survived. I'd say happiness wasn't really a concern in those days, not here, you were doing well enough if you had food on the table and clothes on your back. Come on, Edith thinks, you can do better than that. We had those, Henry says, a nice house and good schools, summer camps. White picket fence, Edith thinks, piano lessons and a cheerful but well-mannered dog, sets of matching towels ironed and folded in the hot press. Airing cupboard. Whatever.

Good, Méabh says, I'd say you probably did better in that regard than we did here, two sisters to a bed we were and rarely a full belly though sure they did their best and I'm not complaining. No summer camps, that's for certain. But it's not everything, is it, a big house and car? He looks out, across to where cloud is caught on the stony hill above the fields. No, he says, it's not. They did love me. Me and my brother almost the same, probably, I expect in every pair of siblings there's a favourite, or you think there is. Or it changes, Edith says, there are phases when one parent finds one child easier and then it shifts. Her and Dad, Lydia and Maman, most but not all of the time. Maybe it works well enough as long as the parents take one child each. Mm, he says, maybe, but you can hear that it wasn't that way, that he wasn't anyone's favourite. Was your brother adopted too, Méabh asks. No, he says, it often happens like that. He's still looking at Méabh, can't take his eyes off her but it's not desire, Edith thinks, he's not looking at her, he's looking for himself in her. Did you all have red hair, he asks, did she – did my mother have red hair? This comes out of a bottle, Méabh says, has done for years, but there's ginger in the family, yes, two of my granddaughters have it, gorgeous on young girls. I'd love to – he says – I had the red hair. It was the strangest thing, growing up, two dark-haired parents and my brother the same, Mom was Italian, see, a generation back, and then me, bright orange, and they'd all tan and I burnt so easily, Mom used to say it was the first sign of spring, my nose peeling. Adapted to the Irish climate, Méabh says, and on cue the rain patters. That's actually true, Edith says, I was listening to a podcast on the BBC, pale skin and red hair helps you make the most of minimal sunlight at high latitudes. Like the unique plants of the Burren, she thinks, bodies shaped by a particular environment, rain-carved and rock-sheltered, cloud-coloured.

Do your kids have it, Méabh asks, your girls? Robyn does, he says, we've always said Katie looks more like her mom though of course I wondered all these years, you're always looking at your children asking who it is you can't see in them. Would you like to see photos? Love to, says Méabh. He takes out his phone and sits beside her on the sofa, an interestingly judged space between them. Oh, says Méabh, oh, she looks just like Caoimhe, like my daughter, at the same age, oh, that's very strange now, something in the way she's holding herself and the shape of her arms, Caoimhe's always had skinny wrists though she's a well-built girl. Would you like another coffee, Edith says, and I'll freshen the pot, and then thinks what a nonsensical phrase that is, as if she were going to anoint it.

She takes her time, rinses the cafetière, wipes a smudge off the chrome kettle before boiling it, notices staining on the teapot lid and gives the whole thing a proper wash, bottle-brush down the spout and then a lot of rinsing to get the suds as well as limescale out. Hard water here, limestone footprints on every glass, across the draining board and down the cafetière, miniature stalagmites forming inside the pipes and taps, infiltration. Probably in their bodies too, bones and stones, here we go again – the rain's settled in. She tips Méabh's scones onto a plate, slices a slab of butter, decides the jam can perfectly well be served in its pot, takes it all through on a tray. Méabh's showing him her phone now, so this is Aoibhinn, wouldn't you say she's the look of your Katie about her now and, well, would you like to see my brother, I suppose I should say your brother, he'd red hair too as a boy – Leave them to it, she thinks, her job's done for now, chaperone, hostess.

Edith recedes quietly. Her bedroom is full of soft grey light, cloud-filtered. She'd like a walk, like to feel the wet grass growing under her feet and hear the birds about their rainy-day business in the hedges, but she won't disturb Méabh and Henry. She settles herself in the armchair, picks up her book. She likes the book, but she's looking out over the pages at the wet hillside, cows resigned under the hawthorn. Lydie's baby will be fifty-four now, into the reckoning years himself, the age-gap between him and her almost the same as between Henry and Méabh's mother. Would he know he started his life somewhere else, as someone else? Would he want to know? There'll be no more secrets, Méabh had said, with these DNA tests, as if biology is the whole and only truth. But humans are narrative animals, apes who tell stories. She's never going to send her genetic code – Lydie and Maman and Dad and Gran's genetic code – to be broken and sold by some American corporation, to have all that they are and were calculated in zeros and ones, but she could tell a story, if she wanted it told. She could leave an account, an explanation – expiation? – for Lydia's son to find if he comes looking when she's gone, and it would give a much better account than any blood test. Would Lydia mind, she wonders, but Lydia is so long gone there's no way of imagining what she might have thought and learnt, who she might have been in her 70s. Would it be too dramatic, is it too unlikely that he'd ever find the trail, a note with her will and a file on her computer, *to be opened in the event of my death*? As if there were some possibility that her death wouldn't happen, as if death were contingent. *To be opened after my death.*

the ways of men

I think this part will be hard to read. I'm sorry. I don't know if it's right, to tell you the truth, or at least what I remember as truth. I might be wrong about any of it, most of it, though I think not all of it. I was young and egocentric as the young are. I'm probably exaggerating my own role, making myself a heroine in ways I wasn't. Signora Pilone and Nurse Rosetti probably did more of the work of your care than I recall, and it's possible that Lydia was less adamant. I don't really believe that. I'm afraid I think that aspect, which is probably the most important to you, is probably right. More or less. Right in principle. It seems unlikely that all the detail is correct, doesn't it, that I really remember how many eggs she ate for her breakfast and when I took a bath? I think I do. In my mind it's all clear.

Lydia stayed in her room all that week, leaving only for the bathroom. It wasn't unusual then, even the bossy book thought it reasonable to keep to your bed for at least a week after childbirth, but she was obviously strong enough to be up. We could hear her feet gliding and stepping and sometimes jumping, and often when we went in with a tray she was over by the window, flushed and breathless. Don't you want to go out, I said, a walk in the fresh air, though I knew that she'd never been much interested in walks or fresh air and it was me who wanted to go out, who wanted to climb high above the snow line, walk over the glaciers into Switzerland breathing in pine trees and Alpine air and not these draughty rooms with the smell of boiling milk and woodsmoke and menstrual blood and baby pee. No, she said, not in the slightest, the only way I want to walk is down to the ferry for the train back to London. You could come downstairs, I said, for meals, if you're well enough to be at the barre. I don't have a barre, she said, and you said the nurse said at least a week of trays upstairs. Nurse Rosetti, I said, probably wasn't thinking you'd be doing jetés before you'd stopped bleeding. I'm not doing jetés, she said, there wouldn't be space, you don't know what you're talking about. And just because – you can't just decide you're allowed to talk about my bleeding, you wouldn't like it if I was nosy about yours. No, I said, fair enough, only, Lyd— No, she said, whatever it is, no. You can take the tray now.

I tried twice more to take you to her, thinking that however angry she was she'd have time and opportunity to forgive me eventually but your hours with us were flowing fast. The only actual hourglass I'd seen was Gran's egg timer, five minutes, and I kept remembering it. A Present from Whitby was carved onto the base of Whitby jet, and the sand in it was black. She and Grandad had had their honeymoon in Whitby, but he bought her the egg timer later, after it had become a joke between them that she was a dab hand with pastry and could turn out a roast dinner without smudging her apron but not boil an egg to his liking. He said to me once, she said, I don't get it, we learnt in the Army, it's not hard, is it? Here's t'pan, here's t'watter, here's t'egg and I know tha canst tell time. If he knew how, I said, why didn't you tell him to boil his own eggs and yours while he was about it and she said ah, lass, it wasn't like that, he was always that busy on the farm, it was a pleasure to cook for him. Only not the eggs, I said. She could do it by then, seven minutes for me, five for Dad, four for Maman when she was there, never looked at the timer, but I liked it, used to play with it, turning it sometimes twelve times for the hour. I don't know what became of it in the end. If I'd thought of it, it's something I'd maybe have kept, small and not useless. I ramble. Maybe you'll be interested. They were your great-grandparents, I suppose. I never talked much to Pat about them, about my childhood. I wanted him to fit in, not to be burdened more than I could help by his English mother and her colourful family history. Anyway, all through that day and night I kept thinking of it, of myself turning it, counting down. We had only one tin of infant formula, because that was all we would need.

Take it away, she said, I mean it and I've meant it all along and I'm not going to change my mind. I won't see it, I won't touch it, I never wanted it and I don't want it now. Take it away.

I held you tight as I carried you back down the hall. It made no sense to me that she hadn't said that six months ago, spared herself the lost months of dancing and the pain and indignity. You could call it love, couldn't you, her choice to give you life? Because the baby's Jewish, I kept remembering her saying, but were you Jewish if you didn't know it, how could you know it?

Was Lydie Jewish, really? We'd never kept Shabbat, Maman wasn't going to be baking challah or boiling chickens, though she did go to the synagogue in Sheffield sometimes and took me often enough that I could muddle through some of the prayers and songs. There was no pork in the house when she was there, though as far as I know all of us ate it at other people's tables. I sat shiva for her, when she died, but I needed the kibbutzniks to show me how and it's only now it occurs to me that we didn't do that for Lydia, it didn't cross our minds. Not mine, anyway. I kept wanting to ask Lydie, shouldn't we get the baby circumcised, at least give him that mark, but by your eighth day you would be in other hands. Other arms. There was so much I wanted to do for you, so much I wanted you to take with you, to pack into your bulrush basket –

Hours passed, the way I'd later learn that they do with babies, seconds and minutes sometimes as if you're wringing them from an almost-dry cloth, as if without the force of your will time might grind so slowly you'd find yourself grey-haired and stiff-jointed and the child still crying, but then it's getting dark again and you still haven't brushed your hair, much less finished the letter you started a week ago or darned your warm stockings. Without Signora Pilone maintaining the rhythm of mealtimes, I doubt I'd have fed myself or Lydia, and indeed fifteen years later when I found myself at home with my own new baby I was daily surprised that Mike came home and expected dinner. Wouldn't porridge do, or a tin of soup? Mike's mother sent a fruit cake and when I noticed I was hungry I ate some of it. I could have done with Signora Pilone in those days.

You were restless, your last night, as if you knew what was

coming, what betrayal we were about to perpetrate. Every time I tried to put you down, however soft and heavy you were in my arms, you startled, stiffened, coughed into tears like an engine on a cold morning, and then took hours, what felt like hours, to accept consolation. I paced, sang, half-anticipating the rest I would take the next night but also wondering who would hold and rock you, who would smell me on your clothes and hair, whose voice would hush and murmur. We dozed a little on the sofa cushions on the floor by the dozing fire, but I couldn't cross into deep sleep in case I rolled on you or one of us rolled off the edge, and every time I moved you murmured and hiccoughed and I woke up properly. You woke again, cried again. It was only two hours since your last bottle so I tried the other things first, all of which seemed to make it worse. We paced the drawing room, which was relatively warm because of the fire. I sang until I was bored and then recited, for which I was better equipped. We'd done Paradise Lost for A-level, and once I settled in I found I could keep going for a surprisingly long time. Of man's first disobedience, and the fruit of that forbidden tree, whose mortal taste brought death into the world, and all our woe. The rhythm seemed to soothe you, or maybe it soothed me and you scented the shift in my breathing and my blood and understood that things were better now, in the drawing room of the villa if not for fallen Man. Thou from the first wast present, and with mighty wings outspread, dovelike satst brooding on the vast abyss – probably not the poem for a Jewish baby on the last night with his own people, but if you were, or were also, an English baby, a Northern Protestant – I may assert eternal Providence, and justify the ways of God to men. I wondered if Milton could still have written like that after the Holocaust, justifying the ways of God to men, though possibly he would have argued that the difficulty was rather and properly with justifying the ways of men to God, as relevant to the Spanish Inquisition or any other of the many examples of man's inhumanity to man as the Third Reich. Regions of sorrow, I murmured, doleful shades, where peace and rest can never dwell, hope never comes that comes to all; but torture without end. No, Milton knew, he'd thought about the architecture and technology of suffering. Shh, I said, shh, baby, and for the first time I realized that we had not named you, that you were just the baby, and I stood still. Rain spattered the windows. Earlier, I had opened one of the curtains la signora liked to close at dusk, because the trees were company of a kind, and a huge half-moon roosted in the bare branches. How could we not have named you? Before I'd really thought about it I was hurrying up the stairs with you and I went into Lydie's room without knocking, but she was awake, sitting at the window.

Lyd, I said, sorry, what are you doing, are you all right? Yes, she said, no. I mean, I'm not ill. Good, I said, Lyd, we never named him, the baby, he doesn't have a name.

She looked away from us, out into the moonlit garden. There was a path of light across the lake, cut off by the mountain's shadow, and I almost expected to see the Apostate Angel hurled headlong flaming. Splash. She didn't say, take it away, or fuck off.

He doesn't have a name, I said again. He's leaving in the morning and we didn't even name him. There's no point, she said, they'd only give him a new name. Whoever. Where he's going.

But he's here now, I said, he's here with us. I've been holding him all these days and I never even thought, I only just noticed, I was telling him Paradise Lost – You were doing what, she said.

He was crying, I said, it calms him, poetry, at least if you walk at the same time, same as singing but I don't know enough songs. She turned her head. It was too dark to see her gaze. Oh, she said, have you been doing that every day? And night, I said, yes, someone had to, you can't just leave a baby.

Except that she could, obviously.

Oh, she said, I didn't know. Well, what did you think, I wanted to ask, who did you think was caring for him? And he needs a name, I said, you should name him, you carried—

Stop it, she said, I know what happened.

Not Igor, I stopped myself saying. What about David, I said, after Dad and it's a proper Jewish name. No, she said, one day you'll have a baby and you'll want to call it after Dad, he'd like that. Anyway, if we're being proper Jewish, Dad's still alive. (She was right, Patrick David after his grandfathers, and Dad was still alive but not, obviously, Jewish.)

I hugged you, brushed your silky hair with my lips. You smelt of yourself, of baby, of me. Gabriel, I said. Maman's father, but I was also thinking of Paradise Lost, the war-like angel calmly reproaching Satan. You might need all the calm, all the readiness, a person could have. She never talks about him, Lydia said. She was still looking towards us and, seeing me, therefore seeing you, if only your face by moonlight. Maman's not the only one, I wanted to say, who doesn't talk about things, but I said no, she doesn't, even less than the other two. We didn't have terms for them. Tante Lydie, I suppose, and Grandmère, but can you be aunt and grandmother to girls who were born after your death? They were mentioned occasionally, the first Lydia's birthday uncannily the day before my sister's, Yom Kippur, sometimes. As far as I knew – and I never went looking, then or later when the terrible archives opened – we had no dates for their deaths. They stopped writing, or the letters stopped reaching Maman in England. They boarded trains. The end. When Maman went looking for an ending, there wasn't one. No anniversaries, though later I'd learn the hard way – what other way is there – that our bodies keep time, lean with the leaning earth, when our minds erase or let go of what hurts to recall. We know the seasons of our losses the way we know the seasons of storm, the shortening days.

All right, she said, if you want, Gabriel. It'll be a name for a few— She stopped, turned back towards the garden.

For a few hours, I said, yes. Lyd, will you not hold him, just for a minute? Only the two of us, no one need know.

But you, I thought, might know. Something in you might know her, the pulse of her blood, the waves of her voice, yours.

Put him down, she said, put him down on the bed and leave.

Lyd – I said. You might hurt him, I wanted to say. He's mine. He's too fragile. You have to be gentle. Don't hurt my baby. Yes, I said, yes, all right.

You cried, of course, when I laid you down.

I walked away.

some other life

Edith's near the end of her book when she hears movement, a change in their voices. The rain has stopped, for now, and the cows are mooching by the wall. The cows were disconcerting when she first came here, the way they were always there, closer to her waking and sleeping and reading and eating than any people, but now she likes their summer company, misses them when they go strangely up the hills for the winter, an inversion of transhumance unique in Europe, because the limestone absorbs the summer sun (what summer sun?) and holds its heat through the cold times. Sleeping with the windows open, she hears their late-night snacks, their middle-of-the-night bickering, occasional laments. Cows dream, she's sure. They get up in the night to pee. She may even have given them names to herself, called them after some of Mike's sisters and cousins –

Edith, asks Méabh, Edith?

Coming, she says. Her legs and back are stiff and she has to push herself out of the rocking chair. Book another yoga class for the weekend.

They're standing together in the doorway. Yes, siblings. At least as alike as Lydia and herself: sandy colouring, something about the set of the shoulders and angle of the head. Edith, thank you so much, Henry says, thank you for opening your beautiful home to me.

She and Méabh catch each other's eye. So American! Ah, it's just a little place, Edith says, it was a pleasure – An honour, really, she thinks, to be trusted, to be allowed to provide a place of safety, but she doesn't know how to say that, not an English utterance, too direct for Ireland, she's not American. I'm very glad you came, she says, thank you for coming. I'm going back to my hotel now, he says, it's been wonderful, I have a lot to process, but Méabh's kindly – I'll be here a few days, I hope, so perhaps we'll meet again? Of course, she says, that would be lovely, I'll look forward – Stop gushing.

Méabh turns and hugs him. A person knows when he's been hugged by Méabh, and you can see him knowing it. Thank you, he says, really, thank you – I can't tell you –

You don't need to, Méabh says, I'll call you later.

They watch him walk down the path, not quite, Edith thinks, the same man who walked up it. Oh, stop, sentimental, no one's transformed in an afternoon. The lights on the big car flash. They see him walk towards the passenger door, remember and turn. He shrugs theatrically at them. Leave him be, Edith says, he'll maybe want to sit a minute, and they wave, smile, go inside. More tea, says Edith, glass of wine, sandwich? I should get back, Méabh says, there's the dinner – twenty minutes, Edith says, they won't starve, take a moment. We can talk or I can leave you be. Yes, says Méabh, all right, thank you. Wine, Edith says again, sandwich? I wouldn't mind a glass, Méabh says, if you've something open, just a small little one, remember I've to drive.

Méabh goes to the bathroom. Edith pulls bottles out of the wine rack. Celebration, consolation, restoration? All of the above? One of few pieces of advice from Maman: keep a bottle of champagne in the fridge, you should always be prepared to celebrate. To celebrate and also to flee the country. Not today, she thinks, we're not quite there yet. A light red that Mairèad brought last time she came to dinner, it'll keep well enough a day or two after opening, not too good for cooking if it comes to that. Wine glasses, which do match, come in pairs. She carries them through to the coffee table, clears the tea, comes back to plump the cushions as Méabh returns, lipstick replenished.

Cheers, she says, sláinte. Do you want to talk about it? Sláinte, says Méabh, thank you, darling.

They sit down. The light outside is beginning to fade; the hills to the west shorten the evenings here. It's not that I don't want to talk about it, Méabh says, just maybe there isn't so much to say. Less than I'd have expected. He's very – very pleasant, you might say. That sounds moderate, says Edith. The wine is good, more complex than she was expecting. It's just, it wasn't really the talking, Méabh says. I mean, you'll have heard it yourself, he seems a nice man, he seems to have made a good life, barring the divorce at least. Divorce, Edith thinks, can be part of a good life, you should maybe try it yourself one day. It was more the fact of him, he's so much like Dermot, he's the look of the girls about him wouldn't you say. I was thinking, Edith says, he looked a bit like you, when you were standing together. Well, says Méabh, he would, wouldn't he, I take after Mam. It's a strange thing, a new brother at my age, and it's almost stranger how he found us, all these secrets coming undone. Poor Mam, all those years.

A good thing, Edith asks, it's supposed to be good, isn't it, to have things out in the open, not repressed, to say the quiet part out loud. Oh now, says Méabh, we don't have to generalize, sure doesn't living in a small place like this teach you fast enough to keep some things to yourself, the town's hardly big enough for everyone to be having opinions. But isn't that, Edith thinks, how you had the untold rapes and the secret pregnancies and the unmentioned trafficking in the first place? Not that other places, places with smaller quiet parts, don't also have rape and trafficking.

Anyway, Méabh says, I didn't ask him yet, I wanted to think about it, but I'm thinking I'll tell the others. He should meet them, shouldn't he?

I don't know, Edith says, uncharted waters, I think you should do what feels right, or at least best under the circumstances.

That must be to bring him back into the family, surely, says Méabh. I mean it's too late, obviously, he won't meet Mam and it's late in the day for all of us, but it's something, maybe it's a lot.

Whatever feels right, Edith says again. There's no *back*, she's thinking, he was never in your family. Life's not a dress rehearsal, Gran used to say. There's no control in the experiment of parenting, Dearbhla says. There's only the choice you made, or the choice that made you, and its consequences. You don't choose your own adventure and you can't go home. The fantasy of restitution sounds odder the more Méabh says, as if there's some other life in which Henry grew up with his half-siblings, married a local woman and raised Irish children, in which case you'd have to think which local woman would he have married and who would she therefore not have married and which children would not have been born. You think I'm being romantic, Méabh says. What I think isn't important, Edith says, what matters is how you feel. She tests this trite statement like a blade against her skin, surprised to find it true enough. And for one thing, she says, I don't see why you should carry all this alone, just because he contacted you first. You always end up being responsible, maybe you want to share it this time. I hadn't thought of it that way, Méabh says, do you think the others will be upset? Not with you, Edith says, you didn't do anything wrong.

peccata mundi

Soeur Mathilde was punctual. I suppose nuns are. She, or maybe the Telephone Sister, sent a telegram, brought by the boy on the bicycle while I was giving you the first bottle of the day, or at least the first bottle after sunrise which was not the first nor the second bottle after midnight. Arriverai au quai 14h. I translated for la signora, who was impressed or alarmed by the fact of the telegram. You must go meet her, she said, you must carry her bags. One of us should go to the pasticceria this morning, why don't you go, you haven't left the house since the baby was born. Gabriel, I said, his name is Gabriel, the baby. Gabriel, she said, you named him? Someone had to, I said. She shrugged. Someone will, she said, soon enough, you know his new family will give him a new name. Sì, I said, capisco. A new Italian name, or maybe, since it was Maman's connection and the nuns were French, a new French name. Probably not a Jewish name. Would nuns handle Jewish adoptions? Were there Jewish adoptions? (You see, I have questions to which you have answers. It's not all one way, the mystery and the guesswork.) Good, she said, you should go for a walk in the fresh air, you're not the one who gave birth. Gabriel – I said. I can look after the baby, she said, remember to take the shopping basket, I don't want the cakes being crushed. But I don't want to give up any time with him, I wanted to say, the minutes are numbered, let me take him with me at least. As if I could go walking around the village with a baby, as if we had no shame. I hugged you tighter and it seemed to me that your gaze fastened on my face, the face you knew best.

In less than a week, the season had changed. The snow line was a little lower, but the air smelt different. There was no softness that morning in Italy, no mellow fruitfulness. The damp had ice on its breath. I thought that it would have been the wrong day for your first outing and then remembered that Soeur Mathilde would not be waiting on the weather. As I pattered down the gravel drive, my feet, which had been cold for weeks in thin shoes on stone floors, began to ache. I curled my fingers into my palms. Did we have enough wraps for you, a hat? I watched the wind come down the lake, where dark birds bobbed still, and I felt the tug of you, your hands moving as if in the currents of a rock pool, your sea-anemone mouth, the mirrored curve of cheek and skull, the warm weight of you against my breast. It was the wrong thing, to go away from you, to leave you defenceless and without words.

The side gate seemed to have stuck or rusted, and after cutting my finger on the casing of the bolt I gave up and climbed over, which was tricky with the basket empty and would be trickier with it full of pastries. We'll burn that bridge when we come to it, Maman used to say; her possibly deliberately mangled versions of English proverbs were often better than the originals. The early worm is breakfast to the bird. Something ripped as I jumped off the top, a new tear luckily at the hem of my dress rather than anywhere that would compromise decency.

I didn't like the increasing distance between us. What if you were crying, what if you needed pacing and chanting? I knew Signora Pilone thought she had better things to do than soothing a cross and misbegotten infant while his mother capered and lounged overhead. I came down to the lakeside and thought of you crossing the water, you in the arms of a nun going further and further away on the boat, on a train, your mother and I not knowing your destination, not even your language and faith and nationality. It seemed that we were carrying out some heartless experiment, setting you adrift in a state of minimal humanity, only potentially a person. And perhaps that was everything you needed from us, the best we could offer you, but we would never know. I still do not know.

There was no one afoot in the village, no old men sitting outside the bar or women stopping to chat at the entrance to the grocer. I could see rain sweeping down the lake, more than a passing shower. I should have worn the smelly coat, though the pastries would give me an excuse to shelter a while. Surely the baker wouldn't want me to take them straight out into the rain? But I didn't like to leave you longer than I had to. The lights were on in the pasticceria, the window under the striped canopy stage-lit gold. Casse-noisette, I thought, nut-cracker, Sugar Plum Fairy. I found myself pausing before crossing the polished floor in my worn and leaky shoes, conscious again of my torn dress, and I was right because as I opened the door

Signora Calle turned and walked into the back room. Something must need taking out of the oven. I waited a few moments. There was a smaller range of breads and cakes than there had been in the summer. A lemon tart lay there with its yolk-gold filling glossy as still water, maybe a blend of simplicity and expense suitable for a nun. I amused myself with the idea of the cream-filled choux buns that are called religieuses in France and probably something less irreverent in Italy. The chances of getting a lemon tart over the gate intact were low and I looked for something more robust. Scones would have been ideal, not that I could imagine Italian ladies seeing the point. Chelsea buns. Fat rascals, parkin, a black fruit cake. Gran would already be making the Christmas cake and pudding. It was the first year I had not been there to chop figs and prunes, to stir and make a wish though I knew Gran thought the wish-making silly. All but praying to a pudding, better get yourself to church. I wish Gabriel could stay, though where and with whom I couldn't say. I wish Soeur Mathilde wasn't coming. I wish the dancers hadn't left, I wish it was still summer. For the second time, I wished for the return of time past. Rain tapped on the canopy outside. There had been more than time to take any number of cakes from the oven. Buon giorno, I called, buon giorno, signora. A selection of the pretty sandy biscuits, I thought, and cannoli should be robust enough if I had to climb the gate. Soeur Mathilde would just have to go round to the main road since presumably she wouldn't be dressed for – oh, and you, carrying you away in the rain, how could we do this, how could we consider – hello, I called, hello, I'd like to buy some cakes, please, but Signora Calle didn't return until the bell over the door rang for another customer's entrance, and then she pretended not to understand my Italian, made me point and mime, overcharged me for broken pastries under the unsmiling gaze of one of the village matriarchs who had attended our dance but did not return my greeting. I dropped the change, left some of the coins on the floor rather than continue my undignified scrabbling, left red-faced and stupid. Better wet biscuits than further humiliation. I thought then that my tatty clothes and wet hair invited scorn; it had not occurred to me that my sister's baby was shameful, or that shame might be contagious.

I could hear you crying before I opened the front door. My fingers had locked numb around the basket and my clothes were clinging, not comforting to a lonely newborn, but I draped a towel from the hall cloakroom over my shoulder and followed your howls to the kitchen, where you lay on a blanket in the laundry basket, ripping the air with desolation. There was a smell of roasting meat and wine. You must have been crying a long time, as if you'd forgotten why you started or how to stop, as if there was no past or future in your unmet need. I picked you up. As your cheek brushed mine you turned and tried to suckle, desperate. I swayed and bounced on my toes, motherdancing. Shh, angel, ssh, come on, let's find you some milk. Shh, baby, shh. You rubbed your damp face into my damp neck, under my dripping hair. I patted us both with the towel as I bobbed towards the sink, now well able to make up a bottle one-handed. Gabriel baby, hush, hush now. I wanted to tell you everything was all right but we both knew that wasn't true. Where was Signora Pilone, and for the matter of that Lydia, how could they have left you so long?

La signora came in when we were settled on a kitchen chair, you feeding and I beginning to shiver. There you are, she said, I thought I heard you come in, where are the cakes? He was screaming, I said, he must have been crying for hours. You were gone forty minutes, she said, where is the basket, I hope you kept the cakes dry. In the hall, I said. She fetched it. A gust of wind whined around the wall outside and threw rain against the window. Your eyes opened, met mine, closed again. I held you tight. The paper's wet, she said, did they have nothing more special than this, we should have something better for the sister. I thought, I said, nuns preferred plain food, I thought they chose poverty. She said something I chose not to understand. I've been cleaning, she said, setting the sitting room right, when you've fed the baby will you go into the garden and find some flowers, there'll be something still. I'm cold and wet, I said, I need to change, anyway I want to stay with Gabriel now. Gabriel, she said, what a name.

I took you upstairs with me when I went to change one set of ragged clothes for another, set you in the middle of the bed where I smiled and pouted and babbled to you. Even my underwear was wet. You were the only person to see me naked since Gran used to bath me. If I picked you up, if I held you to my breast – Oh, I said, oh, baby, oh, Gabriel. I put on my clothes. If I'd had an outfit to annoy a nun, a little dress like the ones Louise wore, I'd have worn it.

We went and listened outside Lydia's door before going downstairs. We could hear her feet sweeping the floor and her murmured counting, un et deux et trois et quatre, port de bras, un et deux et trois et quatre. Perhaps she would be on stage by

Advent. Maybe you'll dance, I told you, maybe you'll be a musician. But you probably wouldn't be a farmer, because you wouldn't have the farm.

We went down the stairs slowly. You were going back to sleep, turning your face to my shoulder, becoming softer and heavier in my arms, as if, awake, you were a little airborne, as if you could almost fly until you needed to sleep. Signora Pilone came out of the kitchen, a draught of roast dinner behind her. Come and eat, she said, you need a hot meal, I killed a chicken yesterday to make sandwiches for the sister, we can have the dark meat. Which chicken, I said, having come to know them. Aren't you a farmer's daughter, she said, don't you cook your father's lambs, come and eat, I'll hold the baby. Your father's lambs, I thought, qui tollis peccata mundi, but hens are distinctly infernal which is one of the reasons I like them. I can hold him and eat, I said, he's asleep, I don't want to disturb him. We sat at the table and I let her serve me, watched her assemble a generous plate for my sister, but I wasn't surprised when she brought it down untouched. Maybe later, I said. Later, she said, is when Signora Lydia's troubles begin.

No, I thought, later is when they end, when things go back to normal, but she was fifty years older than me and of course she was right.

fragmenting

The weather forecast is unreliable round here, in this miniature ecosystem with its miniature climate, at the end of an inlet from which there's a straight run to America (but she's checked, Méabh's right, it's Newfoundland so Canada). It's the wet coast of a wet North Atlantic island off a bigger wet North Atlantic island, the last edges of Europe fragmenting into the sea. The answer is always that there'll be rain, and then less rain, and then more rain, and so it has been all morning. She swam anyway, because she swims daily from May Day until the spirit quails which is usually late September but presumably, if she lives long enough to observe a trend, likely to get later over the years. How far into the end times is it desirable for an old woman to survive? I'll die tidily at the beginning, thank you, she'd used to say when Pat fretted or fantasized about post-apocalyptic survival skills, and most of her friends had agreed. Come the apocalypse, it seems, the lefty bourgeoisie will tidy themselves away before anyone's roaming the land with guns and supermarket trollies, would rather die than try to exist without coffee shops and HRT, or more charitably, have no desire to outlive civilization, which is something of a self-fulfilling prophecy or a plan for self-sabotage, at least as long as you think that the right-wingers are the barbarians. Let them, the Fascists, have the end of everything, the poisoned air and the drought and the flames. You should always leave with regret. If there's no regret, you stayed too long. It was all well and good, that kind of thinking, in Pat's scenarios, in the event of mutually assured destruction or aliens or zombies or malign AI taking over the planet, but this gradual ending, the creeping deterioration, might require a different approach. We – northern Europe, first years of the second millennium if you count the Christian way which in northern Europe you might as well – are boiling frogs noticing discomfort when it's already too late. We must endure our going hence even as our coming hither, old ladies like everyone else. And meanwhile what has looked for an hour now like the edge of the rain is approaching, creeping up the inlet, a moving line across the water between green and grey. A weather front, she thinks, remembering how when they first had a television at the farm Dad used to watch the cut-out clouds jerking across the map, the sky's intercontinental swirls made visible to the masses for the first time, but a 'weather front' sounds too much like a battle front, as if land taken will be held. All quiet on the western front. Here the fronts dance and turn, chase each other up the valleys. Weather wisps, she thinks, weather moods, no sooner come than gone, no sooner gone than returning. The point is that there is sunshine coming and come what may, sunshine in this place is a command to go out.

Raincoat, all the same. Waterproof trousers in the backpack.

Her boots, newspaper-stuffed, are still damp from yesterday, but with wool socks that won't matter. She drives up the hill, trusting the weather's mood to follow her, parks outside the primary school that might have had to close if the Ukrainians hadn't come and saved it. It's a Gaelscoil and there were concerns that two new languages might be too much for traumatized children but also that if the Ukrainian kids were allowed to speak English the Irish kids wouldn't speak Irish, and apparently it's all working out fine, if you're a child bombed out of your house and your town making a new life thousands of miles from home in a different climate and landscape and culture, leaving your dad and your uncles and your older brothers to fight, an extra language makes no odds, might even provide useful distraction. It's not that she didn't try to learn Irish herself, several times, partly to help Pat who was still young enough for compulsory Irish at school when they came from London and partly because it seemed only polite, to learn the language of your new country whose passport you hoped to carry, but she didn't try hard enough, not as hard as a traumatized child trying to look to an unexpected future, like for example Maman arriving in England in 1941. Like the young men in the old hotel.

She is rewarded for getting out of the car in pattering rain by the sky clearing as she sets out up the track. Deep puddles, of course, she has to hop and jump, but as the path rises it dries and soon she is where she wanted to be, in the stonescape, out on the limestone slabs. They're slippery when wet, you do have to be careful, but the astonishingly clear light that follows rain is taking hold of the air and will soon dry the stones. Pulling her coat down over her behind, she perches, watches. It's as if steamy glass is clearing, like watching a car windscreen de-misting, seeing the weather clear, feeling the rain-rinsed air fill her lungs. She breathes down her spine, into the rings of her trunk. The hillfort on the next summit materializes, some friend or fellow to the stone circle to which this path leads. There were more people on this land in the Iron Age than in the decades after the Famine, and the Iron Age buildings outlast those of the nineteenth century, at least apart from the barracks and poorhouses in the towns. Maybe the weather was different, two thousand years ago, but the fragmenting edges of a continent are always wet. Deerskin coats, maybe, but even so, she thinks, not for the first time, give thanks for living in the era of waterproof coats and boots. It's just a pity, if not entirely a coincidence, that they come with mutually assured destruction and the end of everything.

Still, onward. If this mood, her mood, doesn't lift soon she might go to Dublin, revisit the old life and friends. It's not as if meditating on the end of the world defers it, not as if you can hold off apocalypse by prayer. The film festival is next weekend and Dearbhla says there's a new restaurant she wants to show her. She walks on, testing the stone underfoot, paying attention.

human decency

She arrived, of course, Soeur Mathilde. I can't hold it off any longer, can't slow time enough to prevent us reaching the hour of your departure. We both know that it happened.

It was before nuns' habits had taken on the form of other uniforms, schools and traffic wardens. Almost from when the boat started to cross from Bellagio, I could see a figure in head-to-toe black. Unnecessarily Gothic, I thought, surely they could have come up with something less forbidding by way of baby-collecting outfits, but you wouldn't care what she was wearing and probably forbidding was part of the point. In her view, I supposed, Lydie was damned to eternal fire for ever going to that party, getting into that taxi, not preventing herself being put into that bed, probably not that she wanted her holy mind sullied with such detail. I had to get my nuns from Gothic novels, though the stories of convent-educated friends I've heard since don't paint a very different picture, but also I needed a villain. I'm trying not to need a villain now, as long as the alternative villain isn't my seventeen-year-old self. I don't want you to think

I haven't thought of you, over the years, haven't thought that I was old enough to take a stand, old enough to bear some of the responsibility. I can't even say that I thought I was doing the best thing at the time, because it was perfectly obvious that none of us was doing the best thing and none of us was happy about it, perhaps including Soeur Mathilde. We were all adults and we all knew with our hearts if not our minds that separating an infant from his mother is wrong and we all did it anyway, for reasons of ambition and convenience and convention.

As the ferry approached I thought of running back to the villa, climbing the gate, wrapping you in your blanket and absconding together, but we'd have had nowhere to go and you weren't mine and also I wanted to go to Oxford and have my own future. I held myself where I was on the damp-slicked stones, found myself dipping a small curtsey to the sister the way Lydie had taught me years ago, though only for stage purposes, neither of us imagined a social application. Bonjour, madame, I said, j'espère que vous avez passé un bon voyage? I hadn't spoken French for months, could hear the English in my r's. Even then, I knew my speech was old-fashioned, learnt from Maman who until the recent venture had not lived in France for twenty years and spoke the pre-war tongue, but a nun seemed unlikely to miss the latest slang. She wore a black veil secured somehow under the chin, like an uncannily stiff hijab, and I took exception to her toe-to-chin sweep of my own outfit. I had never aspired to be une jeune fille bien rangée, any more than later I would feel inclined towards the South Dublin lady-uniform of trousers and cardigan the colour of concrete and hair the colour of bananas, the kind of elderly but unripe bananas sold here on this island so very far from banana trees, though I'm not sure my rebellion ever extended much beyond fashion. You're kind to come and meet me, she said, using the informal 'you' for which I was, I felt, just about too old. And 'gentille' can also mean 'well-behaved'. Di niente, I said, I mean, de rien. I swallowed, not wanting to say what I knew I should. As far as I could tell under her habit, she seemed perfectly capable of carrying her own bag. This way, I said, and may I take your case? Thank you, she said, passing it to me. And you must be Miss Braithwaite's sister? Yes, I said, I'm Edith, I've been here with her since the summer. I was there, I wanted to say, at the birth, Gabriel has been in my arms all his life. Her brisk step paused. And how old are you, my child? Seventeen, I said, I'm going to Oxford next year. So you are not married, she said. Don't be daft, I wanted to say, but actually two girls from my class at school had married that summer and only one of them, so far as I knew, had been pregnant. No, I said. Then you are too young to be here, she said, under the circumstances, your mother should have known better. Really, I thought, what authority did this woman think she took from her absurd garb and absurd promises to a deity in whom, it seemed to me then, no rational person could believe? I'm not too young anymore, I said, and my mother knows far worse things than a baby in a nice villa by the lake. You are very sure of yourself, she said. So are you, I would have said, had it not occurred to me that I wanted her to be well-disposed towards you more than I wanted to be right, which might also have been a symptom of my being no longer too young for the circumstances. Forgive me, I said, I am sad for my sister, and for my nephew, it has been a tiring week. Yes, she said, one would suppose so.

I bent my head into the sharp wind coming off the lake and through my clothes. I had outstayed the summer too long and it was time to go home, back to the kitchen range beside which we would be nursing lambs in a few weeks, or at least Gran and Dad would be nursing lambs while I started again in Paris. But for a little while I could be at home, sleep in my own bed against the chimney stack passing from the kitchen to the roof, wear the jumpers Gran had knitted with growing room it was now clear that I wouldn't need, read my own books and begin to shape what I had learnt in telling my adventures to Nancy. And you were also going home, if anywhere is home the first time.

Soeur Mathilde appeared impervious to the weather, even her habit apparently supernaturally unruffled. I wanted to ask her, didn't dare, wanted to. Spray was blowing off the little waves on the lake. Do you know, I asked, where he's going, Gabriel? My voice sounded odd, unused. Gabriel, she said. We named him, I said, my sister and I, he needed a name. And he needs a birth certificate, it occurred to me for the first time, his existence needs to be recorded. His parents will name him, she said. Do you know who they are, I asked. She looked at me. Yes, she said, but I cannot tell you. French doesn't distinguish 'can' from 'may' as clearly as English. You are not permitted, I said, to tell me. Precisely, she said, the rules forbid it. Thank you, I said, for telling me the truth. I meant thank you for not pretending that you don't know, for not pretending that there's anything humane or gentle afoot here. Naturally, she said, and we continued in silence. I felt as if I were bringing a priest to sacrifice you, kept thinking of Abraham and Isaac which has always seemed to me more of a test of human decency than of faith and therefore a test that Abraham fails. If your god tells you to kill a child, find another god. But it was life, of course, that you were to receive, the new life beginning before you knew the old, these days with me and your mother and la signora a false start, at best the tuning of the orchestra before the music begins.

Here, I said, this is the main gate, let me open it. La signora had made sure I had the key, a lump of iron the size of my hand that had done nothing for the line of my – Louise's – cardigan. They are kind, Soeur Mathilde said, the baby's parents, kind and rich, he will have a good life. Are they Jewish, I asked. I caught a flicker of surprise. She must have known, surely, that Maman was Jewish, and she was certainly old enough to understand what it might mean, to be Jewish in Europe twenty-three years after the liberation of the camps. I cannot say, she said, it is not permitted to tell you such things. It's up here, I said, we can take the shortcut, if your shoes are sturdy. Trail your habit through the wet grass, witch, I meant, let's get mud on your white stockings. I might have accidentally banged her valise against the retaining wall as I led her up the slope.

I couldn't hear you from the hall, and felt an irrational pulse of fear. What might they have done to you, my sister and Signora Pilone, while I wasn't there? Where's Gabriel, I said as Signora Pilone came from the salon. She had changed her clothes, still all black but tighter and smarter, and put on lipstick. Good afternoon, sister, she said, we are honoured by your visit. Almost, not quite, a curtsey. Soeur Mathilde smiled. Translate, la signora whispered to me. Italian to French, I thought, bloody hell, and at least for now no translation could possibly be required. Welcome, come in, how was your journey, please sit down, eat what I have prepared. I could have translated it from Japanese or Hungarian, what hosts say to guests. Where's Gabriel, I said again. Tell the sister she is very welcome, la signora said, ask her if she wishes to wash her hands. Tell me where the baby is, I said. She glared at me. Asleep, she said, in the kitchen, now tell the sister— I went through the kitchen door and there you were, swaddled in your blanket, your face turned to a three-quarter profile of moon-cheek and eyelashes. You were too small, too innocent, to give away as if unwanted, and I picked you up and you stirred and murmured. Let's go, Baby Gabriel, I said, let's run away, and I held you against me and rocked, rocked us. The porcelain teacups I hadn't seen since the dancers went away were set out on a tray. I could hear thumps from the other side of the house, Lydia dancing.

La signora came in. Put the child down, she said, we must serve tea to the sister, put the kettle back on the stove, it was just boiling. I turned away from her and went on rocking.

I was so very tired.

Edith, she said, he's not your baby. He can't stay. He will have a good life, in a good family.

No, I said. No.

I heard the kettle beginning to boil, her movements as she made the tea. I bent to kiss you, to inhale you.

He's not yours, Signora Pilone said, he will have a good life and you will have a good life, you are children both, you have crossed each other's paths for a week.

I would remember, later, when I held my own baby, that she had given me the words to forgive myself. I would not be, am not, wholly convinced by them.

She asked me and then told me to take the tea tray into the salon, where I don't doubt she had set out the full panoply of afternoon tea, sandwiches from the chicken sacrificed to Soeur Mathilde, the biscuits bought in shame, probably something she had made to compensate for the dry brokenness of the pastries. No, I said, no, and I let her bustle while I sat in the kitchen nursing you as you slept, memorizing the swirl of your hair and the whorls of your ears and the way your eyelashes were already dark and heavy, quite unlike Lydie's which were invisible without mascara. You were a prettier baby than my Pat, who looked well enough as a toddler but was a formless infant.

La signora brought back the tray. The sister must have been hungry after her journey, she said, she has eaten well. Edith, it is nearly time. You should take the baby upstairs, so Signora Lydia can say goodbye.

I looked at her. She nodded.

I stood up and carried you up the stairs. You began to wake, small bleats and turns of your head.

We stopped outside Lydie's door. Your eyes were open, fixed on mine, but you didn't cry. Soeur Mathilde in the room below must have felt as if she was under the stage, because despite the villa's solidity we could hear from the landing that Lydie was dancing at full scale on her wooden floor, centre work including jumps for which the boards were not intended. Between jumps she was humming phrases and talking to herself. I couldn't hear words but I knew it was the dance teacher in her head talking, giving instructions one step ahead. I waited a moment before I shifted you onto one arm and tapped at the door, and when there was no answer we went in anyway.

She had somehow moved the bed to the wall and rolled up the rugs. I saw that she had brought her pointe shoes here, even though she was weeks from giving birth when she arrived. She wore them with bare legs and a short nightdress over her bra and knickers, not unlike some of the costumes I'd seen on stage but she looked both thin and saggy, noticeably out of condition. I remembered Dad saying once that keeping a dancer was like keeping a racehorse, all nerve and muscle and appetite. She wasn't like that now. She paused, en pointe, arms in fifth. You shouldn't be on your toes, I wanted to say, you'll hurt yourself and how will that help, you can't dance the Nutcracker with injured feet. Lyd, I said, Lyd, I'm sorry but it's time. The nun's been here a while and she needs to go.

She leant forward into an arabesque but I could see her ankle shaking.

I brought Gabriel, I said, for you to say goodbye. He's awake.

She kept tilting as one hand floated up, her gaze following towards the ceiling, and after a moment I understood.

In a cramped and creaky room, on her weakened feet, your mother was dancing you goodbye.

invisible flower

Edith still thinks of 'getting out' for a walk, as if there were some resisting force to overcome, as if she still lived with someone who might present objections or resentment. She puts her foot in her boot, takes it out again, shakes grit onto the floor because she can't be bothered to open the door right now and it's her floor and she'll be the one living with the grit or sweeping it up. It will take her years, she thinks, more years, to re-learn autonomy, and maybe autonomy isn't a natural human condition anyway, maybe we're supposed to be in each other's way, under each other's feet, hampering. Is Gunter right, that autonomy is the opposite of belonging? She thinks of Priya, living with her daughter, of several of Pat's British Asian schoolfriends whose elderly grandparents lived with their adult children as a matter of course, were around to care and be cared for; thinks of her Dublin friends and their timetables of family obligation, cousins' birthdays and grandchildren's First Communions (because even if you don't like the Church it still runs the schools and anyway the neighbours expect it and sure don't the little girls like to dress up in white lace). She ties the second boot. Nope, she thinks, no thanks, I'll take autonomy, I'll make my own bed and lie in it, I'll die alone on my blue linen sheets. Coat? Just her cagoule, in case. That's part of where her marriage went wrong, neither of them in the end willing to put themselves out for the other, the autonomy they gave each other eventually what divided them. And now she need put herself out for no one, and it's not getting out but going out to walk, exactly when she feels like it. She locks the door, sets off.

It's a bright day, spring taking hold in the twigs of rowan and hazel and in the cups and cracks of the rocks. It's the season to look for the invisible white flower, and warm enough to stop moving and pay attention. Gentle wind, a scattering of high cloud, a good growing day. Birdsong, and still in those precious weeks when the lambs' call is met by their mothers' response, when the calves potter and nose beside the cows. Her shadow lopes beside her, sun on her back, in her hair, benediction.

She stops at the place where she and Méabh once convinced each other they'd seen the invisible flower, crouches and peers. Tiny gardens, she thinks, in the cracks and cups of the rock, but they're not gardens, not cultivated, just the world making itself despite everything, roots thin as hair, leaves small as eyelashes but there they are, photosynthesizing, sunlight into energy, and yes, insects, ants, something smaller than ants and there are ticks here, that's why she sits on the rock and never in the grass. She cranes forward. A couple of the cups hold last night's rain still, ponds the size of her curled hand mirroring the sky. She holds her spread fingers between the sun and the water, eclipse. Remembers one afternoon with toddler Pat, at a restaurant for Mike's parents' anniversary, must have been their fortieth, making shadow puppets for him with her fingers, a duck talking to a crocodile and her doing the voices, under or over one of those endless conversations about people she didn't know and didn't want to know. She makes the shape again, can't quite close the beak between her finger and thumb but if she angles her hand right it doesn't matter. Someone probably did do that, or similar, for Lydia's baby. Someone remembers his childhood.

She makes the ballet shape with her hands, third finger and thumb slightly inside the others. Different companies, Lydia told her once, hold their hands in different ways. There's a Balanchine shape and a Royal Ballet shape, and if you change jobs you have to learn the new way. She moves her arms, sitting there on the hillside beside her shadow. First, second, third, fourth, fifth. She always liked fourth best, one arm around someone and one reaching away.

There's a disturbance in the nearest pool, a prickle in the surface tension. She leans over, darkening the water. A blonde moth, small as all creatures here are, has made a mistake. Its legs are still paddling, but the wings are sealed to the water's surface. As flies to wanton boys, she thinks. One does not need to be that kind of god. She looks for a leaf, some form of rescue craft suited to the delicacy of the job, but nothing so big grows near here. One finger would displace half the pond and she is afraid that the wet wing would stick to her skin. She feels in the pocket of the cagoule and finds a shopping list written on the torn-off flap of an envelope, ideally stiff and thin. Yogurt, ?fish, coffee, toothpaste. The question mark means, if you find fish that is both sustainable and affordable, buy it, as if she didn't know that such a thing no longer exists. She folds the paper to make a shelf for the moth, to minimize the scale of the intervention, squats low, takes a deep breath to steady her hands and then slowly scoops. The wings stick to the paper, but it's glossy white paper, probably around something better than a bill – some of her friends still send Christmas cards – maybe at least a little water-resistant. A bird-shadow flickers over them, her and the blonde moth, and above, a raven calls. What have we here, it's narrating to its sky audience, a woman playing god? She sits back carefully, holding the moth on its paper stretcher in the sun to dry. Old fool, she murmurs to herself, either way it will be food for birds, but aren't we all, in the end, food for birds, food for worms for birds?

The moth doesn't move, still doesn't move. She doesn't want to leave the paper here, the kind that takes forever, probably more time than we have, to decompose, and taking the moth along on her walk seems wrong, as if it should be left where it was found, as if she should limit her intervention to heroic measures. She tilts her face to the sun, waiting for resurrection. She has time, still some time, enough to wait.

sooner or later

And so here we are, here I am, at the end.

Here I am in Italy again, with Cassie and Priya, Tuscany, nowhere near the lakes and Igor's villa. I looked up the villa; it's aptly enough an artists' residence now, owned by an American foundation. The barn is a studio for sculptors, but on the website the drawing room and dining room look much the same, even the furniture, the pool and grounds just as I remember them, which I mention because it suggests that at least in that regard my recollections are accurate enough. I would have liked to see a photo of the marble bath.

I said yes to Cassie. I look back and I am pleased by the number of times in my life I have said yes, though mostly women are advised to say no, to learn and practise saying no. Perhaps mostly women are asked other questions. I said yes to this other villa, in Tuscany, and so here I am, beside a different pool under the hotter modern sun, and it's all just as it should be, just as we were promised, sunlight spangling on water held dark by Moorish blue tiles, the sky a colour unknown to the North

Atlantic, the stone table at which I sit probably scratching my laptop, the edges of the metal chair pressing through the cushion into my bones, the skin on my forearms beginning to tingle under the sun but I sit here anyway, peering through sunglasses at the screen only half-shaded by the vines trained across the pergola overhead. Not a bad place to finish.

Afterwards – do you want afterwards? Better to leave you in my arms, perhaps, to leave Lydia dancing. But the show must go on.
    She did dance in the Nutcracker. Not the Sugar Plum Fairy, I think she had the sense to know that she would never be the Sugar Plum Fairy. I gathered later there had been some murmuring about her casting, but I didn't see that production. I didn't see her dance again until my final year at Oxford, when she surprised me with two tickets to the last night of Les Sylphides. It was inconvenient, I'd had other plans, but the boy of that term had never been to the ballet or the Opera House and I didn't want to reject her approach, so we went, walked from Paddington on a pretty spring evening and took sandwiches to eat on a bench in Covent Garden because the train tickets had exhausted our resources. I'm no great judge and our seats were far from the stage, but she seemed good to me, strong and brave, though not, apparently, enough to rise any further in the company. After that I was in Paris for a couple of years, and by the time I came back to London she was in New York and then Chicago. Going to America in those days was a major undertaking, still cheaper to take the boat than to fly, and it never really occurred to either of us that I might visit. I thought she'd come back, sooner or later, and as you know other than those weeks in Italy we'd lived

far apart since she was twelve. I won't say I didn't miss her, but I was used to her not being there.

She didn't come back, though I was half-hoping she would for my wedding. And also half-afraid that if she did she would upstage me, she and Maman in their French and American elegance. We scaled back the wedding after she died, not the fairy-tale scene of Mike's mother's dreams which was anyway unfashionable in the late seventies, among people like me, or at least people I had been like: liberated, feminist, graduates of elite universities and the summer of love. Maman didn't come, though sent a Kenwood mixer which was a comment on the choice she believed – not entirely erroneously – that I was making. I thought, you see, that Mike and I were liberating each other, that I was freeing him from the stultifications of the Dublin bourgeoisie and he was giving me safe harbour after years in which I'd more or less sought turbulence, that with him I could avoid becoming Maman. I went on trying so hard for so many years not to be Maman that perhaps I forgot, forgot how, to be myself, and when I remembered – well, this isn't about me. I'm not the one you're interested in.

It was a car accident. You probably could have guessed, no? She lived fast and glamorously to the end. You can look it up, there were obituaries for the violinist who was driving her from the Opera House in Chicago back to his lakeside home after too much champagne and cocaine. Not for her. The police told Dad that the tape of him playing Schubert was still ringing through the woods when they found them at dawn, and I thought oh, trust Lydie, trust my darling sister, to die at the hands of a man who plays himself playing, and I wished Maman had been there, had been able to be there, when we were growing up, had been able to show my beautiful sister how not to do such things.

She was, is, buried in Chicago. I can give you the place, if you want to visit, if you're that way inclined. Maman went to the funeral. She said Igor was there, that he came from New York, but Dad and I stayed in England, because if we couldn't afford to travel when Lydia was alive, what point was there in travelling for her dead? I have a few of her things still, if you want them, but honestly I believe that if I were you, and if you had a good enough childhood, I would leave all this now. None of us is truly autonomous and none of us truly belongs. There are no border guards at the chambers of your heart. It's only the immigration officers who might care, where your mother was born, what passport your father carried. If history grants you the chance, be free of all that, that's my advice. You'll belong by caring for people and places. You can't go home, wanderer. You come from where you were last.

That's why I leave you your story, instead of spitting in a tube or scraping my cheek or whatever it is you do to sell or give your genetic codes, lighting fuses for the comeuppances of people you'll never know. I don't understand why people don't worry more about the lists someone could make from those databases. Wouldn't it have saved the Third Reich some work, to be able to pull us all from a spreadsheet? It's not a light-hearted act, to let them code your blood. You don't write a person in zeros and ones. Don't think it can't happen here, wherever you are, don't ever let yourself think that, that's how we get caught, feeling safe, feeling at home, trusting our neighbours. We're all wanderers. We all live dangerously; the brave thing is to know it.

It's not that your adoption doesn't matter. Of course it does, if it didn't there would be no need to label babies in hospitals, each as good as the next, certainly no need for me to write this account for you. But your past, my past, is irreparable. Storytelling isn't mending. To be alive is to be in uncertainty, which suggests to me that Keats was right, that certainty is death.

If you're reading this, you came looking, somehow found Pat who will have – has, I suppose, if you're reading – my passwords with my will. But I find, foolishly, as I come to the end, that I hope you're not reading, I find that I hope all this writing has been in vain, the egocentric testament of an old woman with time on her hands, making sense of herself as much as of you. This story doesn't make you English. I suppose it does, by some lights, make you Jewish, but unless you were already that way inclined, so what? You have always been who you really are.

This is the only reality: the atoms of each of us come together for a brief while here and now, the pump and flicker of our hearts dancing our bodies and our brains on the surface of our broken planet in this moment. Everything everywhere is already real, the beating of the squirrel's heart and the growing of the grass, the grapes I am about to pick and eat, to burst sun-warm and still ripening between my teeth and tongue, the ache in my back from sitting here too long and the cool water that will soon lick my hot skin; food and water, pain and comfort, what mattered at the beginning of life and the world also what matters at the end, and you, real wherever you are, real in your body, however it is, all of it happening this moment, life.

Yes.

SOURCES

I grew up reading ballet books, with the fascination of a child who couldn't tell left from right and had a body more earthly than airborne. There is a more critical, adult literature for us too, including:

Chloe Angyal, *Turning Pointe: How a New Generation of Dancers Is Saving Ballet from Itself*, Bold Type Books, 2021
Deborah Bull, *The Everyday Dancer*, Faber & Faber, 2012
Guy Cools, *Imaginative Bodies: Dialogues in Performance Practices*, Antennae, 2015
Annie-B Parson, *The Choreography of Everyday Life*, Verso, 2022
Georgina Pazcoguin, *Swan Dive: The Making of a Rogue Ballerina*, Picador, 2021
Jenifer Ringer, *Dancing Through It: My Journey in the Ballet*, Penguin, 2015
Alice Robb, *Don't Think, Dear: On Loving and Leaving Ballet*, Oneworld, 2023
Lyndsey Winship, *Being a Dancer: Advice from Dancers and Choreographers*, Nick Hern Books, 2015

I found the online resources of World Ballet Day excellent for showing some of 'the part of ballet you don't see when you go to a ballet'. https://worldballetday.com

ACKNOWLEDGEMENTS

This book was years in the research and dreaming, but I wrote the first words as a Hawthornden Fellow at Casa Ecco in spring 2023, and the ending as a guest of the Danish Writers' and Translators' Centre at Hald Hovedgaard in summer 2024. I thank both foundations for the gift of writing time and a room of my own. Between the summers, I was teaching at University College Dublin, where I thank the students of the MA and MFA programmes for asking good questions.

I thank the friends who accompanied me to the ballet and listened to my thoughts about dance and writing: Deborah Lee, Elanor Dymott, Chantal Wright, Finola O' Kane, Éireann Lorsung.

I thank Sinéad Mooney, Margaret MacDonald, Anne Gallagher and Colette Redington for reading drafts and making suggestions. They saved me from myself all over Ireland and the twentieth century. All remaining errors are my responsibility.

As always, I am grateful to and proud of my publishers at Picador in London and Farrar, Straus, and Giroux in New York, and especially to my editor, Sophie Jonathan, her assistant, Daisy Dickeson, and my publicist, Camilla Elworthy; in the US, to my editor, Jenna Johnson, and her team.

Thank you to my agent, Anna Webber at A. M. Heath, who understood this project from the beginning as always and was a companion in my return to life's pleasures.

I thank Colette Redington and Anne Gallagher, who introduced me to the Burren and continue to be my guides and companions on adventures there. This book is for them, and in loving memory of Katharine MacDonald, 1976–2022.

A Note About the Author

Sarah Moss is the author of the novels *The Fell*, *Summerwater*, and *Ghost Wall*, the memoir *My Good Bright Wolf*, and many other books. Her work has been listed among the best books of the year in *The Guardian*, *The Times* (London), *Elle*, and the *Financial Times* and selected for *The New York Times Book Review*'s Editors' Choice. A fellow of the Royal Society of Literature, she was educated at the University of Oxford and now teaches at University College Dublin.